The Lord and the Frenchman

Neil S. Plakcy

Samwise Books

This book is a work of fiction. Names, characters, places, and incidents either are products of the author's imagination or are used fictitiously. Any resemblance to actual events or locales or persons, living or dead, is entirely coincidental.

Copyright 2023 by Neil S. Plakcy All rights reserved, including the right of reproduction in whole or in part in any form.

Cover design by Kelly Nichols. Editing by Randall Klein.

There are two books in the Ormond Yard Series:

The Gentleman and the Spy

The Lord and the Frenchman

Chapter 1

His Father's Summons

The summons from his father couldn't have come at a worse time. John Seales was exhausted, bleary-eyed, and cranky after an all-night effort revising his latest broadside. It reviled the House of Lords for their opposition to Anthony Mundella's Nine-Hours Factory Bill, and he felt the stress of his own work as much as that of the women and children the bill was intended to protect. Assuming the messenger was from his printer, eager to get John's words out on the street, he yelled to his valet, Beller, "Tell them I'll be ready when I'm bloody well finished!"

Beller answered the door and moments later brought a cream-colored envelope with "John Seales, Lord Therkenwell" elegantly inscribed on it, clearly the work of his father's clerk.

His essay was due at the printer's by noon to enable it to be printed and distributed to the hawkers who would retail them on London streets and he needed to polish it further. He was sure that his determination to protect those at greatest risk from the worst horrors of factory work was making his prose too florid, too foolish. He didn't have time to waste on a social call to his father, who knew nothing of his work and disdained him as a lazy fop.

Beller cleared his throat with a light cough. "The boy from your father's house waits for your reply," he said, standing across the table from John.

"What can the old man want now?" John demanded, as he opened the envelope and glared at the missive. It had been written on the letterhead of Briar House, his father's home in London. With a sinking heart, he read the summons to meet with Earl Badgely that afternoon at high tea.

His first thought was that his father had discovered his connection to Janner, the alias he used in his writing, and his heart raced.

"Deep breaths, sir," Beller said, and John realized that Beller, who knew him better than anyone, had recognized his distress.

He did as his valet said, inhaling and exhaling, and his stress began to dissipate. There was no way his father could have connected him to the author of the broadsides which criticized factory owners, Earl Badgely included.

Since his father supplied John with an income, allowing him to devote his efforts to his essays, he felt it impolitic to refuse. Taking care to write as neatly as possible, he accepted the invitation and then slid the letter into his father's envelope.

Beller took the envelope away. It shouldn't have been a surprise to receive such a summons; Earl Badgely had come up to London for the opening of Parliament, after spending the Christmas holidays in Cornwall. The Season, a round of parties hosted by and attended by families of the nobility and landed gentry, would begin shortly.

But it was damnably bad timing. He still had to polish the last few phrases of his essay, then send Beller with it to the printers'. He'd have to bathe and dress and make it to Briar House in advance of teatime, or else be berated by his father for his louche habits. Little did the old man know that though he attended his share of parties, he had another career entirely.

As a child, he'd visited his father's hosiery factory in Nottinghamshire, and been appalled to see boys and girls of his own age employed there. As he grew older, he learned that his father's premises were not unique; crowded and unclean factories, a lack of safety codes, and long hours were the norm.

He felt guilty that his family's wealth and his own life of ease were made possible by the labor of children. After graduation from Cambridge, he had devoted himself to this cause, eventually finding a printer who was willing to publish his essays as broadsides, under the name Janner.

He'd adopted the name because it meant an English person born within ten miles of the sea, and he thought it suited him, as he was a Cornishman through and through, connected to the peninsula where he had been born and raised, until he was sent off to school. Though he preferred London now, his heart would always be in that rugged land.

Beller brought him a fresh pot of tea and he returned to his work, slashing out inadequate phrases and rewriting them, dripping ink on the paper in his eagerness to get every word exactly right. He had to be simple enough for the common man to understand, persuasive enough to touch even the hardest heart, and present the deft phrasing readers had come to expect from Janner.

"You will need time to bathe and dress for tea with your father," Beller said, as John was fussing over the closing sentence of the essay.

"I know that!" John snapped. Then he looked up to see Beller, and his voice softened. "Sorry, my good man. You know the pressure I am under."

"From two directions, sir," Beller said. "I know how much you care for perfection in your writing, but you cannot be late for your father."

"Fine," John said. He pushed the paper aside, then waved his hand over it to let the ink dry. "I will have this ready to go in a few minutes. Do you think my pale gray would be suitable for high tea?"

"I should think something darker," Beller said. "You know how conservative your father is in matters of dress. An unexpected summons like this might be something grave."

John recalled his first thought, that his father had discovered his identity as Janner. There was no substance behind that, and he did not want to worry Beller, who tended to fret. "I doubt it. Probably to discuss the arrival of my mother and sisters, and what I shall be required to do to entertain them. But you're right, perhaps the dark gray with the pale pinstripe? I am not going to a funeral, after all."

"But no lace collar or cuffs," Beller said.

John sighed. Earl Badgely had often accused his only son of being a fop, criticizing his oversized cravats and lacy cuffs.

"You are correct," John said. "My father puts up a fuss whenever I dress too much like a dandy. I am sure you have heard him say that I dress like a woman in a man's body."

"I couldn't say, my lord." He bowed slightly and left the dining room.

Beller was marvelously discreet, and John felt that he did a fine job, given that he was both valet and butler. John's budget extended to a cook and a maid of all work, but it was Beller who kept the household running.

Beller had been with John for four years by then, since John had come down to London from Cambridge. He was an amiable young man, able to keep his mouth shut when necessary. John had found him as a footman in a friend's stately home, and recognized that he wanted desperately to get out of Cornwall and to the big city.

He was relatively sure that Beller was interested in women, which was fine with him. Eventually he saw Beller married to a housekeeper, managing Briar House once John inherited. For the time being, Beller was a good man who knew how his lordship should be dressed.

And that was what mattered most.

Chapter 2

A Difficult Translation

Blanton's Coffee Shop was a dismal place, down several uneven steps from the street, with a low, smoke-darkened ceiling and an air of misty gloom. The narrow oak tables were smutty and ringed with the marks of ancient coffee-drinkers. The walls were decorated with hat-pegs and battered advertisements. It was miles from the cafés Raoul Desjardins had come to appreciate during the two years he'd spent as a junior attaché in the Paris bureau of the *Ministère de l'Europe et des Affaires étrangères*, the French ministry for Europe and Foreign Affairs, before his transfer to London.

In France, drinking coffee was an art, and each Parisian café had a unique way of presenting it, which Raoul had come to love. The coffee in London was sludgy and bitter and no matter how he wrapped his heavy, scratchy scarf around his neck, and layered shirt and undershirt beneath his thick wool jumper, it was never hot enough to keep him warm.

The food and drink at Blanton's was even worse than the surroundings, and its sole advantage for Raoul was its proximity to his miserly single room at Bryanston Mews West. He sat glumly at a rear table and stared into the nearly empty depths of his coffee cup, hoping to find some inspiration there. He had spent the last hours poring over a German work that stubbornly refused to give up its secrets to his translation.

The apron-clad proprietor passed by, taking a cracked glass bowl of sugar to another table, and carrying with him the aroma of the slaughterhouse. Raoul kept his head down, afraid he'd be forced to order another cup of the foul-smelling brew. In addition to his problems with the German, and his dislike of the coffee shop, he felt homesick for the seascape and the rolling fields of his native Charente-Maritimes, on the southwest coast.

As a boy, he'd been groomed to leave the small town where he grew up, to make something of himself in Paris or the wider world. His father had handed over his education to the village priest, Father Maurice, who had used Raoul for his own pleasure and directed him to achieve. But was any of it what he really wanted, or was he just following another man's dreams?

Fortunately, some joy arrived in the person of his friend Silas Warner.

"The party last night was memorable only in that I met a man with the most wonderful fireplace, right in his bedroom!" Silas said, as he landed, much like a fantastical bird, in the chair across the table. Raoul almost expected him to bury his head under one arm. Instead he called insistently for a cup of tea and a currant bun.

They lived in rooms side by side in an old house, and the coal-fired boiler in the basement was touchy at the best of times. On a bitter January morning like the one they were experiencing, sunlight glaring off the accumulated snow and ice besieging the London streets, their rooms were about as toasty as the Brighton seashore. At least Blanton's was warm, thanks to the blazing oven in the rear, which contributed to the sooty ambiance.

It was clear to Raoul that his friend had not returned home the night before, as he still bore traces of the charcoal he brushed over his eyelids to make himself look more seductive. His outfit, flamboyant enough for a Saturday night, was out of place on a Sunday morning. The ends of his white lacy cuffs were dirty, and his red and orange waistcoat was buttoned incorrectly, as if he'd scampered quickly from someone else's bed early that morning.

Raoul stared at his first English friend. Silas was more robust, his pale cheeks red from the cold, while Raoul was slim and of a more Mediterranean complexion. Though no one would call Silas handsome, he exuded a joie de vivre that Raoul, whose looks were better, could only admire.

They had met in the hallway of the house only a week after Raoul had arrived in London for his first overseas posting, situated at the French Embassy. Raoul had been eager to sample British cock, and Silas had been more than willing to accommodate him.

Quickly they had discovered that while Raoul was open to a variety of different positions, Silas's equipment was on the small side and not enough to satisfy him at either end. They had become the best of friends instead.

They were of similar height, though Raoul's hair was dark and curly while Silas's was corn-yellow and as flat as if it had been ironed. They were the same age, though, twenty-five, and both on their own in the world.

"And what of you, my little cabbage?" Silas asked. "Did you step out last night?"

Raoul shook his head. "I have been given a German document to translate by the undersecretary. I was up late poring over my dictionary trying to make sense of it."

The server brought Silas's tea and the currant bun, which he dropped on the wooden table with a clatter, then stalked away. "Perhaps I can help you with that," Silas said, before he began to devour the bun.

Raoul looked curiously at his friend. "But you don't speak German at all."

Silas nodded. "But last night I heard about a man who is a tutor and translator in foreign languages. I am told his German is excellent. You could go to him for help."

"I don't know," Raoul said. "The undersecretary expects me to be able to translate even the most complicated documents."

"I am sure that Mr. Marsh can help you with the utmost discretion," Silas said. "The rumor is that he is some kind of diplomat himself, of course on the QT."

"What does that mean, 'on the QT'?"

"It's a new phrase I heard recently. In confidence, or just between us."

"On the QT," Raoul repeated, though his French accent was much different from the broad vowels of Silas's northern dialect.

"Mr. Marsh and his lover, a titled gentleman if you please, host an occasional soirée at their home in Ormond Yard." Silas leaned forward confidentially. "And I have it on the best of authority that Richard Pemberton is a regular guest there."

Pemberton was a barrister at Gray's Inn, one of the four Inns of Court and a mainstay of the British legal profession. He was also the subject of Silas's current obsession. Raoul had heard many descriptions of the finery of his haberdashery, of the elegance of his robes, and how handsome he was in his white wig. "You know, some of the elder barristers look like they have chickens perched on their heads when they head off to court. But not Richard Pemberton! He is the very embodiment of British jurisprudence."

"And you wish to fuck him," Raoul said.

"Have you not listened to me, you silly bird?" Silas demanded. "I only want him to employ me as his clerk. He is too fine a cloak for me to wear. I prefer to be able to look at it regularly." He smiled. "Plus, he pays the best wages of any at Gray's Inn, or so I have been told. And I have heard that his chief clerk is leaving for a position in the halls of Parliament, which means each of his staff will move up."

"How does your employment issue relate to my translation problem?"

"You must seek out Mr. Marsh for help with your German," Silas said. "And while you are there, use your boyish charms to gain an invitation to this Saturday evening's soirée."

He looked satisfied, but Raoul was still baffled, so Silas continued.

"And of course you must bring your very best friend in the world, whom you will assure Mr. Marsh will provide the appropriate adornment for his salon. There I will encounter Richard Pemberton, and use my boyish charm to gain an interview for the position in his office."

"And what if instead he offers you a position in his bed?" Raoul asked with a smile.

"Then I am sure he will have a fireplace in his rooms!"

Raoul returned to his bedroom, but after spending several more hours with his German *Wörterbuch*, there were still several passages that had him baffled. He knocked on Silas's door late that evening. When Silas answered, he was shirtless and his feet were bare. He wore only a patch of purple and yellow Indian silk tied across his midsection like a sarong, a style he had adopted after bedding a Hindu sailor passing through London.

"I didn't mean to interrupt," Raoul said, even as he tried to peer around Silas to see if there was a man in his bed.

"No interruption. Just airing out the goods," Silas said, and he flapped the sarong in the air a few times. Raoul felt a stiffening in his loins even as he knew it was not a good idea to pursue it.

"I wanted the name of that translator you mentioned, if it's not too much trouble."

"Of course not." He backed into his sitting room, decorated with similar fabrics hung on the walls along with a few naughty photographs of male athletes, in and out of their sporting costumes. Raoul wondered if he would ever be open enough about his desires to display such images publicly.

Silas bent over to write the name and address out for Raoul, and the sarong slipped aside to reveal the deliciously round globes of his ass. It would only take a moment, Raoul thought, to drop his trousers, grab the jar of ointment from beside Silas's bed, and plunge his stake into his friend's ass.

But some relationships were better to remain chaste, he reminded himself. Silas turned around and the sarong replaced itself as he handed the paper to Raoul. "Remember, don't leave without an invitation for the both of us for next Saturday evening's soirée."

Raoul was not sure it would be so easy. He had to admit to his boss that some of the German he'd been asked to translate was beyond his comprehension. And that could result in anger, and perhaps penalties or a demotion at his job. If he couldn't handle what he was directed to do, did he even belong at the embassy?

Chapter 3

Distant Relations

After responding to his father's summons, John went back to his essay and spent the next two hours polishing it. After he handed it to Beller to be sent to the publisher, he yawned and climbed into his bed for a nap.

As he lay in the liminal space between wakening and sleep, he considered a visit from his mother and his sisters. He was fond of Vanessa and Lizzie in an offhand way, as one might be of distant relations. Vanessa had been a baby when he left for Eton and Lizzie made her appearance two years later. It was not until he'd spent a summer at home between Eton and Cambridge that he'd passed any time with them, and his connection to them was more avuncular than fraternal.

Many of his Eton and Cambridge friends had similar stories. Little connection to their families, childhoods without much love. When he was growing up at Shorecliff House, he knew small children from tenant farms or whose parents worked on the properties, and he was envious of the way they ate dinner together, the way mothers would often kiss a child on the forehead, the way fathers, some of them who had worked hard all week, still found the energy to play with a child on a Sunday afternoon.

Was it strange that he longed for that kind of affection? He would never be able to get it from his parents, that was certain. And he was not aligned toward women. But another man? Was it possible to find someone who would want more than a quick encounter, who might hold him close and whisper sweet things into his ear?

His mother's health had always been poor, and he had few memories of her from his childhood. Though as he picked up his box of letterhead to return it to the desk drawer, he remembered very clearly the first time his mother had taken him to a stationer's shop, in Truro, shortly before he was to leave for Eton.

She had allowed him to pick the cream of the paper, and to choose among several sets of type. It had his personal crest embossed at the top, followed by *Lord Therkenwell*, and then below that *Shorecliff House, Cornwall*. He was to use it, she explained, to write regular notes home from school. "Always with your best penmanship, John," she had said. "Remember, a lord is noted not only for his words but how he expresses them, in speech and on the page."

When he came down to London from Cambridge, and his father bought him this flat where he was to reside until marriage, one of the first things he had done was order new stationery. *Russell Square, Bloomsbury, London* replaced the Cornwall address.

Now he reflected that his mother must have always known he would leave her, for school and then college, and then his own life. Perhaps she had favored his sisters because she would have them around for longer. And because girls needed tutelage in things their mothers knew, like deportment and dress and table manners.

In any case, she had spent little time with any of them, leaving their nurturing to a series of older nannies who were often as harsh as the taskmasters John wrote about in factories.

He yawned deeply, and the next thing he knew was Beller waking him at four o'clock to dress for his appointment. He smelled the eucalyptus and mint bath salts that rose from the adjacent bathroom where Beller had already prepared his tub.

Beller stood by his bed as he removed his nightshirt and donned the loose linen robe. Silly, for such a short trip, but it wouldn't do to parade naked in front of his valet. He walked into the bathroom and removed the robe, then settled into the warm bath.

The thought of tea with his father was like a black cloud over him. Even though he had a warm place to sleep and food in his belly, he was as unhappy as the ragged children who worked in his father's factory. But his only choice was to do what he could to improve their lot through his words.

He was constricted as much as those factory workers, though his cage was more gilded. Until his father passed and he took his hereditary place in the House of Lords, he must make the world better by continuing his anonymous writings.

And it wouldn't hurt to find a lover, he thought. As he sat in the tub, his cock rose, and he recalled how much fun it had been to play with other boys at school. They had no worry about anyone getting pregnant, so they were free to wag their cocks around, placing them in other boys' mouths or buttocks, purely for pleasure.

He found sex quite enjoyable. In rooms late at night, he and other boys had played at naked games, wrestling each other while coated in grease. The loser had to offer up his buttocks to the winner for penetration, and though he was a decent wrestler, with long arms and legs to wrap around an opponent, he'd often lost those matches on purpose.

Alas, those days had passed, and many of the boys who'd been quite happy to be sucked at college had changed their ways after graduation, focusing on the pursuit of the fair sex. Thus he had tried to find replacements through molly-houses.

He loved the beginning stages. The first delicate kisses, often enhanced by a man's moustache. The tentative gropings, a hand on his cock, another on his buttocks.

And then the ultimate disappointment. Either a man thought he was the best of all cocksmen—and wasn't. Or for whatever reason he found John's sucking technique lacking, when he had it on good authority that he was aces. Some men disdained him because of his fey manners, or the ornament of his clothing.

He sighed. He longed to find a man to converse with, stroll through the park with, and then come home to bed with. He realized that he was tired of these transitory relationships anyway—what he really wanted was a man to love and cherish. But his parents had provided poor role models in that regard, and he did not know if he had the ability to love necessary to sustain a relationship.

Thinking of his failures shrank his cock, so he roused himself from the tub. He dried himself thoroughly, donned his robe once more, and walked out into his bedroom.

Beller was hunched over the bed, using an oxhorn brush to remove any dust from the shoulders of the dark gray jacket. When Beller stood John was reminded of the difference in their body type. He was tall and slim, while Beller was short and stocky. With a pang, he realized that the cost of that suit would have paid Beller's wages for a month.

He had no idea where Beller got his clothes—certainly not from John's tailor. And they were all similar, white shirts and bull-denim trousers, with a close-cut black jacket and hand-tied black bow tie.

Beller had laid out the suit, shirt and cravat on the bed, along with clean drawers. "I have pulled out the dark gray pinstripe suit we discussed," Beller said. "With a white shirt, and perhaps a pocket handkerchief to add a spot of color."

"I like the way you think, Beller." John stood there like a dressmaker's dummy as Beller outfitted him. John noticed once again that Beller avoided seeing his own face in the mirror.

John used various creams and nostrums to keep his skin fresh, something he had learned from watching his mother at her dressing table when he was a young boy. Beller's face was marked with scars from an attack of the pox as a child.

When Beller was finished, John surveyed himself in the cheval looking glass. As usual, his valet had done a stellar job. The tight points of the blood-red handkerchief peeking from his pocket fortified him for what he was sure would be a difficult encounter.

He donned his topcoat and went out into an afternoon of meager sunlight, which glinted off the snow piled at the edges of the pavements in a way that was almost painful to bear. The trees were bare, the air was noxious and sooty, and the streets stunk of fresh horse dung. At least the great sewer network, completed perhaps five years before, had reduced the stench of cesspools. He still had to scrub his hands and face every time he returned from a walk, though.

As he looked down the street for an available hackney, a ragged boy approached him. "Please sir, I'm a respectable boy, I work in the wine shop down the road, but my master won't let me sleep in the back on a cold night, and I'm perishing. Cold as a frog, I am. Could I have a tuppence to get me something hot?"

John dug into his pocket and handed the boy a coin, glad to do something positive on such a grim day. The boy bobbed his head and gave him a gap-toothed grin then ran off, bouncing on his feet to avoid sliding on the icy pavement.

He was fortunate to have a home, he reminded himself. He could have lived at his father's stately pile on Eaton Square had he chosen to do so. But his father had been spending more and more time in London, as he grew increasingly involved in schemes to create British colonies in West Africa, and both he and his father valued their privacy.

Instead, with his father's approval, he'd chosen this suite of rooms on Russell Square. He liked the Bloomsbury area, with its concentration of writers and free-thinkers. Several pubs in the area were lively of an evening, with discussions of art and politics.

A hackney pulled up and he gave the driver his father's address. The interior of the carriage was chilly, and he rubbed his gloved hands together as he stared out at the wintry streets.

Though it was most likely that his father had summoned him to discuss his mother and sisters, he thought back over the last few weeks in case he had done anything that might have reached his father's notice and caused his ire. Yes, he had visited a molly-house near Covent Garden where he had rung in the New Year in the company of a rowdy group of like-minded men, and men dressed as women. Several of them had performed a rakish pantomime.

Other than that, he had kept a low profile of late; surely he had done nothing to cause his father any embarrassment. And he had kept well within his allowance, gambling only occasionally, adding to his wardrobe sparingly.

Unless, of course, his father had discovered his identity as Janner.

As he descended from the carriage in front of his father's house, he brushed that thought away along with a few light flurries of snow that dared to land on the shoulders of his topcoat. He had been careful, and he was not about to stop.

The earl's ancient butler, Samson, answered the door. He was like a cadaver, tall, wizened, and with a distinct lean to his posture. "Good morning, my lord," he said. "Your father awaits you in the sunroom."

Samson took his topcoat and silk hat, then cleared off the flakes with a wire brush. John walked past a line of portraits of his ancestors, from the very first Earl Badgely to his father's father, a stern old man he had been frightened of as a child. His grim visage reminded him uncomfortably of his father's.

John knocked lightly on the frame of the open door, then said, "Good afternoon, pater," as he entered.

"Therkenwell," his father said. "Have a seat." He rang a tiny bell, and almost immediately a housemaid appeared with a tea service on a tray, along with a meager platter of cheese and bread.

He supposed that when he was a small boy, before his grandfather had died and his father had moved into his seat as the new Earl, he had been called John. But it had otherwise been Therkenwell all his life, except to his sisters, who had been unable to form the complicated name as infants and been granted the intimacy to use his Christian name. Even the nannies had called him by his title.

"Terrible weather, isn't it?" John said, as he took a seat at the table across from his father. The city had been besieged by a heavy fall of snow several days earlier, followed by a cold and bitter wind. The trees in the small yard behind the house were barren, the grass withered and brown.

The maid, a small, mousy girl whose name John kept forgetting, poured them both cups of tea, then curtsied and hurried out of the room without speaking.

"I did not call you here to discuss the weather," his father said with a frown, as he poured a smidgen of milk into his cup, barely enough to lighten the brew.

John said nothing, but dropped two lumps of sugar and a healthy dollop of milk into his cup before he looked up at his father. His heart thrummed with all the complaints the old man might make. Since he knew nothing of John's essay-writing, he believed his only son to be a rake, idling his days until his father's death.

"Do you read the broadsheets they sell around the Houses of Parliament?" the earl asked.

John's heart rate sped up. "Occasionally," he said.

"There is a man in particular called Janner whose words I despise." The earl set his teacup down with a clatter. "He clearly has no understanding of the ownership and management of a factory. And yet he employs details that must come from an intimate knowledge of operations such as my own in Nottinghamshire."

John took a deep breath, trying to calm the race inside him. "Surely there are other similar hosiery factories to yours," he said.

"Oh, I don't believe that he has singled me out, or he would have been even more specific. But the demands he makes for what he calls 'worker safety.' Indeed!"

"Has it not been proven that the longer one works, especially when the employee is a child, the greater the chance for an accident with the machinery?" John said carefully. "And thus it would be more cost-efficient in the long run to work even one hour less per shift, with the corresponding savings on down time from a broken machine."

He deliberately avoided the human cost of lost limbs and early death, choosing to focus on the economics.

"I have heard of studies that demonstrate that," the earl said. "But my factory manager says it would be impossible to meet profit projections with a nine-hour shift as Mr. Mundella suggests."

"Have you been there yourself of late?" John asked.

The earl shook his head. "I have been spending increasing time here in the city, working with the Committee for British West Africa I chair, which has important decisions to make regarding the very future of the kingdom. I must trust those I have placed in power beneath me."

He picked up a crust of bread and added a daub of cheese. "Which brings me to the reason why I summoned you here. You must begin to assume your responsibilities with regard to Shorecliff," Earl Badgely said. "It is imperative that you are able to help shoulder the load of managing the estate."

Competing thoughts raced through John's brain. Had the Earl known of Janner's existence, he surely would mentioned that. So half of him was relieved, while the other half annoyed. Though he cherished his Cornish heritage, generations of fishermen, farmers and eventually soldiers, he hated the isolation of the family seat. The winds that swept in from the English Channel to the south or the open Atlantic to the west. The smell of sheep shit and the endless bleating of the lambs.

During his childhood there, he had wanted nothing more than to get away. His only refuge in those times was reading, books supplied to him by a tutor engaged by his father to prepare him for Eton. He couldn't imagine going back there to live.

"You know I have no interest in such things, pater," John said, sipping the oolong tea his father preferred. "Surely Hetherington can handle things on his own."

Hetherington was his father's estate manager, a gruff man more at home with crops and cows than with people. He frightened John, who avoided most contact with the man.

"Hetherington is an employee," the earl said. "You are the heir to the estate. It is your responsibility."

He sipped his tea. "Your mother asks for you, as do your sisters. It would do you well to spend some time with them."

"Vanessa should be ready to make her debut soon," John said. His older sister was seventeen, and though she was no beauty, she had a lively mind and was more interested in education than in entering society. Still, it was a way to get her out of Cornwall. "Surely it would be better for mother and the girls to come to London, rather than have me go there to visit them."

"Your mother's health is parlous," the Earl said, putting his teacup down on the saucer so hard it shook. "She is not fit to travel. It is incumbent on you to make the trip."

John made one last salvo. "Surely not in this weather."

"If the weather lifts in early February, that would be the appropriate time for you to make the journey. You can take the train to Truro, and a carriage will pick you up and take you to Shorecliff."

His brain raced. Could he prepare a broadside or two in advance of departure? In general he tried to time his essays to the latest news from the House of Lords or the House of Commons, but it was possible to write something of an evergreen nature—perhaps even a rant about the muck in the streets or the need for better snow removal.

He picked up a crust of bread and generously applied cheese to it. "This cheese is from Shorecliff, is it not?"

"It is indeed. It is made by a Mrs. Fields, one of the tenant wives, from our own milk."

"Shorecliff cheese always tastes better than any other," John said. "The grass has a special tang to it, from the proximity of the salt water."

"Your trip," his father reminded him.

There seemed to be no way out, so John agreed. Perhaps the weather wouldn't cooperate, or his father would change his mind.

He left Briar House soon after, feeling a heaviness in his chest. Could he claim illness? Or perhaps he should just suffer through the visit quietly, and hope that it would not result in the need for more regular attention to Cornwall. If it did, there was a danger that his printer would find someone else to compose broadsides and John's voice would be silenced.

Chapter 4

African Gold

"What do you know about British interests in West Africa?" Toby Marsh asked his lover, Magnus Dawson, one January morning over breakfast at their house in Ormond Yard, a few blocks from Regent Street.

Magnus shrugged. "I don't hear the drumbeats of war, if that's what you're asking," he said.

"You spent some time on the West Coast of Africa station when you were in the Navy, so surely you must know something of the area."

"I know that over a hundred years ago we built Fort James in Gambia," Magnus said. "That was the first permanent British outpost in West Africa. Right now the whole territory is under the control of the British Governor-General in Sierra Leone. The boundaries of the colony are still under dispute with France and the native tribes, and I believe that is part of what this Committee is attempting to resolve."

Magnus leaned back in his chair. His long legs, flecked with light brown hair, stretched out from below his morning robe. "Why do you ask?"

"The Foreign Office has given me some documents to translate," Toby said. After an adventure with Magnus that had involved the Foreign Office some time before, Toby had been able to establish himself as a tutor and translator of foreign languages, with the understanding that the Foreign Office would send the occasional work his way.

"And what is the substance of those documents?" Magnus asked.

"Each on its own is relatively innocent," Toby said. "They are reports of French adventurers in the area, and their interactions with the native tribes."

"But when put together?"

"I am beginning to see a pattern," Toby said. "There are several documents regarding the growth and export of gum Arabic, groundnuts and other raw materials originating in the interior regions. It appears that rather than concentrate on the slave trade, as we and other European nations have done, the French have been expanding their interests into the savanna regions of the interior under the auspices of merchants and traders."

Magnus reached for his glass of orange juice and drained it. "From what I can see, in a larger sense, there is a battle going on for the control of the riches we believe are located in the dark continent. The Swedes, the Danes, the Prussians and the Belgians are all jockeying to establish a foothold. I don't know much about the agriculture you have been reading about, but I have heard of deposits of gold in the territory of Ghana to the east of the French territory of Cote d'Ivoire."

"That certainly makes it an area of interest for her majesty," Toby said. "She has quite an assortment of tiaras, rings and bracelets and is acquiring more each year."

He had a tutoring client arriving at nine that morning, so he had already bathed and dressed, in a pair of serge slacks and a green loden cloth jacket, with a white shirt and a bow tie. He thought he looked very professorial.

"It will not be as easy as heading to Asprey's," Magnus said. "The

African climate is quite debilitating to the white man. Its rivers are difficult to navigate and horses may only rarely be used, so most exploration must be by foot, with the aid of local porters. As there are great differences between the tribes in areas of behavior and language, it is difficult to cross tribal boundaries without violence. And there is a profusion and variety of wild animals such as white men have never seen."

"Thus the interest by the Foreign Office in these documents by explorers," Toby said. "Now I understand."

He stood and pushed back his chair. "Mr. Brakespeare will be here shortly to go over German chemical terms so that he can understand what exactly he will be importing. What is on your agenda?"

"I have to visit the bank to deal with the latest draft from my brother's investments on my behalf, and then I plan to head to the club for a spot of fencing." As the third son of a nobleman, and a former naval officer, Magnus belonged to two clubs. The London Thames Fencing Club provided him exercise and the British East India Club was quite useful for socializing.

Though the Foreign Office was most interested in Toby's linguistic skills, they recognized that Magnus had entrée to certain posh circles, and part of the stipend they received went to support his occasional contacts with London's elite. And as two men living openly together, they also cultivated acquaintance in London's artistic circles and among men and women of similar proclivities.

When they'd set up their establishment they had hired Will, a houseboy from the home of Magnus's late father, and were teaching him to be a butler and valet, and his boyfriend Carlo, an Italian ruffian who had proved to be a dab hand at cooking and the running of a household. So far, the boys had done a capital job.

When he and Toby reconvened for dinner that evening, Magnus said, "I nosed about this afternoon in search of answers to your questions. After fencing I dropped in at the club. It appears that the French have begun a major push eastward into the savanna regions under the direction of General Louis Faidherbe, the Governor of Senegal."

"Did you discern a purpose in this push?"

"The wealthy women of Senegal, called signares, wear very fine jewelry made of gold filigree. That leads me to believe that the discovery of where that gold comes from is Faidherbe's intent."

"Interesting," Toby said. "Perhaps African gold will be all the fashion in Paris soon."

"And looked down upon as savage by the British," Magnus said. "It will be interesting to see if the Foreign Office continues to send you documents about African explorers. Perhaps the next time Gervase Quinn assigns you such things you might inquire in the most delicate manner why his office is interested."

"How would it serve us to know?" Toby asked.

"My dearest love," Magnus said. "By implicitly condoning our living arrangements, and encouraging us to associate with various other louche individuals, the Foreign Office has placed us in a position of information gathering. And as long as we do not violate any restrictions that might be placed on what we learn, such data could be useful in the way of trade."

"You are a sly one, Lord Dawson," Toby said. "That is a characteristic of yours I find very attractive."

Magnus grinned. "And you may demonstrate that attraction this evening in our bed."

Chapter 5

A Special Boy

Raoul's was one of four desks in a large room on the fourth floor of the French embassy in Knightsbridge, and though he and his co-workers were fortunate to have a window to provide natural light, it looked out on the striated brick wall of the building next door rather than the greenery of Hyde Park.

Morvan's office, on the other side of the building, faced that way, though when Raoul went in there to make his request, the trees outside the window were barren and dabs of snow remained on the highest branches.

As he had expected, Morvan was loath to approve his request to involve an outside translator. "You were brought here from Paris on the strength of your language skills," he said.

The undersecretary was a tall, lean Breton named Georges Morvan and an intimidating figure. He had been an officer in the French army, serving most notably in Algeria under General Louis Faidherbe, before transitioning to the diplomatic service, and he had retained some of that military bearing. His graying hair was short and matched the trimness of his goatee, and his suits were always immaculately pressed.

"There are quite a number of passages that are very colloquial in nature," Raoul said. "My studies were all in Standard German, while I believe the parts I cannot comprehend are more likely to be East Pomeranian."

"Our adventurer was raised in Stettin," Morvan said. "So it makes sense that he would speak a Pomeranian dialect."

Raoul had been given a series of notebooks written by a German man who had traveled extensively through West Africa, particularly in Senegal, which was under French control. He wasn't sure what purpose there was to a translation, for it seemed largely an inventory of his supplies, the troubles he had with his laborers, and the occasional meetings with tribal leaders.

"Let me see the part you do not understand," Morvan said.

Raoul knew from experience that Morvan spoke much less German than he did, but perhaps he had some insight into the Pomeranian dialect that Raoul did not possess. If so, it would be humiliating.

He handed over the journal he had been working with. He had bookmarked each page that had material he did not understand.

Morvan pulled a pair of pince-nez from his waistcoat pocket and balanced them on his nose. He peered down at the text, making mumbling noises.

Then he stopped. Raoul watched Morvan's eyes as his boss looked down the page, then to the next. Then Morvan looked up.

"I can see the difficulty you have been having." He handed the notebook back to Raoul, and returned his pince-nez to his pocket. "You are sure this translator can help you?"

"He comes highly recommended," Raoul said, neglecting to add that the recommendation had come from his one-time bedmate.

"Make sure that your translator can handle the Pomeranian dialect, and that there is nothing confidential in the material you are giving him. Nothing in the work that would compromise French security, or Franco-German relations."

Raoul did not bother to remind Morvan that if he couldn't understand the writing, there was no way he could judge if it was confidential or not. And plus, there had not been anything even remotely confidential in the information about gifts given to tribal leaders. It wasn't as if the man was negotiating treaties, simply exploring the landscape.

It was a small victory. Ever since he was a boy, Raoul had felt he was under the domination of older, more powerful men. For once he'd achieved something against a superior man's wishes and it made him feel stronger.

He sent a messenger to the address on Ormond Yard that he had been given. He introduced himself and his position at the embassy. Did Mr. Marsh have familiarity with East Pomeranian, to assist with a translation?

A response came back almost immediately that Monsieur Desjardins was welcome to call that afternoon.

He left for his meeting soon after hearing from Mr. Marsh. Despite his anger at Father Maurice, he was still an ardent Catholic, and whenever possible he tried to stop at his favorite church in the city, the Catholic Church of the Immaculate Conception on Farm Street.

It was a glorious Gothic building with a magnificent stained glass window over the apse, and as he stepped into the cool nave he crossed himself. Then he sat for a moment in one of the hard wooden pews, pushing away the cares of everyday life to let the sacred slip into him.

Unfortunately, a priest passed by, leading a coterie of young acolytes in white blouses, and he suffered a visceral memory of his time as one of them.

His father, who worked in a vineyard, didn't know what to do with him. Why he always asked questions. Why he preferred to stay indoors and read books instead of coming out to the fields to help with the harvests. His mother's parents had been wealthy merchants, until they were both struck with influenza and died, leaving her and her sisters alone. She considered herself lucky to have married at all, and to have such a handsome, smart child. So she spoiled him when his father wasn't looking.

Then he met Father Maurice, the man who was to become his mentor in all things.

Raoul rose quickly from the pew and hurried outside into the chill January air, hoping the cold would push away those memories, but he was unsuccessful.

Father Maurice had transferred to become the prefect of the École des Pères, the Catholic school every boy in Souvigné attended, when Raoul was ten years old. He was much too young to know that Father Maurice, who had once been a promising priest of renowned intellect, had been transferred to this small village in Charente-Maritime because of his attraction to young boys.

Raoul had been frightened to meet this new priest. He was smarter than all the other students in Souvigné, and worried that the new priest would not recognize this. But after only a few moments, Father Maurice had reassured him, tousling his hair and stroking his shoulder. "You are a special boy," he had said.

Father Maurice provided everything that Raoul's own father did not. Books, intellectual challenges, and then an introduction to the pleasures of the flesh, as he called them. That was strictly between the two of them, the priest had cautioned. If anyone discovered their special relationship then both of their lives would be destroyed.

For many years, he simply accepted the need for secrecy—it protected the only male affection he felt. As he got older, though, he began to recognize that he had been the victim of abuse. It wasn't right for a priest, a man of respect and responsibility in the community, to engage in sexual relations with anyone, no less a young boy. Yet he could not break free of Father Maurice, because to do so would have required an explanation, and he knew that no one in Souvigné would believe him over the beloved priest.

And so his last years as a teen, he suffered, until Father Maurice helped him escape Souvigné for university. He finally broke free in

Nantes, falling in and out of love with a professor and with other students. Then in Paris, where he had been stationed for two years he had an unsatisfying love affair with a married neighbor.

Finally, as he approached Ormond Yard after a walk of some forty-five minutes, he was able to push away the memories of his childhood and relish the freedom of London.

So far in the city, he had found ample opportunity to engage in carnal pleasure, though of late he had found his connections somewhat lacking. They were often crude men who spoke no French, who had no appreciation for art, who wanted nothing more than a quick fuck or wank.

Perhaps if he was able to insinuate himself into the salon that Silas described, he might find men more to his liking. Ones who were of his age, who did not seek to exploit his youth or his body, but were willing to express emotions and share love with him.

As he approached his destination, he surveyed the home ahead of him. It was a simple building, close in with its neighbors, and nothing from the outside advertised it as a place where evenings of ill repute were hosted.

A boy in his teens, in simple yet well-made clothes, answered the door. Raoul presented his card. "I am here to see Mr. Marsh."

The boy's accent was rough but his manners were polished. "Just a moment, please," he said, and he knocked lightly on a side door and then entered the room, closing the door behind him.

Raoul took that time to look around. The first thing he saw was a family coat of arms on the wall. Three red balls at the top, and below them a stag stood on a green mound. Underneath was the Latin phrase "Amatus ab hominibus."

Marsh stepped out of the door where the footmen had gone. "Do you know any Latin, Monsieur Desjardins?" he asked, as he stuck out his hand.

"Many years of study with the priests," Raoul said, accepting the gesture. "Though that is an interesting motto. Loved by men?"

"It's my housemate's family crest," Marsh said. "As far as we understand, the first Duke of Hereford led a contingent in the War of the Roses. His men were exceedingly loyal to him, hence the phrase chosen for his crest when he was granted it." He smiled. "Though it might have a different connotation today."

Marsh was quite a pleasant man, only a few years older than Raoul himself. In other circumstances, Raoul thought, they might become friends. The Englishman was quite handsome, with sandy blond hair well-cut, a dimple in the middle of his square chin. An example of the kind of man Britain turned out with great regularity—sturdily built, a shade under Raoul's height.

They released hands. "How may I assist you, Monsieur Desjardins?"

By then, Raoul had begun to grasp different English accents. Toby's was educated, yet still had some of the flat vowels belying a country youth. "I am quite conversant in German, but as I mentioned in my missive to you, there are certain phrases in a document I am translating that appear to be in an East Pomeranian dialect. Perhaps you could take a look?"

"Of course."

Marsh led him into room which had been fitted out as a study, with a desk that looked out onto the narrow street in front of them. Raoul took a seat beside Marsh and the scent of the man's lime cologne drifted toward him. He opened the folder he had brought, laying out the original pages and then beside them his translation.

"You can see where I am having trouble," Raoul said.

"Ah, yes. East Pomeranian is an East Low German dialect, and with a use of the old first person ending. Can be quite confusing sometimes."

While Marsh focused on the text, Raoul looked around the room. The furnishings were solid but not fancy. There was none of the ornate carving that he had seen in elegant houses, and the sofa across from them was plush but not overly so. It was quite a comfortable room, with a few bookish touches such as the tall mahogany case lined with scholarly texts, and the framed diploma that certified Marsh as a graduate of Pembroke College at Cambridge University.

Marsh began with the first section Raoul had experience trouble with, and it was quite enjoyable working through the complicated German with him, though occasionally Marsh looked at him in a way that made him wonder if Marsh was more familiar with the text than he let on.

It took them the better part of an hour, and Raoul understood why Marsh had such a good reputation as a tutor and translator. He was careful, referring to his own *Wörterbuch* to verify words, and stopped periodically to make sure that Raoul was following.

Mindful of his assignment from Silas, at one point when the traveler mentioned another man accompanying him Raoul said, "I wonder at the relationship between the two men. Do you think they are more than simply friends?"

Marsh looked up at him, his expression bland. "I couldn't say without reading the entire work."

Raoul was frustrated. How was he supposed to introduce his request for an invitation to the soirée?

He tried once more, when the traveler attended a party on his last night on the dark continent, one that appeared to be exclusively male. "It's nice to know that even in faraway places a group of similarly inclined men can gather," Raoul said.

"Indeed," Marsh said, but did not follow up.

When they finished, and Raoul had paid Marsh for his time, he finally had to ask bluntly. "I am given to understand that you host parties occasionally where men of a certain interest can meet others. Would it be possible to obtain an invitation to such an event?" He looked down. "I am only recently arrived in London and have found it difficult to meet other men for friendship."

Marsh stared at him for a moment, and then said, "Well, if you feel you might mingle well with the artistes and boulevardiers who attend, Lord Dawson and I would love to have you. This Saturday, perhaps? Any time after nine in the evening."

"That would be delightful," Raoul said. And then, just like that, he had the entrée Silas had told him to request, which could help his friend, and might be the beginning of a new era in his life in London.

Chapter 6

Encounter

The day after his meeting with his father, John went for a walk. Because the day was relatively pleasant for January, he chose to stroll down Oxford Street toward Hyde Park and the Crystal Palace. The street was busy with store clerks making deliveries, shoppers carrying boxes and bags, and visitors staring up at the architecture.

It was London's best side, he believed, as the vast glass bulk of the Crystal Palace appeared ahead of him. Even the air was cleaner here than in the outlying quarters of the city, where sewage still collected in the streets and the dung of horses remained uncleared.

As he turned past the Cumberland Gate, he was reminded of the Arch of Triumph in Paris, which it was based on, and which he had seen during a trip to France. His father owned numerous operations in the country, and John had accompanied him to inspect them during a break from his schooling.

He stopped to admire the marble and was surprised to overhear a mother and her young daughter. Once when he was home from school he had eavesdropped on a conversation between his mother and Vanessa. She must have been twelve or thirteen then, just coming into her womanhood.

She had said, "You must be very wary of boys," and the woman repeated that very expression, clutching her daughter's gloved hand. As he walked forward, he remembered more of that incident.

His mother and Vanessa had been in the sunroom at the back of Shorecliff House with the windows open. He'd been about to cross the lawn in front of them when he stopped to listen.

"Why?" Vanessa had asked. "John is pleasant enough."

"John is your brother. He must be pleasant to you. But other boys will only be interested in one thing—taking your virtue."

"What do you mean?"

He'd listened, embarrassed, as his mother had explained the sexual duties of a wife, and how contact with a man must be endured for the sake of procreation.

He could see, from the posture of the girl ahead of him, that her mother was explaining the same things to her.

Such was the way of the world, he thought. Instead of entering the park, he turned up Gloucester Road toward Regent's Park. It was a habit of his to notice how dark the sheep there were. Their coats were originally white, and the longer they remained in the capital the darker their coats became from the noxious air around them.

Ahead of him he spotted a young boy selling broadsides. He hurried closer to see if it was the latest Janner. And indeed as the boy called out the headline, he recognized it. He felt warm inside—until a portly man in a heavy overcoat grabbed one of the pages from the boy without paying.

"Here, mister, that's a penny," the boy said.

The man glanced at the headline. "I don't pay for trash!" he said.

When the boy grabbed for the paper, the man pushed him, and John felt obliged to step in. "It is theft to take something without paying for it," John said. "Either return that page to the boy or pay him, or I will call the bobbies on you!"

The man turned on him, his mouth a snarl. Then his eyes

opened. He looked at John, taking in the cut of his topcoat, the ruffled sleeve that stretched over his wrist. "A molly, are you?"

"Even I were, I would have no interest in such as you," John said coldly. "A pork pie stuffed in a sausage casing, and a thief to boot. I reiterate, sirrah. Give the boy his coin or his paper."

Huffing, the main pulled a coin from his pocket and handed it to the boy. He folded the paper under his arm.

John tipped his hat and said, "Good day." Then he turned and began to stride back toward Russell Square, his heart beating rapidly. The nerve of the man, a commoner in cheap clothing, to insult him, a member of the gentry. Usually his outrage led him to write as Janner, so when he got home, he pulled down an empty notebook from his shelf and wrote out the incident, indicating, time, place and what the man was wearing. Those details would be useful at some point, he was sure.

As he closed the book and put it back on the shelf, he wondered if other boys suffer the same conduct when selling his work? The idea remained with him, and became the substance of the next Janner broadside, about the value of work. Regardless what readers might think of broadsides, they were the result of work by writers, editors, printers and salesboys, and each of them deserved to be compensated. To snatch away a page, as the man had done, was a theft against all involved in the production.

He worked all week on this essay, taking quick trips out to spy on the salesboys and see if anyone else tried to take advantage of them. He witnessed hectoring and even one man who spit, and he used those examples as well.

By the time Saturday night arrived, when he had an invitation to a soirée at the home of Lord Dawson and the man he shared a house with, Toby Marsh, he was tired. He was still angry about the injustices perpetrated against the salesboys, and unhappy over his father's demand that he head to Shorecliff.

"I don't know if I shall go out tonight," he said to Beller as evening darkened.

"You have worked hard this whole long week, my lord," Beller said. "See how ink-stained your fingertips are? They are a mark of your industry. Whether you go out or not you must let me work on them."

John sat at the small table in his kitchen. Beller sat across from him with a bottle of rubbing alcohol and a worn cloth, and John stretched out his right hand. Beller grasped it with one hand and used the other to brush aggressively against the ink stains.

"You take very good care of me, Beller," John said, even as his fingertips stung against the abrasion.

"God calls every Christian to glorify him in our work," Beller said. "According to Saint Luke's account in the Bible, Mary Magdalen washed the feet of Christ with her tears at a banquet in the House of Simon." He looked up at John with the hint of a smile. "At least I may use rubbing alcohol instead of my tears."

John laughed. "You are a rogue, Beller," he said. "And that is why I enjoy your company so much."

"And I yours, my lord." When he finished cleaning John's fingers, he said, "and now, are you ready to reward your hard work with some entertainment?"

John smiled. "I am, my good man. Thank you. Shall I wear the tweed suit?"

"I think it is appropriate for the January cold," Beller said. "With a wool scarf and top hat, and your greatcoat over it. Will you need a carriage?"

"No, I have only about a half-hour's walk," he said. "The exercise will give me time to think about my father's summons."

"When are we to leave for Shorecliff, my lord?" Beller asked. "I will have to make preparations."

"My father says in a month's time. But I am loath to press him for a specific departure, in the hope that he will keep postponing it."

Once Beller had completed John's ensemble, John struck out for the walk to Ormond Yard. The night was chilly but clear—or as clear as sooty London could be. He even managed to spot the North Star above him, though it was quickly eclipsed by wafts of smoke coming from chimneys he passed.

Cornwall in February would be quite dreary, he thought, as he turned onto Great Russell Street, past the enormous pile of the British Museum. It was closed, of course, but he gave a nod toward the Egyptian sculpture gallery, one of his favorites. When he came down to London occasionally from Cambridge, he had often strolled through those galleries, peering at the Rosetta Stone as if it could decipher his future for him.

He had so much good fortune in his life, he thought. An allowance from his father that enabled him to live in comfort, his writings as Janner that gave him a purpose. He had Beller for companionship and service. Though he longed for a male companion he had to resolve to continue until such a man arrived in his life.

Two elderly men passed him, one holding the other by the belt so he would not topple, and John tipped his cap at them and wished them good evening. Seeing their connection made him smile all the way to Ormond Yard.

Chapter 7

Appeasing Silas

Saturday evening, Raoul stood nervously at the corner of Ormond Yard and The Duke of York Street. He had dressed in his best frock coat, tight-fitting slacks, and a shirt of fine French linen he had bought with his first paycheck in Paris. He moved anxiously from foot to foot as he awaited Silas, who was to meet him there.

He had gone out on a limb for his friend, after all. He had broached the subject of his sexual inclinations to a stranger and requested, nearly demanded, an invitation to a party at the man's home. Marsh could hardly have refused him, after he'd been paid a significant sum for his translation, with the promise of more work to come if there was additional writing in that infernal dialect.

How would he be received? Marsh had mentioned that his guests were artistes and boulevardiers. Suppose they shunned him as provincial, working class? And even worse, what if Silas's information about the party was incorrect, and the guests were all ordinary men and women, and scorned him or called him names? He thought he might die of embarrassment.

By the time Silas arrived, Raoul was ready to flee, and only his friend's beautiful attire made him feel like he could enter the party, regardless of who was there. Silas looked as much like a peacock as he ever did, with a smart black suit and a waistcoat of lavender brocade and a cravat of royal purple.

"I was about to leave," Raoul said, as they embraced, their cold cheeks touching lightly.

"I had some questions about my toilette," Silas said. "If you had not departed Bryanston Mews so early you might have advised me."

"When I left, you were entertaining, quite noisily," Raoul said. "I did not want to appear to make light of Mr. Marsh's invitation after I had worked so hard for it."

"I had to take the edge off my hunger for male flesh," Silas said. "Had I not done so, I might have propositioned the first man I met inside, and ruined my opportunity to meet Richard Pemberton."

Raoul shook his head. "You are a satyr," he said. "I wonder you can work at all, around satisfying your desire for men."

"It's a challenge," Silas said. "But you might always surprise me. There will be older, powerful men in attendance. Perhaps like your priest? Do you prefer a man to take charge of you?"

"I want a man who is nothing like Father Maurice," Raoul said. "I am a man, and can stand on my own. I no longer need the direction of someone older and wiser."

"And yet you work for just such a man, don't you? You are at Morvan's beck and call, even if not in his bed."

"That is a matter of necessity," Raoul said. "I have much to learn about the diplomatic service, and I can do so by observing Morvan." He frowned. "Though at times I do chafe under his restrictions."

"So the man you want will let you make your own decisions," Silas said. "Understood. I will keep an eagle eye." Then he looped his arm in Raoul's and tugged him down the street.

Two men passed them, both appearing to be mollies, and Raoul was sure that they formed the same opinion of him and Silas.

The two disappeared inside Marsh's home, and he and Silas climbed the steps moments later. The door was opened by the same young footman in very casual dress, who addressed Silas. "Sir?" he asked.

Raoul stepped forward. "Raoul Desjardins. I was here to see Mr. Marsh the other day and he invited me and my guest to come this evening."

"Oh, yes," the footman said. "Please come in."

The party was ongoing in the salon on the other side of the entrance from the office where he had met with Marsh. In attendance were perhaps a dozen men and three or four women—he couldn't be quite certain of two of those in fancy clothes.

They handed their coats to the boy, and Marsh immediately came over to them. "Monsieur Desjardins," he said. "Welcome."

"Please, call me Raoul." He introduced Silas, who received an appraising eye from Marsh.

"And I am Toby, and this is Magnus." He used an arm to pull his lover close. Lord Magnus Dawson was quite a tall, handsome man, with a military bearing. Raoul was struck, as he had been on arriving in Paris, at the diversity among those men who preferred the company of other men.

Some were large and hairy, as Father Maurice, while others were slim and fey. Still others looked like they could be farmers or cart haulers. And yet there was something in the eyes of each one that betrayed them.

Not that all those in the room were men who preferred to bed other men—at least two Raoul recognized were painters, both renowned for romancing their female subjects. Two of the women were quite mannish, while others appeared very feminine.

When Toby and Magnus turned to greet the next guests, Raoul asked Silas, "Do you see your man?"

"Indeed I do. Over there by the fireplace, the man with the velvet lapels."

Raoul was startled to see that the man Silas noticed was not nearly as handsome as his friend had indicated. Indeed, he was at least fifteen years older than they were, closer to forty-five than forty, and heavier than he should have been. A few gray hairs nestled amongst the black.

But then, Silas hadn't intended to bed the man, merely gain a position in his office. "Shall we go over there?" Raoul asked.

"I'll try this on my own," Silas said.

Raoul accepted a glass of gin and found himself in conversation with one of the more masculine of the men. He was an amateur pugilist and sometime fencer, and since Raoul had fenced while he was at Nantes, they talked of sport. He could tell the man was interested in him—sly glances, a hand on his shoulder.

But then he caught the eye of a handsome young man across the room, and his stomach fluttered and his loins tightened. Perhaps there was more purpose for him this evening than merely appeasing Silas.

Chapter 8

That Soirée

John Seales arrived at Ormond Yard somewhat latish, as was his wont. He liked to make an entrance, after all. He had met Lord Dawson at a party soon after graduating from Homerton College at Cambridge, and while they did not become friends, as such, he had a standing invitation to the soirées he and his lover sponsored.

There was always good food and drink and interesting company. Several of the Pre-Raphaelite artists were often in attendance, and one evening he had met the painter Frederic Leighton and his lover, the poet Henry William Greville.

For the most part, though, the soirées attracted men of loose character and often looser pants, which pleased John. There was often dancing, when no one cared about the sex of one's partner. Late in the evening, some young man would undoubtedly shuck his shirt and invite admiring glances.

John could not help noticing, once he was ensconced in a corner of the salon with a glass of gin, that a handsome young man with wavy black hair, heavily pomaded, was trying to catch his eye. They traded glances for several minutes, and then John lazily began to move toward him. He made for John's direction as well.

They met halfway, "You have beautiful eyes," the man said then, the opening salvo in a conversation that would eventually lead them to bed together. *"Les yeux sont le miroir de l'âme."*

"The eyes are the windows of the soul," John translated. He was flattered. His eyes were green, flecked with gold, and his lashes were as long as a girl's.

"I am Raoul Desjardins, from Charente-Maritime by way of Paris," Raoul said. *"Parlez-vous Français?"* The Frenchman's voice sent a tingle to John's loins. And the way he stared soulfully at John didn't hurt.

"I am John Seales," John said. "From London by way of Cornwall. I spent some time in Paris after I left college." John was reluctant to tell the truth, that he was as fluent as an Englishman could be, so instead he added, "I can order a meal and ask where the water closet is, but that's about it."

"I could teach you," Raoul said. "That is, if you would be a willing pupil."

John swooned. He would follow this handsome man anywhere—as long as it led to a bed. He stuck his hand out. At such a party, there was no need to add his title. Better that casual acquaintances didn't know he was a wealthy earl's only son.

Their hands met, and Raoul's grip was strong. It sent flares through John's body. "And what do you do here in London, monsieur?" he asked.

"I am on the staff of the French embassy. A very minor role, to be sure, but at the moment I am very glad that my career has brough me to your city, and to your presence."

John shivered with pleasure. He'd had several French lovers during his year in Paris, and he loved the way the language rolled off their lips. And he loved their lips as well, especially when pressed against his own.

"And what do you do, Mr. Seales?" Raoul asked.

John could not admit his essay-writing to a stranger, so he said, with a sly smile, "I have interests in the arts. Particularly in the art of presenting myself." He put his hand over his breast pocket. "This handkerchief, for example. I find the plum tones a way to bring out the colors of my suit."

"I am quite fond of that color myself." Raoul leaned in close to John's ear. "I have silk drawers in just that shade."

John felt himself hardening at the idea of seeing the handsome Frenchman in his drawers—and out of them. "How very interesting," he said. "I find the contrast of dark," and he motioned to Raoul's groin, "and light," his hand moving back to his own, "to be quite interesting."

"It is clear we share some interests in common," Raoul said. John noticed a certain hardness pressing against Raoul's pants when he motioned there.

"I would agree." John had found that when he took a man to bed without knowing anything about him, their parting was quick and unemotional. There was something about Raoul, however, that made him want to draw out their acquaintance before their cocks did battle.

"But what of other arts beyond fashion?" Raoul asked. "Do you have a taste in painting, for example?"

"I have made something of a study of the male nude," John said. "I would like to point out to you that bearded gentleman in the corner, with the Romanesque curl dangling over his forehead. That is Sir Frederic Leighton. I have seen some preliminary sketches of a sculpture he plans, of an athlete wrestling with a python. He has quite a talent for presenting the musculature of the male form. Have you seen the David of Michelangelo?"

"Only in books," Raoul said. "You have seen it yourself?"

"And observed it for quite some time," John said. "He is quite well endowed for what is supposed to be a mere boy. And his hands! You know what they say."

"That the larger the hands, the larger the—as you would say, endowment?"

"Indeed." John reached over and held up one of Raoul's hands against his own. "My goodness. Our fingers are quite the same length, though yours are somewhat thicker and meatier than my own."

John felt desire resonating through Raoul's hand like the notes from a bass violin, deep and strong. The rest of the room seemed to fade away as they connected, and John could not say how many glasses of gin he drank—but his intoxication was altogether of another sort, having nothing to do with liquor.

"My rooms are simple," Raoul said eventually. "But they are not far. Would you care to see them?"

John let his hand brush casually down Raoul's front, generating only the lightest touch on the Frenchman's groin. "I think there is much I would like to see."

"I must say good night to my friend," Raoul said. "Would you convey my regards to our hosts?"

"Indeed." He watched Raoul move across the room to speak with a man of their age, and felt a momentarily pang of jealousy. Raoul had called the man a friend, but of what sort? He was clearly their kind of man, from the way he held himself and the manner in which he and Raoul kissed cheeks—though he knew that was a French custom.

He said goodnight to his hosts, who both smiled knowingly as Raoul crossed the room toward them. To avoid any embarrassment, John turned to the hallway, where he retrieved his coat and top hat. Raoul joined him there, gathering his own coat and hat, and they walked into the chill of Ormond Yard together.

John felt no chill as he walked close to Raoul, holding his gloved hand in the darkness. His cock pressed hard against his pants and he was filled with the exquisite pain of longing.

"You are from Charente-Maritime, you said," John said. "I have only passed along that area of the coast but I recall it as lovely."

"I am from a small town called Souvigné, not far from the

Atlantic coast, on the outskirts of La Rochelle," Raoul said. "I had no desire to work in the vineyards, as my father did, and his father before him. When I was a teenager, I used to cycle out to the *Plage du Roux* and sit on the rocks there to do my schoolwork. It was a place of lonely beauty in those days, particularly in the winter. It forms a curve, and if I sat in the center and stared forward I felt I could see all the way to the Americas."

"I, too, grew up in a small town," John said. "My home, Shorecliff House, overlooks the Carrick Roads, a tidal estuary that runs into the English Channel."

"I was fortunate that our priest, Father Maurice, recognized my eagerness to learn and encouraged me to continue my studies in the university at Nantes."

"I had no choice in my education," John said. "I was sent to Eton as a boy of ten, as my father, and his father before him. I was eager to get away from Shorecliff House, even though there was no ocean anywhere close to Eton, just the Fellows' Pond and the River Thames. I did some punting as a schoolboy, though as often ended up in the water if we got into boat-fights."

He smiled. "Much as the men of your family toiled in the vineyards, I toiled in the fields of learning. I could not envision myself as far away as you, but I did find the salt water and the movement of the tides soothing as a boy, and I still feel connected to my home in Cornwall. Though I would not care to live there now."

He looked at Raoul. "For one thing, there is a severe shortage of handsome Frenchmen there."

"Just as there are no handsome Englishmen in Souvigné," Raoul said, his words forming a cloud which merged with those John's speech created.

By the time they reached Raoul's rooms in Bryanston Mews, John was chilled to the bone, yet ravaged by an inner fire that could only be quenched by intimate contact with his new acquaintance.

Raoul warned him before he put the key in the lock that the building might be cold, but it was warm compared to the outdoors.

They both shucked their heavy coats and stood by a radiator that brought a waft of heat through the house. Raoul took John's hands in his own. "Let me warm you, *mon cher*," he said.

John's hands tingled, and he pulled Raoul towards him. Their cold lips touched briefly, then again, as they both fell into the kiss.

John put his hand against the back of Raoul's neck and held him close, and their bodies swayed together in an unheard rhythm. Very quickly, the warmth of the room penetrated them, and they moved awkwardly to disrobe each other.

"You have so many buttons," Raoul complained with a smile.

"I usually have my valet undo them," John said. "But then, I had no idea that this evening I would meet a handsome man who would wish to undress me. Had I realized, I would have worn something easier to remove."

"I do not mind," Raoul said. "I find it erotic to reveal a lover's body, piece by piece. Especially one as handsome as you."

John did not consider himself particularly handsome. His face was angular, his thin brown hair sometimes unruly. But he did revel in the perfection of his body. It was slim but muscular, the result of regular bouts of fencing. He eschewed the rich foods that had caused his father to suffer from gout. His stomach was flat, and he carefully trimmed the hair around his cock to make it stand out. Though it was only of average girth, it was long and allowed him to penetrate men with impunity.

Once they were naked, they continued to kiss and rub together until John could hold back no longer. "I would like to feel myself inside you," he said. "Would that please you?"

"I am usually the dominant partner," Raoul said. "So I am not accustomed to receiving. However, if that would please you, I will open myself."

"I shall be very careful," John said. "Do you have grease?"

"In a jar in the cupboard." Raoul lay his long, naked body on the bed, crossing one leg over the other to expose his buttocks. John sat down beside him, taking a fingerful of the grease and using it to massage Raoul's opening, which soon blossomed, exposing his rosebud. "You are so beautiful," John said, fingering the hole. "I am like a bee probing the opening of a delicate flower."

Raoul groaned with pleasure. John inserted one finger, then two, feeling forward for the Frenchman's prostate, and was rewarded by deep moan as he found it. "There you are," he said, his voice husky with lust. "And there I shall be."

He lay down beside Raoul, cock at buttocks, and gently pushed forward. He met only the barest of initial resistance, which implied to him that Raoul was not such a virgin to anal intercourse as he might have said.

John pushed forward, his cock enveloped by warmth, as sweat trickled down his back. He pulled Raoul close, pushing his cock farther in, and then built a slow rhythm that had the Frenchman bucking and moaning beneath him. As he neared his climax, he reached around and roughly grabbed Raoul's cock, jerking him as John spilled inside him.

It was truly a delightful culmination to an evening he had at one time been loath to enjoy. Thank goodness Beller had prompted him.

And then, all thoughts of his valet fled as Raoul leaned in to kiss him once more.

Chapter 9

Priapic Adventures

As the evening wore on, Magnus was intrigued to watch the way pairings occurred. The lovely young man who had accompanied the Frenchman had made a beeline for Richard Pemberton, with whom he enjoyed a spirited conversation. But then Pemberton had been beckoned away, and spent the rest of the evening with a fey young sprite who danced in one of the vast ballet spectaculars at the Alhambra Theatre. The sprite left cuddled beneath Pemberton's ample arm.

The Frenchman's friend had spent some time with the artistic crowd then, and eventually left with a nondescript young man who seemed frightened of his own shadow. The Frenchman had been quickly appropriated by Lord Therkenwell, and before the two of them drowned in each other's eyes, they had slipped off to bed somewhere.

Magnus and Toby didn't intend the soirees they hosted to be a dating service, but when men paired off together he was happy. Even more, he was delighted when people made new acquaintances outside their circle and discovered common interests.

He had been particularly intrigued to meet Edwin Strong, a

reporter for the *Morning Post*, who had recently returned from an expedition to Sierra Leone. He was tall enough to speak above the crowd, with a thatch of brown hair and a matching mustache.

He regaled the group with tales of endless miles of swampland and jungle. "Crocodiles as long as I am tall were our constant companions, along with swarming tsetse flies that killed our pack animals. Several of our porters abandoned us mid-journey, and I suffered from a case of dysentery. I was cured by a black man who had learned medicine in Bristol and then been repatriated back to Africa."

"Are the Africans as violent as we have been led to believe?" asked a fetching young woman who was on the arm of the painter Dante Gabriel Rosetti.

"They are very tribal," Strong said. "And if a neighbor tribe should encroach on their territory, they will be met with violence. They are also fond of taking members of opposing tribes as their slaves. Indeed many of those brought to British traders are captured by their fellow Africans."

The young woman shivered, and Rosetti wrapped his arm around her shoulders.

Other questions were asked and answered, and it was not until late in the evening that Magnus could draw Strong apart. "What do you think of Britain's chances to increase its foothold in Africa?" he asked.

"We are making a mistake by anchoring ourselves with slavery," Strong said. "The French are doing a much better job by establishing trade."

"And gold?"

Strong shrugged. "I saw little gold while I was there. Mostly crushing poverty in the main port of Freetown, which occupies a peninsula overlooking the bay, and an agrarian lifestyle in the countryside. The whole country is barely larger than Ireland, and half of it is covered in hills and high mountains. My understanding is that gold is more prevalent in Senegal, far to the east."

"Could gold be a motivating factor in British interest in conquering those territories?"

"You know about the Golden Rule, don't you?" Strong smiled and the edges of his mustache rose. "He who has the gold makes the rules."

Magnus laughed. "Much truer than the one we were taught in chapel."

"Indeed. The British have an outpost in the Gambia, while the French have staked out Senegal since 1659. If there is gold to be found, the French will claim it."

After the last guest left he and Toby trudged up the stairs to their bedroom, leaving the chaos below for Will and Carlo to clear up. "I spoke with Strong further about Africa," Magnus said, as they began to remove their clothes. "He believes that the French have a lock on Senegal, which is where the gold is reputed to come from."

"That might explain why the Foreign Office is interested in West Africa," Toby said. "First, because there might be other deposits of precious metals in the unexplored interior."

"And second to keep the French from whatever riches Senegal might yield," Magnus added.

"As usual, we are two minds of the same thought," Toby said. "However, the letters I have been translating have little or nothing to do with gold. They are more like reports of general conditions on the ground in West Africa. The names and addresses of the recipients, as well as the senders, have been removed, and I have the feeling that some of these might be messages that were intercepted by the government before being sent on to their intended audience."

"Why do you think so?"

"I believe that the future of British exploration in Africa is an issue of great concern to her majesty's government. The Committee on British West Africa was convened last year by Earl Badgely of the House of Lords, and it is said to be considering moves to thwart French expansion on the continent."

"Every colony that France gains is another square on the global chessboard," Magnus said.

"And it would not please her majesty to see the *Tricolore* erected where the Union Jack might otherwise triumph."

"Interesting," Magnus said, and he yawned. "Please do not consider my expression as a lack of interest in your ideas, my love. Merely that at this point in the night my thoughts lean more toward sleep than discussion, or any priapic adventures."

In unconscious imitation, Toby yawned as well. "Though I am ever at your disposal when it comes to priapic adventures, I will agree with you. Tomorrow is another day."

Chapter 10

As I Am

Raoul was pleased to wake on Sunday morning to find John's naked body beside him under the quilt. He pulled himself close to his sleeping lover, and his cock hardened as he pressed against John's buttocks.

Sadly, John turned on his side to face Raoul before he could gain any purchase. But then John said, "What a lovely way to awaken," and kissed him deeply.

That kiss was enough to convince him that the night before had not been a fevered dream. John swung his leg over Raoul and pressed their bodies together, leaning his head back and offering his neck for kisses. Raoul obliged.

"I believe I owe you a debt from last night," John said, as they frotted beneath the eiderdown.

Raoul paused in his attack on John's pale neck. "And what is that?"

"You opened yourself to me, but we slept before I could return the favor." He reached down for Raoul's stiff cock. "I believe you are ready now."

Raoul tossed back the quilt and the cool air of the room sent tingles across his naked flesh. He grabbed the jar of grease and returned to the bed, where John lay wantonly, his legs open and his cock stiff as a flagpole. Then John lifted his legs to his chest, wrapping his arms around them and offering the winking rosebud of his hole. "I should very much like to see your face as you fuck me," John said.

"Then I can but oblige." Raoul greased his fingers first, pressing them to John's hole, which welcomed them eagerly. He could see John was no virgin to the reciprocal role. Quickly, then, he greased his own pole and knelt by John's legs. He held his cock with one hand and pushed at John's hole with the other, and quickly inserted himself.

John gasped for breath.

"I do not hurt you, do I?"

"Not at all," John said. "But I do call your attention to the width of your fingers, which I noted last night, and compared them to what I believed might be your cock. Its width is quite welcome. The last man there was slim as a pencil and hardly caused any feeling."

"And does that excite you, to talk of your other lovers as I fuck you?" Raoul said, pushing forward.

"The intense look on your face is enough excitement for me," John said. "You are even more handsome when you have a purpose before you."

"And you, too are more beautiful from this angle," Raoul said.

He pushed back and forth as John said, "Yes, there, and there, oh."

They panted, seemingly in unison, as Raoul thrust and John received, clenching his muscles down there to hold Raoul in place, then releasing him. It was a remarkable joint effort, culminating first in John spending over his own chest a moment before Raoul felt his own relief.

"I rarely spend like that," John said, when Raoul had removed his cock and slid up beside John on the bed. "We are a good match."

"Game, set, match, I would say," Raoul said. "Are you a fan of tennis?"

"I am if it means more of what we have been doing," John said. Then he pulled himself up. "I have been known to play a game of tennis now and then. But never before have I had such a worthy opponent."

He pulled his watch from the side table and looked at it. "Oh dear, Beller will be quite worried that I did not return home last night."

Raoul pulled away from him. "You have another lover?"

John laughed. "Beller is my valet, *mon cher*. And as far as I can tell interested in marriage with a woman at some point. I would never invite someone from downstairs into my bed."

"I am not familiar with that phrase."

"I was not complete in my introduction to you last night." John held out a hand to Raoul. "John Seales, Lord Therkenwell, if you please. My father is Earl Badgely of the House of Lords, and I am his heir."

Instead of shaking his hand, Raoul took it and kissed the top of it lightly. "*Enchanté*," he said. "Sadly I have no corresponding title to reveal. Does that make me—downstairs—of you?"

John laughed. "No, you are anything but my servant. I could tell that last night." He sat up. "I must find my clothes and return home before Beller sets the bobbies on my trail. May I see you again?"

Raoul stood naked before the bed and opened his hands wide. "Exactly as I am."

He was conscious that spend was caked in his pubic hairs, and his cock had not yet recovered from its exertions, but there was something about John Seales that made him want to be received that way.

John stood and came to him, kissed him and grasped his buttocks. "And you may see me again, exactly as I am," John said. "Though perhaps if we meet in public we shall have to begin the evening in clothing."

"I would not mind that, as long as we do not remained clothed the entire time we are together."

They agreed to meet two nights' hence at a chop house in Russell Square, near where John lived.

John was surprisingly incompetent when it came to dressing himself. It was the result, he said, of too many frills and fripperies, and being spoiled by having a valet. But Raoul donned a silk dressing robe, and between the two of them they got John respectable enough to go outside and hail a carriage. Raoul stood at his doorway and watched John descend the stairs to the ground level, and just before he walked out the front door John turned and blew Raoul a kiss, which he made to grasp with one hand and plaster against his cheek.

Chapter 11

The Wine Shop

Despite the chill of the carriage as it drove away from Bryanston Mews, John felt suffused with warmth.

He realized it was the first time he had spent the night with a lover, away from Russell Square, and he hoped that Beller had not been too worried.

Unfortunately, when he arrived at home Beller was in a state. "I am glad you are all right, my lord," he said, when he appeared as John entered the flat.

"No need to worry," John said, as Beller took his coat and hat. "I simply had too much to drink and decided to stay over with a friend."

He looked at Beller's face, which was etched with worry. "I am sorry to have caused you distress."

It was time he took Beller into his confidence. "I learned early in life that there was no keeping secrets from the domestic staff," he said.

Beller stowed his coat and hat in the wardrobe. "The best of help take a vow of silence when they enter into service." Beller returned to John to undo his cravat, which he had hastily tied himself upon leaving Raoul's bed.

"Then you know the kind of man I am."

"I know you are a good man, kind to me and the rest of the staff," Beller said.

"But you also know I prefer the company of men to women."

Beller was silent as he removed John's shirt and folded it carefully. John undid his own trousers and stepped out of them, and Beller bent down to retrieve them.

"I have been aware of your proclivities for some time, my lord," Beller finally said. "And though I have been raised to believe that such choices are directed by Satan, rather than by God, I am confident of your character, after these years together." He paused. "I have decided that your choice of bed partners should not be my concern."

John could not help smiling. It was such a relief to be his true self for a moment, and be accepted for it. Just as he had felt with Raoul, he thought his life was coming together.

His heart beat strongly in his chest. "Oh, Beller, you have no idea how much that means to me. To know that you are in my corner."

He realized that he cared for Beller as a friend and confidante as well as a manservant, and that this was the first time that a person who really knew him, and cared for him as well, had been open and accepting. The years of pain, being called names by his father and ignored by his mother, washed away. He could not help smiling broadly.

"If I may be so bold, sir," Beller said. "I am aware that men who ... share your interests can get into trouble of a night. There are dangerous parts of the city, and the bobbies are not always sympathetic to a man of your ilk." He looked up at John. "That's why I was worried."

John clapped him on the shoulder. "You may feel confident that I am aware of places where I could be in danger, and do my best to avoid them. The friend I stayed with last night is eminently respectable and lives in a safe area."

"Very good, sir."

In for a penny, in for a pound, John thought. "Would it upset you, or the household, if my friend were to visit here? Perhaps stay the night?"

"I can only repeat what I said earlier, my lord. The best of help take a vow of silence when they enter into service."

John got the sense that he had pushed Beller as far as he could when the man said, "And now, if you wish, I will prepare your bath."

"Thank you, Beller." John watched as his valet left the bedroom. He felt like a steeplechaser who'd conquered the first few hurdles. Of course there was still a long race left to run. He could never imagine bringing a man home to meet his family, or introducing a lover into casual company. But there were secret corners of the city where he could share time with Raoul, and now he felt that his own home was at last one of those places.

John did not attend church, but he did consider Sunday as the Lord's day, and one of rest. And after his exertions of the night before, he found rest eminently desirable. He napped for part of the afternoon, and read until supper. Then with Beller's help he dressed and went out to a café nearby, which was bright and cheerful against the January gloom. Most of the patrons were of the artistic or political bent. Such freethinkers dressed simply, with long, flowing hair and loosely-fitted dresses, compared to the tight-fitting bodices his mother and sisters wore.

He settled at a table and told the proprietor he would begin with the *croûte-au-pot,* toasted bread with cheese and duck fat in a poultry broth, accompanied by a bottle of French wine in honor of his new acquaintance.

He spied the naturalist and adventurer Alfred Russel Wallace at a table, surrounded by a crowd of admirers, and as he ate he listened closely as Wallace spoke about his book, *The Malay Archipelago,* and his adventures and discoveries.

John began taking notes, almost ignoring a roasted breast of chicken with scalloped potatoes in his eagerness to learn about

Wallace's ideas of natural selection. He was particularly piqued when he heard Wallace say, "Men as a rule ornament themselves more than women, and they do so to be admired by their fellow-men quite as much as by the women."

He leaned in closer, sipping his wine. "There are animals which practice polygamy, where the most dominant male breeds with multiple females," he said. "This has in my observation led to the less dominant males having no outlet for their sexual urges other than that found in the attempt to breed with the least aggressive males of their tribe."

"Do you think that is a reason today why some men choose sexual intercourse with other men, rather than women?" one of his acolytes asked.

"I think it is dangerous to apply the habits of one species to another without considerable research," Wallace said. "Though that is not an area I personally wish to pursue."

His acolyte's face turned red as the crowd around Wallace laughed. John had been wondering if he might write a broadside defending the man's work, but that comment pushed the idea away. Yes, at Eton he had provided sexual service to stronger, more dominant boys—but in some of those cases he had been the penetrator, rather than the recipient, so he knew that Wallace's ideas could not be applied so easily.

By the time he was brought a small wheel of delicately flavored cheese, Wallace and his acolytes had departed, and John focused on the completion of his supper.

The rich meal led him back to bed, allowing him to rise on Monday morning to face the blank sheet of unlined letter-paper, ready for his next missive.

He stared at the page for quite some time, unable to muster up his usual anger against the oppressors. He simply felt too good. The memory of Raoul's lips, his fingertips, the smooth skin of his legs, all transported John into a feeling too good to push away.

He recalled Wallace's ideas that men who preferred sex with other men were merely those who were not strong enough to attract the attention of a woman. Clearly not the ideas of a man who'd never had his cock sucked by another!

And yet, he recalled Beller's worry for his safety. Perhaps that could be the subject of Janner's next broadside. That men who loved other men should be safe in their pursuits, neither fearing the hand of the mob or the long arm of the Queen's men. He could avoid the issue of whether any of them would prefer to be with women if that possibility was available.

He began to write. "Why should the government care what goes on between men? What gives the Queen the right to enter into a man's bedroom and criminalise what he does with another?"

He crossed those lines out. Even for a broadside writer such as Janner, those were impossible sentences to put forward. He tried several other contexts, slicing through each with the nib of his pen. Beller approached several times with offers of tea and cakes, but John pushed him away each time.

How was it that he could write about the miseries of others so eloquently, but the problems that were closest to his own heart remained impenetrable?

He was not the first to raise the issue of worker rights, particularly those of women and children. In a sense, he had, as the American P.T. Barnum had put it, merely jumped on the bandwagon of others. There he could wave his flags knowing that he was surrounded by others who felt the same way.

No one else had yet taken up the flag in this case. And he knew that while there were those who valued his words, they would be as Isaiah wrote of John the Baptist, the voice of one crying in the wilderness.

It was a miserable day. He had begun on such a high note, with the memory of Raoul piercing him providing an inner warmth though a slight discomfort as he sat. But more time on the hard wooden chair combined with his inability to express what he wanted. He became surly as his shoulders ached and his heart sank. Janner had always been the outlet for his deepest thoughts, the armor he donned to fight the world's battles, but this was a fight he could not win. He could not even begin the first salvo.

Then he recalled the boy from the wine shop, and how the owner would not let him sleep in the building on a cold night. That was unjust and cruel. And that, perhaps, was a cruelty Janner could lacerate.

He stood up hurriedly. "Beller!" he called. "I need to go out."

Beller appeared in his nearly soundless way. "Should I draw you a bath?"

"No. I don't intend to go far, or to socialize with anyone I might know. Bring me a shirt and trousers and a woolen jumper."

Beller raised his eyebrows. "You do not have a wide selection of jumpers, my lord. And none of any distinguishing color."

"Just a jumper, Beller. I need to go out."

Beller left the room, and after scribbling a few notes, John went to his bedroom. Beller had already laid out a pair of wool trousers, a shirt of heavy cotton, and a jumper he remembered wearing in Cornwall. "Excellent," he said. "I apologize for being short with you. It's just I have an idea."

"I am aware of your moods, my lord, and I take no offense from them."

He dressed John and handed him his topcoat and a black Homburg hat. "Where would I find a wine shop nearby?" he asked.

He did not normally buy his own wine; Beller took care of that, along with all the other provisions of the house.

"There are two," Beller said. He wrote down the addresses. "We purchase the bulk of our wine from Hambly's, but Steingrob's has a better selection of the Rieslings that you like."

"Excellent." John took the paper and strode out into Regent Square. He quickly found Steingrob's, where an elderly Jew with a white beard and a skullcap presided.

"What can I get for you, sir?" he asked, with an accent redolent of Eastern Europe. "I am Samuel Steingrob and this is my shop."

"I shall browse for a moment or two," John said. He walked the dusty aisles, alert for the boy he had seen on the street. But the only help seemed to be a woman in a floor-length dress and apron, and a young boy with a skullcap like the old man's.

"Do all your boys dress so?" he asked Steingrob. "With a cap on their heads?"

"It is a custom of our people," Steingrob said.

So the boy did not work for Steingrob. He was embarrassed to simply walk out, so he chose several bottles of the Riesling he liked and handed them to the boy, who carried them up to the front of the store.

"My house has an account here," John said. "Lord Therkenwell, Russell Square."

Steingrob nodded. "Yes, of course. It is an honor to have you here."

"Please," John said. "You provide good wine for my table. Please have these charged to my account and delivered."

"Certainly, my lord," Steingrob said.

John left and walked to Hambly's, a few streets away. He did not even have to go into the shop; the boy approached as he did, towing an empty cart. "Boy!" John called, and the boy looked up.

"Do you recognize me?" John asked.

The boy looked down at his feet. "I ain't got the shilling to give back to you," he said. "Spent it, didn't I, to be able to sleep in the stables at the pub."

"I don't want the shilling back," John said kindly. "And I have more to give you, if you will only talk to me for a moment."

The boy shook his head. "Got to get back, or the master will dock me pay."

"What about when you finish work. When the shop closes?"

"I work seven to seven," he said. "And sometimes later, if there is stocking to be done."

"Fine. I shall return here at seven this evening. I will take you to dinner at the pub, if you will only talk to me."

"I ain't do funny stuff with men," the boy said.

"I won't ask you to," John said. "Now, hurry back to the shop. I will return at seven."

Chapter 12

Lederhosen

Monday morning after his weekend adventure with John, Georges Morvan reminded him of a dinner that evening at the Austrian embassy. "The Ambassador's wife has exacted a promise from me, that I will bring all the unmarried men from my staff."

"I will be there," Raoul said. When Morvan had gone into his office and closed the door, Raoul pivoted his chair to address his three colleagues, Alexandre, Hugo and Gabriel. "Are you all attending?"

Upon his arrival in London, Raoul had been notified that he would be required to attend various diplomatic functions, from meetings to formal dinners to balls. As he was an accomplished dancer, and already owned the requisite attire from his stint in Paris, he had no problem with that.

He had learned from embassy gossip that Morvan did not dance, and that his wife, a woman reported to be what the French called *une jolie laide*, had remained in Paris. It was a polite way of saying she was unattractive—or least had unusual looks. Further gossip had revealed she had come to her marriage with a substantial dowry, which enabled Morvan to live the way he did on a public servant's salary.

Alexandre was dating a London girl who worked in a millinery shop, which appeared to interest Morvan quite a lot. He was a dull young man, a mathematician by training, who handled all the numerical analysis regarding trade between France and Britain. "Do we have a choice?" he asked.

"Clearly not," Gabriel said. He was the office peacock. He dressed the way that Raoul longed to, in expensive suits with satin waistcoats. There was never a loose thread or missing button, and his shoes were always perfectly polished. He was quite the Lothario, a charming conversationalist, and single women flocked to him at these events.

Hugo sat at the desk closest to Raoul, and it was never clear to him what Hugo's role was at the embassy. His father was a wealthy industrialist in Marseille, and he had been sent to London to acquire some polish. He was a poor dancer and had few social skills, but he was handsome and exuded wealth, from his gold signet ring to his elegant watch. He often had private conversations with Morvan, at which Raoul assumed he was assigned work, but he never discussed it with the rest of them.

"I hate to dance," Hugo said, when he must have realized the rest of them were staring at him. "And the scent that women wear often irritates my nose."

Raoul had his suspicions about Hugo, who despite his wealth never seemed to be very interested in women. Raoul was very careful not to become too intimate with Hugo in case his officemate should demonstrate an interest in him.

That evening the four of them met on the street in front of the embassy for the short walk to the Austrian Embassy. Raoul wore a black suit, a white shirt with a single pearl stud, a white neckcloth and gray gloves. And while his clothing was serviceable, and similar to Alexandre's, Gabriel and Hugo outshone them both in the quality of their attire.

Raoul hoped that the women would congregate toward those two, leaving him and Alexandre to speak in French in a corner except when they were pressed by their hostess into dancing.

Though he enjoyed dancing, and was quite good at it, as soon as the first round of dancing had concluded, he usually tried to make his escape.

It was not to be, however. Once they had been introduced, several young ladies swarmed around them, having been introduced at a previous event, and Alexandre, Gabriel and Hugo were all peeled away quickly, leaving Raoul on his own. He noticed the *chargé d'affaires* across the room, engaged in conversation with a woman whose solid body matched his, both of them bedecked in medals. The *chargé* often took the ambassador's place at such functions if the ambassador was away, and Raoul worried that the *chargé* would notice him on his own and complain to Morvan that he wasn't doing his job. He turned away and moved over to the table where the punchbowl was set.

He had just helped himself to a cup of punch when a man appeared beside him. He was shorter than Raoul and plumper, and he spoke English with a German accent. "Not a fan of the ladies?" the man asked.

Raoul turned. He hoped that he had not shown any disdain toward the female sex that might have caused someone to see his true inclinations. "My colleagues had admirers from previous balls," he said. "I shall have to wait to be introduced to a dance partner."

"I am Otto," the German said, holding out his hand.

Raoul shook it. "Raoul."

"In my country we have many opportunities for men to dance with each other, without bothering with women," Otto said. "The Schuhplattler, for instance. Do you know it?"

Raoul smiled and lifted his left foot, smacking his heel with his right hand. "Though I believe I should be wearing lederhosen," he said.

"Ah, the smooth feel of the leather against one's skin," Otto said.

"Do you know that it is the custom to wear those without anything beneath them?"

Raoul felt his face flush. Was Otto flirting with him? He could not appear to entertain any advance from another man at a political function. And it was bad enough that he had invited an Englishman to his bed—a German cock would mean treason!

"I have not explored such a situation," Raoul said. He looked around for his colleagues but could not see anyone.

"I own several pair of lederhosen," Otto said. "I wear them when the nasty London weather allows." He smiled lecherously. "Or indoors, of course. But then they are usually removed quickly."

With relief, Raoul heard the announcement that the dancing was to begin. "I must excuse myself," he said. "My boss has promised the ambassador's wife that we will dance."

He put his punch cup down on the table so hard that it spilled over the side and he hurried off to join a line of gentlemen.

He attempted to avoid Otto's glance for the rest of the evening, but sometimes during the turns he could not avoid it. Fortunately his cock, which had risen during their brief encounter, had subsided, and he concentrated on his steps, and on the partners passed to him in the dance.

As soon as the first interval was called, he hurried to the cloakroom. "You don't leave so soon, do you?"

He turned, and saw that Otto had followed him.

Thinking quickly, he said, "My fiancée awaits me, to hear the details of the ladies' dresses," he said. "I cannot keep her waiting or I will forget too much. Good night, sir."

He was afraid that Otto would follow him outside, and he nearly stumbled hurrying down the marble steps, beneath the flag-bedecked portico. Fortunately Otto did not, and he was able to walk home at a pace that befit the soft soles of his dancing shoes.

When he returned to Bryanston Mews, he went immediately to Silas's room. "How can I make myself less attractive?" he demanded, as soon as his friend opened the door.

Silas laughed. "That is not usually a request. Come in."

He walked in, relieved to find Silas alone. He appeared to have been reading by the light of a candle on the bedside table. "Why in the world would you want to be less attractive?" Silas asked. "You have not decided to become a monk, have you?"

Raoul sat on the wooden chair by the bed and described his encounter with Otto.

Silas laughed. "A man flirts with you and you complain? Was he that awful?"

"He was short and round and German," Raoul said. "But more than that, we were in public. At an official function. Suppose my boss had spied me flirting with him?"

"Did you flirt back?"

Raoul felt his face flush. "I might have, a bit."

"Then you can hardly complain that the man pursued you. You are fit enough, and comely of face."

"But I cannot have such a thing happen at an embassy function."

"Then you must practice disdain," Silas said. "You accept only the most commonplace pleasantries. Tamp down your native Gallic charm. Give your name, shake a hand, but refuse to engage in conversation. Smile tightly, nod, and ease away."

"But what if I can't tell at first what his intentions are?"

"Then follow my advice as soon as you do. As it seems you did this evening. Though without the reference to lederhosen."

"He brought them up!"

"But you almost asked him to take them down!" Silas said.

Raoul hung his head. "I believe you are right. I must be more careful in the future."

Silas used his finger to tip up Raoul's chin. "Now, now. You have an Englishman on the hook, so nothing to feel despondent about. And a titled one, at that!"

"The title is his worst feature," Raoul said. "He is much too likely to be recognized. And whenever I am with him I must remember to keep my distance, lest either of us be compromised."

"When do you see him next?"

"Tomorrow evening, we meet for dinner."

"Then you shall be distant during the meal, and close afterward," Silas said.

If only it was that easy, Raoul thought.

Chapter 13

No Better Lie

To make sure the boy did not slip away, John returned to the street across from the wine shop at ten minutes to seven. Through the leaded-glass window he saw the boy moving crates of wine, then the owner locking the door.

Blast, he thought. There must be a back door. He hurried to one side and spotted the boy stepping out into the alley. He watched as the boy bid good night to the owner, who walked in the opposite direction.

John waited until the boy had reached the end of the alley to step into view. "Cor blimey, you scared me," the boy said. "I was coming to meet you, you know. Takes a lot to scare me off a proper meal."

John reached out his hand. "I'm John. What do they call you?"

The boy laughed harshly. "I could tell you evil words, but me parents named me Sid."

"Well, Sid, let's get a meal into you."

They walked to the pub, where John allowed Sid to order whatever he wanted. He choose an eel pie and a jar of whelks, while John ordered the fish and chips—and gave Sid more than half his chips.

He took out a small notebook and a pencil and began making

notes as Sid spoke. In between mouthfuls, he described his working conditions. Long hours of labor, irregular mealtimes, no half-holiday or any time that might be spent bettering himself.

"Did you ever go to school?" John asked.

"Just as a boy. I started to work when I was ten."

"You look hardly older than that now," John said. Indeed, the boy was scrawny and short, though he already had a workingman's muscular arms.

"I'm thir'een now," Sid proclaimed. "Almost a man."

"Indeed. And what are your working conditions like?"

Sid frowned. "The backroom has a low ceiling and always smells of gas," he said. "There's no washroom, either. Old Enoch, what owns this pub, allows me to use the facilities here but only when I buy summat."

John cocked his head. "What do you do when…"

"A public lav if there's one available. Otherwise I find a corner out of sight," he said.

No wonder the streets smelled so foul, if working boys were forced to piss and shit in hiding. That was an important point he could mention in his broadside. Surely even the richest could not complain about better-smelling streets.

He discovered, as Sid talked, that the boy worked close to eighty hours a week, more at the holidays as people entertained and ordered more wine. John shuddered to think of the parties he'd attended where the wine had flowed like water, and some poor boy like Sid had worked overtime to deliver it.

"How much do you get paid?" John asked, as Sid downed the last of the chips. Both their plates were as clean as if a scullery maid had scrubbed them.

"Supposed to be twenty shillings a week, but often me pay is cut for broken bottles or late deliveries."

"Would you take a different job if you could get one?" John asked.

Sid shrugged. "Ain't none to be got. Lucky to have the one I got."

John wrote house boy with several question marks after it. He knew that such jobs were often grueling work, though they usually came with food and roof over his head. He only employed Beller and a maid who came in by the day, taking Sunday as the Lord's day, but he knew many with bigger houses, such as his father's, who kept boys and young men.

At Shorecliff, they had employed stable boys who grew up to be grooms and house boys who carried coal and waited on the other servants. They become footmen and perhaps even butlers. He knew where to find Sid if an opportunity arose to help the boy to a better life.

He pulled a card from his pocket. "This is my calling card," he said. "If you find yourself on a cold night without a place to sleep, present this to my valet and he will give you a coin."

As Sid took the card, John noted how grubby the boy's fingers were. His life could not be a healthy one, perhaps even worse than the ones lived by factory workers. Well, there was something he could begin to do about that.

The next morning he was energized to begin drafting his next broadside. He poured out his indignation on the page as he spelled out the lives of boys living right under his own nose and those of his family, friends and neighbors. It was important that they not be forgotten whenever Parliament got around to drafting a bill.

He worked all day, then relaxed in a bath before dressing for dinner with Raoul. He was unaccountably nervous, though, as he left home that evening. The chophouse was only a few streets away from Russell Square, patronized by many of the Bohemians who lived in the area. He worried that Raoul might not be comfortable there. It was one thing to consort with artists and the more flamboyant members of society behind closed doors, and another to be seen amongst them in public. Raoul had an image to protect, as an embassy employee. He represented his country in everything he did.

And if he admitted to himself, he was worried that the connection that had flourished between him and Raoul at the party, and in bed afterward, might have dissipated. What if Raoul didn't show up? Or if he had some awful excuse about why he had to leave early and wasn't willing to accompany John back to his flat?

By the time he reached the chophouse he was a bundle of nerves, but his anxiety quieted when he saw Raoul approaching along Woburn Place. It was already evening, but in the light of a streetlamp John could see that Raoul wore a broad smile.

John held out his hand, but Raoul said, "May I greet you in the French manner?"

John withdrew his hand and thrust forward his face, and Raoul kissed first his left cheek, then his right. His lips were cold against John's cold cheek, but warmth rose inside his chest.

"It is so good to see you again," John said. "I did worry that perhaps we had burned our candle out on Saturday night…"

"But it flames again," Raoul finished for him. He rubbed his gloved hands together. "This restaurant, it is good?"

"I am happy to show you," John said.

One of the reasons the Woburn Arms was so favored by the local populace was the dimness of the interior. John and Raoul were shown to a table along a side wall, lit only by a lamp hung from the ceiling. From their vantage point they could see only the outlines of individuals—a long dress here, a scarf over the shoulder there.

"I like this place," Raoul said, as they settled. "I feel quite incognito here."

"I believe that is the idea. One can be more of what one is here, without fear of censure."

Raoul picked up the menu, and John said, "I can recommend the porterhouse steak, or the filet of sole. I have had both, depending on my appetite, and both are prepared well. I would stay away from the sausage, though. Its origins are dubious."

"I expect to have sausage later," Raoul said with a grin. "That is, if I am not too bold in my assumptions."

John laughed. "No, you are not too bold. I too hope to have some sausage later."

The proprietor came by to take their orders, and both decided on the filet of sole with a side of haricots vert, and John ordered a flagon of white wine for them to share.

"I had a talk with my valet on Sunday morning," John said, between sips of the dry wine. "He was quite concerned when I did not return home Saturday night. Afraid I'd been caught in a raid somewhere, or that some villain had lured me into an alley and knocked me out."

Raoul looked at him. "He said that?"

"Not in so many words. But I took that chance to take him into my confidence. There is no hiding from one's valet, after all."

"I wouldn't know. I have never been in a position to hire a servant."

"Yes, well, you're traveling in the upper berth now," John said. "Best get accustomed to it. I made sure Beller would not object on any moral grounds if I were to bring you home of an evening."

"You gave him the option?"

"Well, I sounded him out. And he was a bit diffident, but agreeable. He is young, and I treat him well, and he has good prospects if I inherit my father's title and property. He can marry, rise in station to that of a butler, and supervise a whole household. That is a great deal for him to aspire to."

He drank some wine. "And I am certainly not the first man of the upper classes to seek comfort outside of marriage, either of the male or female persuasion."

"I imagine you are correct," Raoul said. A seafood chowder was delivered as an appetizer, and Raoul dipped his spoon and brought it to his mouth, a movement John found unaccountably erotic.

"Quite good," Raoul said.

"How have you fared these past two days?" John asked.

"I work," Raoul said. "My day is filled with correspondence, contracts, and the occasional translation. The undersecretary has taken an unusual interest in the prospect of commerce in Africa, and he has many closed-door meetings, some of which result in more documents than I can manage at once. I was lucky to be able to get out of the office on time this evening."

John was uncertain about whether he should reveal his own occupation, but he dove in. "I write the occasional essay which is published as a broadside," he said. "My last went to the printer on Saturday, and I was at sixes and sevens as to how to follow it up."

"Sorry, I do not understand that phrase. At sixes and sevens?"

"Confused, uncertain," John said.

Raoul nodded. "And what did you decide?"

In a rush, John told him about meeting Sid and giving him a coin, then tracking the boy down and interviewing him about his working conditions.

Raoul smiled. "You have such passion," he said. "I am pleased to see that you can extend that emotion outside the bedroom." He tilted his head. "You and this boy, you only talked?"

"Of course. I would never… oh, no. I am interested in men, not boys."

Raoul said nothing as the fish course arrived, but quickly shifted talk to his childhood, and John discovered that they had both grown up near the sea, both were avid swimmers, and both loved the romance of the open ocean and what it could mean.

By the end of the meal, John was sure that the affection that had sprung up between them was still there. John insisted on paying the bill, and then he led Raoul the few blocks to his flat. "You're sure it's all right that I come up?" Raoul asked.

"Quite sure." John took Raoul's right hand in his, and with his left opened a middle button on his greatcoat. He brought Raoul's hand inside the cloth to feel the hardness beneath his slacks.

In the lamplight, Raoul's eyes were merry. "Well, then, lead on."

John opened the door to the flat, grateful that Beller was not there to greet him. The man had a good deal of discretion, which was pleasant to know.

He hung his own coat and Raoul's on pegs by the door, and left both their hats on the table. Then he quickly led Raoul into his bedchamber, locking the door behind him.

Raoul took him by the shoulders and leaned in for a deep kiss. Their lips and noses were still cold from the January air, but they warmed up the longer they remained in the embrace. "I have been wanting to do that since I saw you on the street," Raoul said at last.

"And I have been wanting to do this," John said, dropping to his knees on the plush carpet. He undid the flies of Raoul's pants and popped out his lover's meaty cock, which he swallowed with great aplomb.

"Oh, my," Raoul said, as John licked and sucked his way along the shaft, pushing aside the fabric to get greater access to Raoul's balls, which he grasped and stroked. "Imagine if we had been able to do this at the restaurant. We would never have eaten."

John pulled off Raoul's cock for a moment. "I could make a meal of this," he said, and went back to sucking.

As he felt Raoul grow close to spending, he pulled his lover's buttocks close and buried his head in Raoul's pubic hair, feeling the tickle along his forehead. Raoul moaned and bucked and then almost without warning spent himself in John's mouth.

John stayed in place long enough to swallow everything, then pulled back, licking his lips and smiling broadly. "That was quite delightful," he said, as he stood up.

Then he began to strip. "I should like to feel that excellent tongue of yours at work," he said. "I bet you can lick my hole in several languages."

Quickly they were both naked, their clothes tossed willy-nilly on the floor, and John was on all fours on the bed, pushing out his hole for Raoul to attack. Raoul was quite willing, beginning with long swipes of his tongue up and down. "This is my impression of an Englishman's speech," he said, between lashings. "All tongue and no sense."

John laughed, even as the sensations rose in him. Raoul sucked in the flesh and blew around the hole. It made farting sounds which made John laugh. "Now I am the German," Raoul said, in the accent of that country.

Then he began poking his tongue into John's hole, in and out, licking his way around. "And this is the way a Frenchman makes love to a man's back bottom."

By then John was engulfed in heat, sweat rising on his brow. He grabbed his own cock and jerked it as Raoul penetrated him with his tongue, and very quickly he found himself spending, the white viscous fluid flowing over his hand and dropping down to the coverlet below.

"I knew I could make you spend that way," Raoul said, laughing, as they rolled onto the bed together.

"With your command of languages," John said, joining in the glee.

They spent another hour together, cuddled on the bed, sharing confidences, until Raoul stood up. "I must go, my love. I have work tomorrow."

John sat up on the bed and watched him dress. "When will I see you again?"

"Friday? You might tell your man you are going out of town for the weekend and spend it in my bed."

"I can think of no better lie to tell," John said.

Chapter 14

Weekend Encounter

Raoul and John spent the weekend together, only going out for meals. "I confess I am more comfortable in my own room than in your more spacious apartment," Raul said on Sunday evening over dinner at the same chophouse where they had first dined as a couple. "When I am with you I am always in fear that your valet should come creeping in on us."

"I had the door locked," John said. "But you are right. Even though I have confessed myself to Beller, a maid comes in to clean, and there are often other tradesmen in and out. It is probably best that the fewer people who knew of our affair, the more protected it is."

They met twice for dinner that week, choosing different restaurants that were equally as dark as the Woburn Arms, and then that Saturday they walked together in Hyde Park. Then on Sunday when the weather was cold they explored the British Museum. John led him to several of his favorite artworks, which Raoul came to realize were all male nudes.

"See this one," John said, as they arrived in front of a sepia-colored print attributed to Agostino Veneziano. "What an unusual scrap of fabric he has on his head."

"Veneziano might have done better to reposition that fabric over the old man's privates," Raoul said with a shudder. "I have no desire to see how I may be in fifty years."

John smiled. "You will still be handsome, I am sure. Look at the detailing of the man's musculature. I'll bet he was still a randy bull at his age."

They moved on to an engraving on pink-washed paper called *Battle of the Nudes*, by the Florentine Antonio Pollaiuolo. "Looks like a fight has erupted in the back room of a molly house," Raoul said.

John leaned in close. "The man on the left with the raised sword is saying, 'My cock is larger than yours!'"

Raoul laughed. "Too bad we can only see the buttocks of his opponent." He pointed to the left. "See there, the man with the axe? He looks quite violent."

"Yes, I think we can agree we have both been lucky to avoid similar events. Though I did attend a party at a molly house on New Year's Eve."

"Did it come to blows?"

John laughed. "One red-faced man with a copious belly wore a stained woman's nightgown and a frowsy wig, and was attended by two other men in nurses' uniforms."

He steered them away from an approaching couple. "As midnight approached he groaned and howled, mimicking the pains of childbirth, and promptly on the stroke of twelve pulled up his skirts and extracted the baby new year. The wooden doll arrived already clad in a Roman toga. One of the wags lifted it up and declared 'It's a boy!'"

"Clever," Raoul said. "I have never seen such a tableau enacted. Only the sight of one man servicing another, or perhaps several in a group."

John shook his head. "I cannot agree to such sharing," he said. "Perhaps because I never had to share any of my toys, I do not have such custom now."

"Nor I," Raoul said. "Tell me, how is Janner's career these days?"

"I have hit a nerve," John said. "The details of Sid's life have outraged many. He introduced me to another boy who works at a tanner's, and another who is an apprentice to a watchmaker. The stories they tell are simply horrific. All I have to do is record them to startle and appall my audience. I have been working hard to prepare enough material to carry through the time I will be in Cornwall."

The following Sunday, after they had known each other for nearly a month, Raoul and John were admiring coats in the window of Farmer & Rogers, a cloak and shawl emporium on Regent Street. Raoul looked up and was surprised to see Alexandre approaching him, with a young blonde woman on his arm. They both appeared besotted with each other.

Raoul tugged on John's arm to turn him away from their approach, but at that moment Alexandre looked up and spotted Raoul.

There was nothing for it but to bull his way through. "*Bonjour, Alexandre*," he said, hoping they would exchange their greetings in French and then be on their way.

But it was not to be. "Hello, Raoul," Alexandre said. "This is Betty. You have heard me speak about her."

Betty was pretty in a classical English way, with blonde curls held tight to her head, dabs of pink on her cheeks, and red lips. She wore a scarlet wool coat over a long dress in a corresponding shade of pink.

"Indeed," Raoul said. He leaned down and took Betty's hand, encased in a white glove, and kissed it delicately. "*Enchanté.*"

When he raised his head, he saw John and Alexandre eying each other. "And this is my friend John," he said. "I am advising him on the French style of a new coat."

"Alexandre always dresses so handsomely," Betty said, giving her beau's name the English pronunciation. "It is a singular skill of the French."

"Betty works for a modiste," Alexandre said. "She is quite the fashionable young woman herself."

"I can see that," Raoul said.

They all looked to Raoul for further introduction to John, but Raoul said instead, "You have an appointment inside, John. We must go," and he steered John toward the door.

"Goodbye," John said, and they all exchanged farewells.

"Who was that?" John whispered when they were in the store.

"My colleague. I did not wish to reveal anything more about you other than your name." He looked at John. "You understand? I am not embarrassed of you, your sex or your title. But I do not want gossip to begin at my office about my choice of friends."

Though he enjoyed spending time with John outside the bedroom, Raoul was still nervous that they might encounter someone who knew either of them. Beyond the obvious complication that they were both male, Raoul knew there were those who disdained any relationship between a Briton and a Frenchman. Tensions were high between the two governments, especially over Egyptian and African issues.

"I understand," John said. "But I do like Silas."

"Silas is one of us," Raoul said. "He understands."

Raoul liked the sense of having John all to himself. He thought himself very clever in keeping secrets, until Morvan called him in on a gray afternoon a week after encountering Alexandre and Betty.

Usually, he walked into Morvan's office, and Morvan motioned him to a seat across from his desk. There they would discuss whatever missives had come in from Paris, or any outstanding issues that required attention.

They walked a tightrope, attempting to develop commerce with another land many of their countrymen considered a mortal enemy, but the conversations between them were always collegial.

That afternoon, though, Morvan did not motion him to sit, so Raoul remained standing. Behind his boss, the windowpane was streaked with rain. Another gloomy London day.

"It has come to my attention," Morvan began, "that you are a *pédéraste*."

Chapter 15

Pineau de Charentes

It was a casual conversation with his father that led John to Janner's next broadside. He joined his father for dinner one evening at his father's club, White's, and as they sat, Earl Badgely called for a bottle of Pineau des Charentes, a marriage between fresh grape juice and young eau-de-vie that John had often seen him drink as an aperitif. It was less strong than Cognac and much sweeter, and John didn't have much taste for it.

But he accepted a glass, and then peered at the bottle after the servant had left. "Why, it is from Charente-Maritime," he said in surprise.

"Do you know the area?" the earl asked. "I have an interest in a vineyard there. The one that produces this bottle." He lowered his voice. "Though we must not bruit that about. My long-standing antipathy to the French might come into question. No matter what I think of their imperialism toward the world, I do enjoy their wines."

John marveled at the coincidence. Raoul came from that very province, and his father toiled in a vineyard. Could it be the one his father had an interest in?

"What do you know of the vineyards there?" John asked.

The earl shook his head. "Dashed bad business," he said. "We've been saved because the vines we grow have been more resistant to a virus that has decimated over 40% of production." He smiled. "The good news is that many of our competitors were put out of business, resulting in widespread unemployment. That has enabled us to pay lower and lower wages and yet maintain production."

John stared at this example of capitalism at its worst. Could this be a story for Janner?

"The French are fools," the earl continued. "The vineyard manager opposed lowering wages on humanitarian grounds. But in a crisis of any kind, it is the strong who survive."

And do so by trampling on the working people, John thought.

"I blame heretics like this Janner," the earl said, and a shock ran through John's body.

"Really?" he asked, his voice a bit strangled.

"He is the talk of the House of Lords," the earl said. "His support of Anthony Mundella's Nine-Hours Factory Bill has caused a number of factory owners to reconsider their policies. That leads to a domino effect, as you can imagine. Why, the manager of my hosiery factory in Nottinghamshire has had to raise wages and cut hours to retain trained staff, who otherwise might migrate to other operations."

"Isn't that good for the workers, though?" John asked. "Surely a few pennies more in an employee's pocket can't hurt the overall profitability of the enterprise."

"Spoken like a young man who lives off the profitability of that factory, and the work of our tenants at Shorecliff."

"I would gladly forego a new suit or an expensive meal if it means workingmen can feed their families," John said, aware he was treading on dangerous ground.

"You're not turning into a damned socialist, are you?" the earl demanded. "The world doesn't need another George Bernard Shaw."

If only my broadsides had his skill, or his reach, John thought, but he did not say anything further, just applied himself to the consommé in front of him.

But he was pleased that his work was getting results, and energized at the idea of exploring the work that went into the wines that graced his table.

The very next day, he went back to the elderly Jewish wine merchant, Samuel Steingrob. The man recognized him immediately. "What can I offer you today, my lord?"

"I am interested in French wine," he said. "But I understand that there has been a virus attacking the vines there. Can you tell me anything?"

Steingrob proved to be very knowledgeable, and within the span of an hour John had learned a great deal about an aphid called *Phylloxera* and the venom injected by it into vines which caused a disease that was quickly fatal to many European varieties. Some vineyards grew a variety called the Ugni Blanc, which was more resistant to the virus, and they prospered.

He mentioned the bottle he and his father had consumed the night before, and Steingrob confirmed it was one of the better ones available on the market. "And it is consistently available," he said, with a frown. "In my opinion, the workmen there are little more than slaves." He tapped the cap on his head. "You can take it from me. As a Jew, I come from a lineage of slaves in Egypt."

Steingrob gave him the name of his importer, whom John tracked down later in the week, and who confirmed what Steingrob had said, and provided John with excellent examples of abuse he had witnessed personally. He requested and was granted anonymity because he did not want to harm his business relationships.

And thus Janner had another subject. With each broadside, he worried that someone might figure out his identity, and then connect him with the earl. Since his father's business practices were increasingly Janner's targets, such a revelation would harm his relationship with his father, perhaps permanently.

Yet, he could not stop. Each stroke of his pen represented a poor unfortunate, a worker driven to exhaustion, a child pulled from school to toil in in the vineyards, a family without enough food because of the father's low wages.

He did not dare to confide the name of his father's vineyard to Raoul, for fear that it might be the very one where his father worked. It seemed doubtful that there would be such a coincidence, and one day he sought out a grand atlas at the British Library. Fortunately, the vineyard where his father's Pineau de Charentes was distilled was many kilometers from Souvigné, where Raoul had been raised.

Such a coincidence would have been all too horrifying for John to consider, and sure to drive a wedge between the two of them. So he did not choose to share the broadside with Raoul, even though he might have provided more details.

Some things were best left unshared between lovers.

Chapter 16

Morvan's Allegation

Raoul's stomach dropped and his mouth became dry. He stood in front of Morvan, in his severe black suit and simple black cravat, and all he could think of was what the undersecretary did in his own bedroom. How would he feel having his sexual liaisons brought up publicly?

"You do not disagree with this accusation of depravity?"

Raoul did not respond, but he hung his head. He was sure he was to be fired, and sent home to Souvigné in disgrace. What would he do there? Work in the vineyard like his father? Perhaps he could learn to be a vintner, work in the caves?

"There is a way you can turn your deviance to the good of France," Morvan said, and that was when Raoul truly knew his fate had been sealed.

"Yes?" he asked timidly.

The undersecretary finally motioned him to a seat. "You are familiar with a British nobleman, Lord Therkenwell?"

"He and I are ... acquainted."

Morvan hmphed. "Acquainted with his buttocks, if my sources are correct."

Raoul felt himself blushing. If the word cock came up in the conversation he thought he would die of mortification.

"Are you aware who his father is?"

They had talked little of their families—whenever John mentioned his father, his cock seemed to wilt. "Earl Badgely, I believe."

"And do you know what role he serves in the British House of Lords?"

Raoul shook his head. It seemed stupid, now, to have engaged in a romantic liaison with a member of the British aristocracy, and not done his diligent research on the man's family and connections. But then, he had been more interested in John's body than his background.

"I do not."

"He is the chair of the Committee for British West Africa," Morvan said.

Raoul permitted himself a small shrug. What was a Briton's interest in Africa to him?

Morvan leaned forward. "You are familiar, of course, with the Suez Canal Company, and our contention with Britain over it."

Raoul nodded.

"Despite British interests in a railroad from Alexandria to Suez, they allowed de Lesseps to finish the canal four years ago. It left both of our countries positioned to explore the interior of the dark continent and explore its riches."

Raoul still did not understand what this had to do with his romance with John Seales, but he continued to listen.

"We are come to a similar position with regard to west Africa," Morvan said. "We have established our footholds in Senegal and Côte d'Ivoire, while the British have theirs in Sierra Leone. It is in France's best interest to stall further exploration of the continent by the British."

Raoul looked out of the window, where a single pigeon huddled against the ledge, trying to avoid the onslaught of the relentless rain.

"Earl Badgely is the prime driver of his country's initiative to explore and conquer," Morvan continued. "Our ambassador has tried to reason with the British and tried to negotiate, but with little outcome. And so the task has fallen to us, to do what we can in this situation."

"Did you wish me to draft a letter to Earl Badgely, outlining reasons why Britain should desist in its exploration?" Raoul asked. "I could research the situation."

"It is already beyond that. It is time for more severe action."

Morvan sat back in his chair and steepled his fingers. "Do you know the penalty for committing sodomy in Britain?"

Raoul swallowed hard. "I do not, sir."

"It carries a maximum prison sentence of life with hard labor."

Morvan was silent for what seemed like a very long time, probably to give Raoul a chance to consider what could happen to him.

All thoughts of exile to Souvigné evaporated. No, he would not return home in disgrace. He would be sentenced to life in a filthy British prison, walking a treadmill to produce grain or some other back-breaking work.

Morvan continued, his tone almost kindly. "Just five years ago, two British men were arrested outside the Strand Theatre for wearing women's clothes. They were charged with conspiracy to commit sodomy with the third son of the Duke of Newcastle. There was quite an uproar. But then, you were in Paris, then, were you not?"

"I was."

"No one could prove them guilty of anal intercourse, so they were sentenced for an offence against public morals and common decency. Instead of imprisonment, they were under government surveillance and control for two years."

Well, that didn't sound so bad, considering the alternative. Would he have to stay in Britain, or would he be returned to France in ignominy?

"The duke's son, Lord Arthur Clinton, was not part of that trial, but he was a suicide later that year, because of the stigma attached to his family."

Suddenly it all became clear to Raoul. This whole charade was not about him at all, but about John Seales and his father. He swallowed hard.

"As you can imagine, it would be quite damaging to Earl Badgely were such charges to be brought against his son. The accompanying scandal might even force him to resign from his position and return to the countryside."

"Are you proposing that I expose myself in an effort to have Lord Therkenwell charged? But surely that would have dire consequences for me."

"Perhaps you should have thought of that before inserting your cock into his ass!" Morvan roared unexpectedly. Then his voice quieted. "Or do you play the woman? Does he penetrate you?"

Raoul's mouth dropped open. "I find the entire subject of this conversation objectionable." He pushed back his chair and stood. "You will have my resignation forthwith."

"Sit down, you stupid boy." Morvan stared at Raoul until he complied. "You are too valuable an employee to be wasted in such a manner. I have other ideas for you."

Raoul's body shook. "What sort of ideas?" he asked.

"A simple threat should do," Morvan said. "A letter on embassy stationery notifying Earl Badgely that it has come to our attention that an illegal and immoral relationship exists between one of our employees—you will not be named—and his son. That unless he resigns from his position on the committee such details shall be posted publicly."

Morvan sat back, a beatific smile on his face. "I think that will do nicely. We remove him, and he avoids the public scandal. You will secure your lover's acquiescence to this plan as soon as possible. And of course you must continue your regular duties as my assistant."

He waved his hand, and Raoul rose and walked back to his desk.

He had no idea how Morvan had ferreted out his secret. He

never spoke of such things in the office. All his encounters in London prior to meeting John had been quick and furtive, and he could not imagine how word of their relationship had reached Morvan's ears. And yet, he did work for an agency that engaged in subterfuge, so he ought to have expected that.

Someone in his own office had spied upon him, presumably at Morvan's direction. How could he continue to work at the Embassy when any one of his colleagues could know such intimate details of his life?

He appeared to be in the same trap which had snared him for Father Maurice. He was at the mercy of a more powerful man—and once again one who was attempting to use his cock to manipulate him.

As he returned to his desk, he looked at each one of his colleagues. Who had betrayed him? Alexandre had his head down, carefully copying numbers from one sheet to another. Was it him? He and Betty had encountered Raoul with John outside Liberty's. Could Alexandre have followed them, ferreted out John's identity?

Then there was Hugo, who never seemed interested in women. Had he spotted Raoul in an indiscreet encounter? He had been to molly houses before meeting John. He and John had been together on the street. Hugo could have spotted them and interpreted the gestures between them. He could not catch Hugo's eye as he was intent on a document he was reading.

Or finally Gabriel, who was Morvan's pawn. Had he been assigned to trail Raoul, to search for a way in which his sexuality could be used against him? He took no notice of Raoul, staring into space as he often did.

He saw the three of them in a different way. They were not friends, certainly, though their work threw them together. Colleagues? Yes, officially. But which one was the spy?

Chapter 17

Unsavory Request

As the days crept forward to John's departure for Cornwall, he hurried to scratch out enough material to keep his printer busy with broadsides while he was away. In addition to his writing about the vineyard workers, trying to tie their plight to the wealthy Briton's consumption of fine wine, he interviewed a boy who tended the fires at a blacksmith's and another who worked at Camden lock on the Regent's Canal.

At the same time, his father sent him a series of missives. His youngest sister Lizzie was showing a great interest in the French language; did he have any books to bring her? His mother felt neglected, after his father's prolonged time in London. Could John stop by Asprey's and pick up a bauble to pacify her?

And finally, one afternoon in mid-February, as he was dressing for dinner with Raoul, a trunk arrived from his father that had to be taken to Cornwall. It sat in the hallway of his flat like a giant reminder that his father took up much too much room in his life, and he stubbed his toe on it as he walked out.

He was still angry about the trunk when he arrived at the

Woburn Arms, but one look at Raoul's desperate face pushed that idea aside.

"My heart, what is wrong?" he asked, as he slid into the dimly lit booth across from Raoul. "You look as if there has been a death in your family. It isn't one of your parents, is it?"

Raoul shook his head. "It is something much worse."

The proprietor came over to take their order, and Raoul said, "May we have a moment, please?"

The man huffed and turned away.

"I am afraid that after I tell you what has happened today, you will not want to eat with me again," Raoul said.

"I very much doubt that. But please, go on."

"I have told you of my boss, Morvan," Raoul said.

"Not a very pleasant fellow, from what you've described."

"No, he is not. And you know, of course, that the embassy staff sometimes uses unsavory means to accomplish their goals."

"Has he asked you to do something unsavory?"

Raoul nodded.

"Oh my heart. You must know that I would never change my idea of you if you were forced to do something that went against your character."

Raoul seemed to be choking on the words. "But it involves you."

John's stomach dropped and he sat back against the wooden bench. "Me? In what way?"

Raoul took a deep breath. "Morvan has learned of my relationship with you."

John crossed his arms over his chest, wanting to retreat into himself. "That is difficult," he said. "And dangerous. Particularly for someone like you, a foreigner, and without the cushion of nobility to protect you. Has he threatened to reveal our relationship to the authorities?"

Immediately he thought of what could happen to him. Arrested, his name thrown into the gutter, his parents rejecting him. Losing his income and title, as well as the friendship of other men who might be in danger. It made his skin crawl and his throat dry.

"He spoke to me of a man named Lord Arthur Clinton," Raoul said. "Have you heard of him?"

John's mouth gaped open. "But of course. Any man who seeks pleasure in the company of other men has. You had not?"

Raoul shook his head. "Morvan said that when this Lord Clinton was exposed as a man who had sex with men he committed suicide because of the disgrace to his family."

"So they say," John said. "But I am confused. Does this Morvan mean to expose you? And me? For what purpose?"

Raoul looked down at the table and explained what Morvan had told him to do.

John stared at him coldly. "Did you know who my father was when you accosted me at the soirée?"

"I did not accost you," Raoul protested. "Our eyes met across the room."

Raoul leaned forward. "Please, you must believe me. I had no idea who you were, or who your father was, when we met. It was only this afternoon that Morvan made these threats toward me."

"And me as well." John could not help the cold tone in his voice. Seeing Raoul's utter despair, he said, "I am not angry at you, my heart. But rather at your evil boss, and all the awful people who would deny our love and keep us apart."

"Then you will continue to see me?"

John's heart melted to hear the tremor in Raoul's voice. He reached across the table and took Raoul's hand in his own. "We will figure out how to face this challenge together. I promise you."

The proprietor came over again, scowling, and they quickly ordered their regular meals. When he was gone, they were both silent, and John's brain raced ahead. "We need time to assess all the possible responses to your Monsieur Morvan," he said. "Do you think he would give you leave to come with me to Shorecliff House?"

"Why?" Raoul asked.

"Because it would remove you from his clutches for two weeks," John said. "You can phrase it to him that the invitation would give you time to assess my relationship with my father and how best to approach him."

"And your family? What would they think?"

"My sister Lizzie has asked me to bring French textbooks to her," John said with a smile. "I shall bring her a French tutor as well!"

They ate, though John had difficulty tasting the food and on the way back to his rooms with Raoul he could not even recall what he had eaten. Then he walked inside and once again stubbed his toe on his father's trunk, still in the hallway.

He yelped and clutched his foot, and Beller appeared. "Is everything all right, my lord?"

"I swear, I do not know how we will manage all my own baggage along with what my father has asked us to transport," John said. "Even with your help." He looked at his valet. "And Monsieur Desjardins will be accompanying us, to provide some tutoring in French to my sister."

"I will help with the bags," Raoul said. He nodded toward the valet. "Under Mr. Beller's supervision, of course."

"It is only Beller," the valet said. "And I will be able to engage a station boy to help."

"I must make one thing clear," Raoul said. "I am not a nobleman, nor have I ever engaged a servant. You need not feel that you must look after me in any way."

"No matter their station, a guest in a noble home is treated the same way as the occupants," Beller said. "Though I will not push my services where they are not needed."

"All will be fine," John said. "As Beller already knows, Shorecliff is a massive pile, and one whole wing is not heated in the winter. Vanessa and Lizzie share a room during the cold months, to avoid setting extra fires. My bedroom is large, with a gorgeous view out to the Carrick Roads. I will ask to have a second bed brought in there for you, to help economize. That will minimize work in looking after the two of us."

Beller nodded, and soundlessly retreated to his own room. John and Raoul went into John's bedroom, avoiding a large suitcase Beller had already begun to pack, and made their way to the bed, where John did his best to shuck off the tension of the evening by applying himself enthusiastically to Raoul's pleasure.

But it was quickly clear that in both cases their thoughts were elsewhere. John retreated to one side of the bed and went back over what they had discussed. What would he do if he and Raoul were exposed? They could flee to the continent, of course, but Raoul would lose his job and his diplomatic connections, and John depended on his father for the largest part of his expenses, though he had a small income from a three-percent consolidated bank annuity left to him by his mother's mother.

Raoul stood up and began to dress. "I shall return to my own room," he said. "We both have a great deal to think on."

"We will be a united front," John said, though he was sure some indecision crept into his voice.

"I believe that," Raoul said. He leaned down and kissed John's cheek, then left the bedroom.

Only a few moments later, there was a soft knock on his bedroom door. It was Beller's custom when John was alone to undress him for sleep.

"Is there trouble, my lord?" Beller said from the doorway. John was naked beneath the sheets, and Beller brought over his nightshirt. "Your look is most unhappy."

"There is. And potentially a great danger. I may be on the road to bringing disgrace to my father and my name. As well as loss of fortune and regard."

"I will stand by you, sir."

John reached out and grabbed Beller's hand and shook it. "Thank you so much," he said. Unaccountably, he yawned, as if Beller's words had lifted a burden from him and now he could sleep. "We will talk more about this in the morning."

"Good night, my lord," Beller said, and soundlessly crossed the carpeting and closed the bedroom door behind him.

Chapter 18

Pawns

The day after his dinner with John, Raoul waited until Morvan was alone in his office to advance his proposition. "I have been invited to Shorecliff House for a two-week visit," he said.

"Two weeks!" Morvan said. "How much buggering must you do before Therkenwell agrees to the plan?"

"I believe an extended visit would cement my relationship with Lord Therkenwell and his family, and make it more reasonable that they should believe any assertions against me and him." He looked down at the floor. "I might arrange for a witness from the family to notice marks of affection between us."

Morvan frowned. "And who is to do your work here while you frolic in this Englishman's bed?"

"I have little on my desk beyond a few contracts to translate. I can get those finished before I leave."

Morvan sighed. "I suppose you can go. I am the one who put you up to this mess in the first place. Well, second place. You are the one who started it all."

Raoul was silent.

"And while you are there look for anything else that we can use against Badgely to force his hand on West Africa. It is extremely important to our government to develop our foothold on the dark continent and control its resources. I am directed by the highest authority to do whatever is necessary to thwart Badgely's commission and force the British to step back their explorations. As well as the vile slave trade. Over fifty years ago, Napoleon established that the French would have no part in such abominations, and it is one of my fondest wishes to see the British be punished for their actions."

Raoul nodded. He was surprised that Morvan was so fervently opposed to slavery, when he worked his own employees so hard.

"Tell Alexandre when you will be away. He will have to pick up what you are not here to handle."

"I'll do that now," Raoul said, and left Morvan's office. He realized that his heart had been pounding during the conversation, and he needed to settle at his desk for a few moments, perhaps with a soothing cup of tea. Morvan disdained all British teas and had Mariage Frères black tea shipped in from Paris.

As he passed by Alexandre's desk, he said, in the French that they always used around the office, "I'm going to make myself a cup of tea. Would you like one?"

Alexandre looked up in surprise. They didn't often make such offers. "Yes, please," he said. "With sugar, if you don't mind."

"Not at all."

The soothing ritual of boiling the water and steeping the tea calmed Raoul's nerves, and he returned to Alexandre's desk with two cups. He laid them on Alexandre's desk and pulled up a chair. "I will be out of the office for two weeks beginning in Monday," he said, as he picked up his own tea.

"Vacation?" Alexandre asked.

Raoul shrugged. He wasn't sure how much he was able to share with Alexandre. "A little of this, a little of that," he said. Then he decided that the only way forward was to be as honest as possible. "You met my friend John the other day."

Alexandre nodded. "We are supposed to create a bridge between our two countries, are we not?"

"Morvan has a different approach to bridges," he said. He lowered his voice. "I have been assigned to learn about John's father through him." He explained about Earl Badgely's committee. "To examine how we might persuade the earl to see things our way about west Africa."

"Intriguing!" Alexandre said. "I wish I had something more interesting to do than accounting. Where will you go?"

"To the family's house in Cornwall," Raoul said. "I have been told it is cold and drafty and that there is a possibility that snow will keep us housebound."

He knew nothing of the sort, but didn't want Alexandre to see this as a vacation, no matter how Morvan phrased it. "You are to watch my correspondence and handle anything you can."

"I cannot speak or read German, as you know," Alexandre said.

"Morvan has some German. Give him anything you do not understand."

They both sipped their tea. "This John, he is your friend as well as the subject of your inquiry?"

"It is awkward," Raoul said.

"I can see that," Alexandre said. "Morvan has asked me to get occasional information from Betty about the clients of the salon where she works. The girls, they overhear so much. But it is uncomfortable to have to ask her."

Raoul looked at Alexandre with a new appreciation. Though he was dull and focused on his numbers, Morvan had him play at the spy game as well. What about Gabriel and Hugo? Were they all pawns in some larger game that Morvan was playing?

For the next two days, Raoul kept his head down and hurried through all his work. But at the same time he watched Gabriel and

Hugo. All of them had occasional conferences in Morvan's office, so that was nothing new. But he noticed every interaction, curious to understand the currents that swept through the office and how they might affect him in the future.

Chapter 19

In Love and War

By the morning, John had resolved not to think about the sword of Damocles hanging over his head, but instead to focus on preparations for his departure for Shorecliff. A noxious fog lay over the city, so he treated himself to a carriage ride to Asprey's on Bruton Street.

It was housed in a lovely building of red brick, and once inside, he introduced himself to the clerk. "I am here to buy something for my mother, on my father's account," he said.

"Let me check the records for your father's past purchases." The clerk rooted around beneath one of the counters and brought out an account book. A page was dedicated to his father, with a list of what he had bought. Several items for his own use, including a gold cigarette case, and a few items John recalled seeing on his mother, including an emerald pendant.

"We have a pin of a similar design that would complement the necklace," the clerk said, and brought it out to display on a velvet cloth.

"I think my mother will like that," he said, though he really had no idea what she would like or not. It was simply a way to complete his errand.

It came in a small presentation box of brown leather, and he carried it out of the store. The fog had lifted, allowing some faint sunlight to appear, and he walked home contentedly. One thing off his plate.

On Saturday, Raoul arrived with a single valise, ready to join John and Beller on the train.

"Oh, good, you are here just in time," John said. "Have you sufficient clothing? We dress for dinner at Shorecliff House. And we may be invited out of a night, as well."

"I occasionally must attend formal events on behalf of the embassy, so I believe my attire will suffice. I do not own a hatbox, though, so I could not bring a top hat."

"I have an extra you can wear," John said. "Beller, you'll arrange that?"

"Of course, my lord," Beller said, and then left the room.

It was a bit embarrassing to John that Raoul, who had only a single case, should see how much clothing Beller had laid out for the next two weeks. Certain items, of course, would be laundered at Shorecliff House, but he needed to be prepared for all sorts of activities. If the weather was clear he would ride, and he and his mother and sisters might call on neighbors or receive them in turn. There was bound to be at least one country dance for which he would need formal attire.

"He is a capital chap, Beller," John said. "He knows that you have spent the night here on occasion, though he would never say anything about the looks I cast your way."

"I would call you a rogue, and perhaps even take you to bed as you are, but right now my mind is occupied with more serious stuff."

John sighed deeply. "I know. But we must take our pleasure where we can. When we can." He stood up. "And now you must help me organize this trunk my father sent over, to see what goods of my own can go inside."

Much of what his father was sending down to Shorecliff seemed to be old files and items of clothing that he no longer fancied. There was, buried at the bottom, a single leather-bound volume whose like John recognized.

"This is the kind of journal my father keeps," he said, holding it up. "Perhaps it will give us some clue as to his feelings about the committee he heads, and how willing he would be to step down from it if we are forced to confront him."

Over cups of Ceylon tea, they looked through the earl's journal. "I am uncomfortable," Raoul said, as they scanned the first pages. "Even though I don't know your father I feel it is an invasion of his privacy to inspect his private thoughts."

"All is fair in love and war," John said. He stared into Raoul's eyes, and thought that while Britain and France were no longer at war his feelings for this particular Frenchman ran very closely toward love.

"Look at this bit," John said. "See how he longs for a bit of female companionship."

"Your parents do not get along?"

"They have had separate bedrooms for as long as I can recall," John said. "And he spends more than six months at a time each year here in London, rather than back in Cornwall."

He sat back against his chair. "My father's title goes back to British nobles of the Middle Ages. Our money came from tin and copper mines, many of which are now closed, as well as from the farms that are part of the estate. When I was a boy, he invested heavily in a hosiery factory in Nottinghamshire, which today provides a significant part of his income as far as I can tell."

He picked up a cup of cooling tea and sipped from it. "The earl does not like to speak of the factory, though. He prefers to be considered a lord of his own manor, rather than a filthy industrialist."

"He does not connect you to the broadside writer Janner?" Raoul asked.

John laughed. "Not at all, though he knows well what the name means, as a born and bred Cornishman himself. He considers Janner a traitor and has railed against his writings to me on occasion. Most recently he mentioned a certain vineyard he owns in Charente-Maritime, where the manager has given the workers a raise in pay to compete with other employers."

Raoul named the vineyard where his father worked. "Not that, certainly?"

John shook his head. "No, I checked as soon as my father told me. His operation is some distance from Souvigné."

He looked at Raoul. "I am certain that if our relationship is exposed, it would not take much for an enterprising writer such as myself to discover the connection to Janner, and further hurt my relationship with the earl. But I must tend to my home fires, as they say. My father wishes me to speak with the estate manager and begin to understand how things work. And use what he calls my educated brain to find ways to keep the people where they are—and of course, in service to him and the estate."

"You will inherit it all someday."

"Yes, but my father is healthy as a horse, despite problems with gout. He is barely fifty years old, and he only came into his title a dozen years ago, when my grandfather passed at sixty-something. I shall have a long time before then."

He sighed. "If I die without an heir, as is likely, the title will pass to a cousin of my father's whom my sisters and I have never met. Which is why it is crucial that I remain in good standing, at least until my father's death, so that I can be sure to provide for my mother and my sisters, should they survive me."

"Why can't your father do that?"

"He is firmly of the belief that they must marry well, as their mother did, and not count on him for support."

"And if you are disinherited, and your father dies before making provisions for your sisters, they could end up with nothing."

"Exactly."

"Do you get any benefit from being the son of the earl? A hereditary tithe or something? The cock of an attractive young field hand?"

"Hardly," John said. "The droit de seigneur only ever applied to men and women." He looked at Raoul lasciviously. "Unless the rules were different in Souvigné."

"Alas, the only seigneur I ever bedded was Father Maurice," he said.

"You must tell me all about him sometime," John said. "But first let us finish with my father's diary."

There was little else to discover, other than that his father was a workhorse when it came to Parliament, with a pervasive sense of loneliness.

"I have always resented him for his sternness," John said. "But now I begin to feel sorry for him."

"Hold back on those feelings," Raoul said. "We must use whatever leverage we have to convince him to change his opinions regarding the committee he chairs, and the need for Britain to combat France by colonizing more of Africa."

"You know he will not step down, or change his mind, on my account," John said. "Of that I am certain. He has already told me numerous times what a disappointment I am to him. Though he has never directly accused me of being a molly, he has come close on several occasions."

"And you don't think the embarrassment would bother him?"

John frowned. "There would be snide remarks made, and he might have to forego visits to his club for a while, but that would be about it."

"And your mother? How would she feel?"

"I don't know," John admitted. "I have not spent much time in her company since I left for Eton ages ago. I believe that she loves me, and cares about my future. But would such a scandal wound her? It would be worse for Vanessa and Lizzie, because it might harm their marriage potential."

He frowned. "All this adds to the burden on our shoulders. I am glad I have you beside me, my friend."

Chapter 20

The Flying Dutchman

Beller appeared at John's bedroom door in his soundless manner on Saturday evening, as Raoul and John were considering what to do for dinner.

"I have purchased the train tickets for tomorrow, my lord," he said. "First-class carriage tickets for your lordship and Monsieur Desjardins, and second class for myself. I have also arranged for a hackney to transport us and our baggage to the station tomorrow morning."

"Very good, Beller," John said. "Why don't you take the evening off, if you wish, since we will be away from London. Perhaps you might wish to visit your family?"

Beller smiled. "That is very kind of you, my lord. It would be good to see my parents and my sisters before we depart."

He left soon after, and John and Raoul had a quick dinner nearby, then retired to John's room for private enjoyment.

On Sunday morning, they took the carriage Beller had arranged to Waterloo Station, where they would take the Flying Dutchman train to Truro. It was a cold day with moisture in the air that presaged snow, and Raoul was glad to climb into the warm carriage while Beller oversaw the loading of the baggage.

"This feels odd," Raoul said, as he looked out the window and watched Beller work. "I have never had a servant before."

"You get used to it," John said. "Beller is very good about fading into the background, and then being there when I need him."

Raoul saw Beller tip the carriage man and dismiss him, and then he disappeared, presumably to find his own seat. People of all ages and backgrounds boarded the train, comparing tickets and lifting cases to the rack above the seats. An elderly Jew, in a black homburg and suit, with a long white beard and white forelocks at his ears, attended by a young woman and a boy, sat across from them.

A group of young boys, all in matching jumpers that identified them as members of a choir attached to a school in Exeter, arrived in a jumble of noise, valises and candy wrappers and Raoul smiled in amusement as they wrestled each other for the best seats.

As everyone settled, Raoul asked, "Do you think we will have any time together at your father's house?"

With a loud belch of steam, the train crept forward. "I certainly hope so," John said. "Especially if we are sharing a room. Do you ride?"

"Only as a means of transportation," Raoul said. "Not for sport."

"If the weather is suitable, we will ride down the coast. It's quite pretty." They sat close to each other as the train racketed through the outskirts of the city, finally reaching the countryside. The views were severe, acres of leafless trees and barren farmland lying fallow for the winter.

The snow held off, and the air seemed lighter, especially as they moved past Reading, then through the rolling downs of North Wessex. They ate lunch from a basket Beller had provided as the Devon countryside passed, talking quietly between the two of them, or occasionally with the boy across from them, who they learned accompanied his sister and their grandfather, apparently a learned scholar, who was visiting a group of his fellow Jews in Plymouth.

They stopped briefly at Exeter, where the rowdy boys departed, and then the train continued through Dartmoor. "Now you will begin to see the true beauty of Cornwall," John said. "We are approaching the Royal Albert Bridge, which was designed by Isambard Kingdom Brunel. It just opened a few years ago, and it is quite a marvel."

It was a high crossing, with quaint villages clustered on either side, and a few sailboats and fishing vessels bobbing in the waves. It did truly appear to be a marvel to Raoul, the more so because it was so far from the city. There were no structures anywhere near as grand in the vicinity of Souvigné. He began to doubt how he would fit in at John's country seat, if even a bridge made him feel inadequate.

In Plymouth, the Jews disembarked, leaving the carriage nearly empty. "I have not been so far from London in my time in England," Raoul said. His feeling of isolation increased as a pair of young people boarded the first-class carriages. They epitomized to Raoul the class of English people that he could not hope to penetrate, and not surprisingly, they recognized John immediately.

"Lord Therkenwell," the young blonde said, as they approached. "How pleasant to see you again." She smiled coquettishly at John, and then Raoul.

"Lady Tyne." John stood and bowed. "And Lord Tyne. May I present Monsieur Raoul Desjardins of the French Embassy in London."

Raoul stood and bowed to both. John turned to him. "The Tynes have a beautiful manor house just outside Truro where my sisters and I have been entertained on numerous occasions."

The Tynes took seats across from John and Raoul. "Do you travel to Shorecliff House?" Lady Tyne asked. Her curls were arranged around her face in a pleasing manner, and she wore a cloak of lavender wool that matched her eyes.

"My father has sent me to handle several errands on his behalf," John said. "And you both? Are you returning home from travels?"

"Only to Plymouth to visit my aunt," Lady Tyne said. She and

John began talk of mutual acquaintances, and her brother turned to Raoul.

"An embassy chap," Tyne said. "What brings you out to the wilds of Cornwall?"

"I am pleased to call Lord Therkenwell a friend," Raoul said. "He wishes to show me the beauty of his home county. And I am to assist his sister with her studies of my native language."

"Dashed difficult," Tyne said. "I have no head for foreign palaver myself. Enough trouble sometimes expressing myself in English."

He laughed, and Raoul felt obliged to laugh with him, though a difficulty in expressing oneself, even in one's native language, did not seem to him a laughing matter.

Tyne pointed out several things through the train window, and eventually they reached Truro. "I shall have Mama send you an invitation to our upcoming ball forthwith," Lady Tyne said, as they all rose. "And you must promise to save several dances for me."

The conductor offered a hand to Lady Tyne as she stepped daintily from the train. Her brother followed, then John and Raoul.

The Tynes met up with their maid and valet on the train platform, and walked off with them, as Raoul noticed Beller descending from the train and heading toward the baggage car. "What was that about?" Raoul asked.

"The Tynes are having a ball, much as I feared," he said. "They had planned to invite my mother, Vanessa and Lizzie, but that would leave them short two men for the dancing. It was most fortuitous for Luella that she spotted us and swooped down on us like a hawk on a pair of juicy mice."

"You make her sound rather predatory," Raoul said.

"She made her debut in London last year, but did not snag a husband from it. This far onto the peninsula we are rather off the map, and good husbands are hard to find for ladies of breeding who do not possess a large fortune."

Raoul smiled. "Does she consider you a possibility?"

"I have known her and Ranulph since childhood. It has always been her goal to marry above her station and move to London, but perhaps if that dream has not come through she will lower her sights."

"And you? Would you marry her?"

"Not for a hundred thousand pounds," John said. In a low voice he added, "Now that I have you."

Raoul was momentarily comforted, until they approached a carriage bearing the crest of the Badgely family. The creature on it appeared to be a badger, over three wavy lines that represented a brook or stream. John's family's motto was Ædificemus.

"You build?" he asked John as they crossed the platform and were buffeted by the wintry air. Raoul adjusted his scarf around his neck.

"Oh, the motto," John said. "Yes, a play on the badger and his building of setts. Though I don't think anyone in this family has built anything in a few generations."

"Perhaps your father hopes to embody the motto by building colonies in west Africa."

John shrugged. "Or he may just see it as a way to line the family coffers."

The coachman and Beller loaded the bags, and then John insisted that Beller ride inside with him and Raoul, rather than up top with the coachman.

"It doesn't do me any good if you catch cold," John said. "Osbert is accustomed to being outdoors in this weather. You're not."

They traveled down a bumpy country road, passing through several small towns, until John announced, "This is Therkenwell."

He pointed out the window at a small hamlet of a half-dozen buildings, including a pub. "My father actually has two titles—Earl Badgely and the Marquess of Therkenwell. Since the marquess is the lesser of his titles, I am granted the use of it as I wait to become the earl."

Raoul peered out the carriage window, frosted with the cold. "It doesn't look like much."

John laughed. "No, it's not. That's why it's only my father's secondary title. Up ahead, now, there's Badgely, along the bank of the Carrick Roads."

"Is that what we're on then, the Carrick Road?"

"Not road but roads," John said. "An old word for river. This is an estuary of the River Fal. Meets up with the Channel at Falmouth. As the crow flies, Badgely and Shorecliff House are very close to Falmouth, but there's no bridge, so our nearest large town is St. Mawes. Which isn't saying much."

Badgely was only marginally larger than Therkenwell, in Raoul's opinion. The ubiquitous pub, in this case The Running Footman. A whitewashed school with a yard behind it where the children could play. A cross street that led down to the water, and a cluster of houses and shops.

Badgely passed by, and they turned down a curving lane. "If you lean over me, you can see Shorecliff House ahead of us," John said. "This is the nicest vista. You get the full effect of the Regency style this way."

Raoul did as he was bidden, feeling John's warmth next to him, but unable to do anything about it because of Beller's presence. The house was built of a pale tan stone, and achieved three levels including the basement, where Raoul presumed the servants lived. The first floor was reached by a short staircase that led to an imposing front door beneath a semi-circular window.

There was little ornamentation beyond two tall rounded pillars at either side of the door, two flattened ones at either corner of the building, and a stone balustrade along the roofline. It did not look particularly welcoming, and Raoul understood why John preferred London.

Once again, he doubted the whole premise behind this excursion. He had hoped it would give him time to find a different solution to the problem posed to him by Morvan, and to enjoy a few weeks with John during which they might deepen their relationship.

Yet the foreboding house seemed to say to him that all his desires would come to naught.

Chapter 21

Shorecliff House

The carriage slowed to a stop at the center of the drive, and Beller opened the door and hopped out, then brought a step around for John and Raoul. The air was cold and crisp, and carried the scent of salt water with it that reminded John with a pang of his childhood.

As Beller and Osbert unloaded the baggage, the front door opened. John was surprised to see his childhood playmate Maisie had been promoted to housekeeper, as her beige linen apron represented.

"Maisie!" John said, and stepped forward to embrace her. "How good to see you again."

She stepped back shyly. "And you too, my lord."

"Come now, Maisie," John said, his breath showing in the cold air. "We were children together! Surely you can use my Christian name."

"I am the housekeeper now, my lord, now that my grandmother has retired and my mother has gone to London with the earl. I have to keep to my place."

John turned and introduced Raoul. "Monsieur Desjardins will be here during my visit to improve Lizzie's French. I have decided that it would be overly lavish to heat a separate bedroom for him, so you may have one of the spare beds brought into my room."

"Very good, my lord," Maisie said. "Your mother awaits you in the drawing room."

"Shall we enter, then, monsieur?" he asked Raoul.

Shorecliff House was very much a working manor house, not nearly as elegant as many John had visited, but he could see that Raoul was impressed. "This is the reception hall," he said, as they walked in. The parquet floor clicked under their heels, and in the afternoon light the walls appeared to have faded since his last visit. "The dining room is to the right, the sitting room to the left."

A footman took both of their coats. Then John steered Raoul to the left, and opened the tall paneled door. "John!" his sisters called in unison, and they rushed over to hug him. Though it was customary for family members to call him by his title rather than his given name, he had been John to them all through his childhood, before his father had become the earl and he had become a lord.

Then he turned to where his mother sat beside the fireplace. She was paler than he remembered, though perhaps that was due to the winter cold, or a reflection of the white linen blouse she wore under a gray woolen jersey. He hurried across the room to her, and knelt to kiss her hand. "Mater," he said. "It is good to see you."

"And you too, my son." She adjusted the lay of her gray wool skirt, which fell to just above her shoes.

He stood and introduced Raoul to her, and then to his sisters. He was surprised at how they'd grown in the year or more since he'd been to Shorecliff. Vanessa's hair was still short and businesslike, just above her neckline, while Lizzie's curls, in the same dark brown, fell in waves from her head. Both had healthy complexions with a hint of red on their cheeks.

"I have brought you a genuine Frenchman to help with your conversational skills," he said to Lizzie. "And he has a trunk of books for you as well."

Lizzie squealed with delight.

"Nothing for me, John?" Vanessa asked. "No mathematics tutor?"

"I have brought you a selection of advanced texts from my college days," John said. "I do not have the head for numbers that you do, but we can spend some time over them together."

Vanessa looked pleased.

"Your sister must be preparing for her debut, rather than poring over musty books," his mother said. "I am glad you have brought another gentleman with you, because I have engaged a dancing master to come several times during your visit to help your sister overcome her ungainliness."

John grabbed Vanessa's hand and twirled her around. She laughed. "My dear sister is anything but ungainly," John said.

Then he turned to Raoul. "I neglected to ask you. Do you dance?"

"I have had to learn, because of the need to attend so many embassy functions," Raoul said.

"Yes, Mater, Monsieur Desjardins is an assistant secretary at the French embassy in London."

"Does your father know that? You are aware of his feelings toward the French."

"My father is concerned with business above all," John said. "If the French stand in his way, then they are his enemies. But if they offer a hand in accommodation, he is willing to accept it."

John remembered the brooch he'd bought at Asprey's for his mother, and stepped out to the hallway to retrieve it from his greatcoat pocket. When he returned, he said, "Pater asked me to bring you this token of his affection," he said, holding out the box.

She took it from him and opened it, and her face softened. "It's lovely," she said. "And it matches a necklace your father gave me." She smiled. "Such a thoughtful man."

Then she glared at John. "You would do well to cultivate such habits."

He tamped down his irritation. After all, he knew little of what really passed between his parents, and it would do no good to reveal the truth of the brooch's acquisition.

They took a midafternoon tea with his mother and sisters. After they finished, he showed Raoul the rest of the house. By then Beller and Osbert had brought a second bed into John's bedroom, and Maisie had seen it furnished with fresh linens.

"What a view you have!" Raoul said, striding across the parquet floor to the large windows, which overlooked the back garden and the Carrick Roads.

"They do call it Shorecliff House for a reason." John joined Raoul there. In winter, the view was even more expansive, as the barren trees opened a broader vista to the water. "That spire you see to the right is St. Just-in-Roseland, our family church. And there, across the water, you can just make out the houses of Mylor Churchtown and the beach along the estuary. Too bad it is so cold—I know a secluded beach where we could swim without the encumbrance of bathing costumes."

He smiled wickedly. "But perhaps we will return when the weather is warmer."

Raoul turned to him. "We are not here to play, John. What is it you think we can do?"

"Why, you must warm my bed for me, of course," John said with a grin. Then he became serious. "We need time to think through the problem with your undersecretary. And you must help Lizzie with her French, as I promised, and we shall dance, and make as merry as possible before the noose slips around both our necks."

Beller knocked discreetly at the door. "When will you be dressing for dinner, my lord?"

"Give us at least an hour or so. Thank you for arranging our clothing in the wardrobe. But monsieur Desjardins and I must go through the rest of the baggage and retrieve the books for Vanessa and Lizzie, and hand around the items my father sent with us."

"Very good, sir," Beller said, and soundlessly closed the door behind him.

John crossed the floor and flipped the lock. "That should give us some time," he said, grinning. "I have been dreaming of you rogering me in my childhood bed all day."

"Who am I to disappoint your dreams?" Raoul asked with a smile. "But I must undress you carefully, because I will have to dress you again after we have finished. When Beller arrives you must show no sign of what we have done."

"I am but a doll in a dress-up play," John said. Raoul came over to him then, and put his cool hand against John's cheek. His flesh rose to meet it with heat, and Raoul's lips moved closer. John opened his mouth to receive those rich pink lips, and they kissed.

The kisses were delicate at first, just touching each other, and then Raoul pulled him close and devoured his mouth, his tongue licking eagerly, John's mouth opening to receive him. "I fear I will not be careful enough," Raoul said, speaking into John's ear. "My wish to take you is so strong."

"Beller will know whatever you do," John said, panting. He opened the top buttons of his linen shirt, feeling the fabric scrape gently across his chest. Then Raoul lowered his head to kiss and lick John's neck. "Oh, god, take me."

Raoul made quick work of the rest of John's shirt buttons, and John slipped it from his shoulders and tossed it to a chair beside the bed. While he did so, Raoul stripped off his own shirt and undid the buttons of his fly.

John did the same, kicking off his shoes and then dropping his trousers, so he remained in his wool undershorts and his socks. Raoul wore silk beneath his pants, and he kept his drawers on as he dropped to his feet, pulled down John's shorts and took his cock into his mouth.

"Oh, my dearest," John gasped at the pleasure of Raoul's velvet mouth. He reached down to run his hands through Raoul's dark curls, feeling a pulsing in himself.

Then he pushed Raoul's head away. "You will not have me so quickly," he said. "Not without my having a taste of you."

He fell backwards on his bed, and Raoul climbed on beside him, heads to cocks. He grabbed Raoul's buttocks through their silk covering, and licked his way along Raoul's body.

"I must," Raoul panted, "must wear these later." He struggled to push them down but John resisted.

"I would love to think of you at dinner in formal wear, with my spend inside, drying against your skin."

Raoul succeeded in wiggling out of his silks, then applied himself to sucking John once again. They both engaged like that, but then all too quickly John felt himself erupting. He pulled back from Raoul to gasp deep breaths as his body quickened and then spent into Raoul's mouth.

Before Raoul could pull away, John was on him again, licking up the outside of his cock, teasing the slit at the top with his tongue, sucking and pulling with his lips, until his lover was wriggling beneath him and muttering in guttural French.

John was not nearly so good at swallowing as Raoul was, and some of the spend slipped out of the corner of his mouth and down his chin. He wiped his hand in it and then rubbed that along Raoul's leg.

"I will need a bath," Raoul said, as he clambered up beside John on the bed. "Or else I will stink of your spend all through dinner."

"My sisters will not know what that smell is," John said, laughing.

"And how do you know that?" Raoul asked. "Are there no handsome stable boys or housemen?"

John pushed his shoulder. "Vanessa is but seventeen," he said.

Raoul leaned on one elbow. "And how old were you when you first tasted of another man?"

"That was different," John protested. "I was at school, with so many other boys. And it was sometimes duty rather than pleasure."

Thinking of it, he rolled on his side. "Can you ride me, horseman?" he asked.

"So soon?" Raoul said. "I must rest a bit."

John pushed back, his buttocks against Raoul's groin, and felt him rising. "Not for long, I feel."

"You are a harsh taskmaster," Raoul grumbled, but he stood up and John watched as he crossed the room to his case, then rummaged through it for the necessary supplies.

His naked body was so glorious, so much a man. Handsomer than any he'd had in London, more experienced in the ways of love than any boy at school or college. His skin was slightly darker than John's paleness, his chest blessed with the dark hair that covered his head and his pubic area. He was as leggy as a colt, and his cock bounced as he walked back.

John lay on the bed, his hands wrapped around the back of his thighs. Raoul climbed onto the bed, his legs dangling off the edge as he licked and kissed the tiny rosette that blossomed around John's hole. Quickly John squirmed with pleasure, feeling each push of Raoul's rough tongue against his tender skin. Then his hole felt empty for a moment, as Raoul prepared a finger coated in oil.

That finger! It plumbed his depths with skill, coaxing the chemicals inside John's body to blossom. Another finger, then emptiness again for a moment. Then the blessed feel of Raoul's cock pushing for entrance.

"Breathe, *mon cher*," Raoul said, his breath hot against the back of John's neck. "With each deep breath I will conquer you further."

"I am your willing captive." John's cock had hardened again as Raoul pushed inside him. He felt a momentary starburst of pain, and then it was pleasure, all pleasure, as he and Raoul were united in an act some decried as buggery, but which they reveled in.

He felt Raoul pushing in and out of him, and he spent a few drops onto the coverlet as Raoul achieved his second release of the afternoon.

Raoul pulled back, and turned John by the shoulder to face him. "Well, then, now what shall we do with the rest of the hour granted to us?"

Chapter 22

Special Friends

Raoul was determined to make a good impression on Lady Badgely. She was his hostess, as well as the mother of his beloved. But hers was a hard shell to crack. He began the process at dinner. "Thank you very much for accommodating me," he said. "I look forward to helping your daughter with her French."

"You are my son's guest, not mine. You may direct your thanks to him."

He tried again, during the soup course. "You have a lovely home," he said.

She shrugged. "It is my husband's ancestral seat. I merely live here."

No matter how polite he tried to be, no matter how many compliments he strewed in front of her like rose petals, she maintained an icy distance.

It was no wonder, he thought, that John's father spent his time in London, and in his private diary longed for female companionship.

John's sisters, at least, were vulnerable to his charms. "John never seems to tell us tales of his social life in London, though we are desperate to hear," his younger sister said. "Can you tell us anything?"

"My most recent social outing was at the Austrian embassy," he said. "There are four of us in my department, and my boss uses us mercilessly as fodder for young ladies who enjoy the attentions of foreign men."

He laid on his French accent. "Alexandre, Gabriel, Hugo and I must represent our country as we dance the quadrille, our arms held high." He demonstrated with his right arm and Vanessa and Lizzie giggled.

"Please, more," Lizzie begged.

He could not tell them much more about the Austrian ball, as he had been so intent on avoiding Otto's unwanted attention. "The invitations usually come to the embassy on gilt-edged paper, at least ten days before the ball itself. They are addressed to Monsieur Georges Morvan, who supervises my area, and after securing our participation he responds on our behalf."

Lady Badgely looked supremely uninterested, but the girls were goggle-eyed.

"The evening of the affair, we leave our coats in the cloak-room and then proceed to the room where refreshments are served. At the Austrian ball they included coffee, tea, and round biscuits with raspberry centers, called Linzer tarts."

"There will be different biscuits served based on the tastes of the hostess," John added.

"Ooh," Lizzie said. It was clear that she was the more ebullient.

"What is the etiquette of asking a young woman to dance?" Vanessa asked. "And must she agree?"

"There is little point to attending a ball if you do not wish to dance," her mother said sharply.

Raoul smiled. "No gentleman is allowed to invite a lady to dance without a proper introduction," he said. "In a public ball, one must seek such from a member of the floor committee. The lady is under no obligation to accept; she may cite a full dance card already, for example."

Vanessa nodded.

"At a private ball, many of the ladies and gentleman have been previously introduced. Such is the circuit of embassy balls, for example. When the four of us entered the room we already recognized numerous previous dancing partners."

He turned to John. "Has that been your experience as well?"

"I am rather out of experience with balls at present," he said. "As the young ladies making their debut are so much younger than myself."

"But you must attend them," his mother said. "However else shall you find a woman of appropriate breeding to marry?"

"Because surely that is the only reason to attend such balls," Vanessa said. "To secure oneself a husband. My mother did so during her Season."

"My family lived much closer to London, and my mother had been presented at her own Season," Lady Badgely said. "It is a family tradition I expect my daughters to follow, even if I am not in good enough health to accompany them. My sister, Lady Rosemead, who lives in London, can stand in my stead."

Vanessa and Lizzie exchanged a look which Raoul could not interpret. Vanessa had a seriousness about her that had skipped her brother and sister. She was more like her mother in that regard. She would have a hard time in her season in London, he thought.

"I should much rather attend college in London than waste a year in a round of silly parties," Vanessa said. "I do not see why I cannot follow in John's footsteps and delay marrying until I am ready."

She turned to Raoul. "I have my sights set on Bedford College for Women, provided that my father will support such an endeavor and allow me to live in his home in London while I study."

"I have met several young ladies at embassy parties who are students," Raoul said. "From Queen's College, I believe. And I had a most interesting conversation one evening with a lady who represents the Women's Education Union. It may be possible for you to satisfy both your mother's ambitions and your own."

That idea seemed to please Vanessa, though Lady Badgely made no comment.

After dinner, he and John and John's sisters made a foursome for whist in the sitting room, while Lady Badgely sat at a desk near the fireplace intent on her correspondence. Did she write to her husband, he wondered? Lady friends or relatives? He had seen how the British were devoted to their letters, calling cards, and party invitations.

At least the four of them chatted cheerfully, criticizing or commending each other's plays. When Lady Badgely decided it was time for her bed, it was clear that she intended her daughters go up with her as well. That left John and Raoul in the sitting room.

"I do not believe your mother likes me being here," Raoul said.

John waved his hand. "It is me she has no interest in," he said. "You are but a side party to an ongoing issue. I do believe she was glad to see me off to school, and she certainly never complained if I wanted to spend my holidays with a schoolmate's family."

"Did you have a special friend at school?" Raoul asked.

"I tended to long for the older boys, who had only one use for me," John said. "Not that I minded. But usually I attached myself to some boy, often one with few friends but a wealthy family, and became his bosom pal. That helped me secure an invitation for a holiday visit. I'd only come to Shorecliff for short stints, to have new clothes made and so on. It wasn't a particularly happy place to grow up."

He turned to Raoul. "And you? Did you have a special friend?"

Raoul shook his head. "Not among the boys. I was always at Father Maurice's hip."

"Did your parents suspect anything?"

"On the contrary, they were delighted that he took an interest in me. My father saw my intellect when I was a boy, and for him there was only one place for a smart lad to go. Into the priesthood, where I could devote myself to learning, and to God."

"You didn't want that?"

"At first I did. But then after I went to college, I realized the inequity in my relationship with Father Maurice. That would be the only chance I ever could have for physical intimacy—with a young protégé. I didn't believe that was right. And the cloistered life of a monastery did not appeal to me, even if I might find a collegial brother. I did not want that kind of rigidity in my life."

"But doesn't your government work give you a similar kind of commitment?" John asked. "Morvan seems to demand as much of you as God might."

"But at least I do not have to wake at all hours to say devotions," Raoul said. Then he grew more solemn. "A duty to one's God is similar to a duty to one's country. And sometimes Morvan asks me to do things that I do not wish to."

"Such as expose me to my father."

"Exactly. Though this is only the largest and most difficult of his demands to meet. Often they are simpler, like attend a certain function and be handsome and charming."

"Surely that's not difficult for you," John said.

"I don't like to feel I am taking advantage of anyone. That I am charming a man or woman and plying them with drink to gain information." He looked down at the table. "Sometimes I have had to do things that your countrymen would not appreciate."

"You French are ever devious," John said, with only a hint of a smile.

Raoul moved his leg beneath the table to touch John's, and felt the warmth of his lover's body surge into his. "I assure you that anything you and I do has been purely for my pleasure, and yours. Not for Morvan's."

"The problem remains. How will we extricate you from this situation? For my part, I care little what my father thinks of me. And I know he already thinks the worst."

"But the shame to your family name? Would you still be welcome in London?"

"Among the men I know, such a reputation would invite a calling card rather than a refusal," John said, though Raoul thought there was more than a bit of bravado there. "My father pays my bills, and though he might stop my allowance he cannot disinherit me without the permission of the Crown, and I doubt he would go that far. I might fall on hard times until his death, but I have survived in the past, and I will survive again."

"That is what I must convince Morvan," Raoul said. "That even if I were to reveal our liaison publicly, it would not cause your father to change his mind about his policies. I will draft him a letter."

"I will help you, if you wish. And then we can post it from St. Mawes."

Raoul agreed, and they went up to the bedroom together. Beller materialized, as if out of the air, and asked if John was ready for bed. "I shall use the washroom," Raoul said, allowing them to complete their ritual together. "And I can take care of my own toilette."

He waited in the tiled room until he heard Beller wish John goodnight. Then he returned, to find John tucked chastely into bed, wearing a nightshirt. "Beller must have his proprieties," John said. Then he quickly pulled the shirt over his head. "Come join me here, my dearest."

Raoul carefully removed his dress clothes and laid them out on a chair by the bedside. He found a nightshirt of his own in the wardrobe and left it easy to reach. Then he climbed into the bed with John, letting their naked bodies press against each other.

He spooned against John's back, his arm over John's chest, and they slept. When he woke as usual, at the first light of dawn, he donned his nightshirt, left John's on the bed beside him, and crept into the other bed, where he fell back asleep.

He awoke to hear John returning from the washroom. They kissed and then, when Beller arrived, Raoul once again gave them their privacy.

That morning, he worked at composing his letter to Morvan, while John and Vanessa went out to meet with the estate manager, and Lizzie did whatever a fifteen-year-old girl in the country did to occupy her time.

It was difficult to find the right words, in French of course, to convey the discussion he and John had gone through during the previous evening. He portrayed the family as cold and distant, none of them that interested in what the others did or thought. That both parents already held John in disdain, and that it would be easy for Earl Badgely to repudiate John without suffering much to his own reputation.

He ended with an encouragement to Morvan to find other means of satisfying his goals.

By the time he finished, he was sure that it was a professional suicide note—in that he would never be able to resume his career at the embassy. Would he be ejected from Britain? Never see John Seales again?

It didn't seem like there was any other choice.

Chapter 23

An Unwelcome Guest

"Raoul has promised to go over French intransitive verbs with me," Lizzie said, as luncheon was finishing. "I am sure Nessie would love to review one of those mathematics texts you have brought, John."

John resisted the impulse to share a glance with Raoul. He joined Vanessa in the small sitting room that adjoined her bedroom and Lizzie's while the French lesson took place in the first-floor morning room that faced out over the back lawn.

"I don't understand why you bother about these things," John said an hour later. "Who cares about the measurement of a circle or the value of pi?"

"I do, and you should too," she said. "You need to be able to understand the work of a surveyor if one comes to handle a dispute over land. And to calculate the area of a field, and how much wheat can be grown there, and how many cows and sheep it will feed."

"That is the work of the estate manager."

"And who is to supervise him? If you are busy gallivanting in London it may be me."

John looked at her in surprise. "Really? That would interest you?"

"After I have some college behind me, perhaps," Vanessa said. "I have already spent quite some time with Hetherington going over accounts. He has taught me a great deal."

John had so far successfully managed to avoid the estate manager. He and his wife and a brood of children lived in a cottage at one edge of the property. He was the one who handled all the business, when the earl was in London, and often even when he was at Shorecliff. Hetherington decided what to plant and what livestock to raise, and managed the accounts of the tenant farmers.

To gather his thoughts about the idea of Lizzie running the estate, he looked through the front window. Under a slate gray sky, a carriage approached. "Are we expecting anyone?" he asked his sister.

She joined him to look out the window. "No. But that is Jacob Lee's carriage. He often picks people up at the railway station."

They watched as the carriage pulled up and a plump young man in a black overcoat stepped out. "That is cousin Marley," Vanessa said. "How odd of him to arrive just now, while you are here."

"Cousin Marley?" John asked in surprise.

The Badgely family tree was a sparse one. The earl was the eldest of three children, two boys and a girl. His younger brother had died of the flu as a child, and his sister drowned as a young woman when she was swept out to sea by a rogue tide. He had only two first cousins, a boy and a girl, and the boy had been caught stealing and was scheduled for deportation to Australia when he died in prison, without issue. His female cousin had died in childbirth, while attempting to deliver a stillborn infant, her first child.

Which meant that the earl had to look farther afield for a successor, in case John could not accede to the title. The next closest was a second cousin, who managed a tin mine and had died of consumption the year before, leaving a son called William Marley.

John had never met the man, though he had become aware of his existence when the earl's second cousin had died. That was when the earl had begun talking to John seriously about his responsibilities.

As he had explained to Raoul, Shorecliff Manor and its estates were entailed to the holder of the title of Earl Badgely. If anything were to happen to John before he had an heir, the property would pass back up the line through his father's second cousin, and then down to Marley.

"Rather presumptuous of him, don't you think?" John asked. "To show up here as if he were already the lord of the manor." He turned to his sister. "Have you met him?"

"He came here over the summer, shortly after his father's death," Vanessa said. "At our father's invitation. I believe the earl meant to look the man over and see what to make of him."

"And what was that?"

"He is rather common," Vanessa said. "His closest connection to gentry was our mutual great-grandfather. I gathered he never met the man, and had never been to Shorecliff, or even knew that there was a connection here, until his solicitors notified our father, who then reached out to him."

Vanessa stepped back from the window. "Mother received a letter from father last week. I assumed it was about your arrival, but Mother would not let me read it. Now I believe that I see our father's hand in this."

"Our father has always been disdainful of me," John said. "I felt that he only tolerated me because I am the heir. But if he is cultivating Marley…"

"We must go down and welcome him," Vanessa said. "And see how Mother reacts when she sees him. That will tell us if he is expected."

"Am I to compete with him?" John asked. "To see which of us is best suited to assume father's title?"

"And his wealth," Vanessa said. "You know, for all her love of fancy dress, Lizzie is not a stupid girl. She swanned around after Marley when he was here, praising his words and quietly coaching his behavior. I believe that she might choose to marry him to secure her position, if you are unable to take care of her."

"Marry him! But she is only fifteen!"

"And you are twenty-six, and show no interest in marrying and providing an heir. She understands how precarious her financial situation is, as well as mine. We are both forced to think of how we could make our way in the world."

"You know I will always take care of you, Nessie," John said.

Vanessa shook her head. "But what if you can't?"

They hurried downstairs, where Maisie open the door. John espied a rather ordinary-looking man standing on the drive. He was already broad in the belly, his frock coat was poorly cut, and he wore heavy boots more suited for field work than visiting a country estate.

Vanessa and John stepped outside. "Cousin Marley," she said. "This is an unexpected pleasure."

The carriage driver handed Marley his valise, and then climbed up on the carriage again and took off.

"My lady," Marley said, doffing his hat. "I am surprised at your surprise, as I am come at the invitation of your mother. She did not tell you?"

"No matter," Vanessa said. "You are always welcome here. May I present my brother, Lord Therkenwell?"

Despite how he might feel about the man in front of him, John had been raised to be polite. "It is my pleasure to meet you," he said, and he extended his hand.

Marley approached and shook it. "The pleasure is mine, my lord."

Vanessa shivered, and John said, "We will all catch a chill if we remain outside. Please, come in."

Maisie hovered behind them, ready to take Marley's valise. "Is my mother in the sitting room?" John asked.

"Yes, my lord."

"Then we shall all take tea there," John said.

Maisie took Marley's valise, and John led his sister and his cousin to the sitting room. "Mother, we have a guest," he said, as she looked up from her writing desk.

"William," she said, and John thought he detected more warmth in her voice than when she spoke to him. "I am so glad you arrived safely."

She made no attempt to explain his presence to John or Vanessa, and they all sat and made polite conversation. John inquired about Marley's journey, and they compared train rides. Raoul and Lizzie joined them, and Raoul was duly introduced as well.

Then the cook, Mrs. Hampden, arrived with tea and cakes on a platter. Those had to have been made in advance, John thought, as his mother poured the tea. So Mrs. Hampden had been notified of Marley's arrival, and probably Maisie as well.

John understood, for perhaps the first time, that he was surrounded by people keeping secrets, and his own secret, kept from his family, was equal to any in the room. He did not know what his parents intended by befriending Marley, whom Lizzie appeared to be enamored with, though he wasn't sure whether it was genuine emotion on her part or merely financial calculation. At least Vanessa made it clear that she wanted to attend college, though how would their parents feel if she wanted to take over the management of the estate.

And what did he want, aside from a few more pleasurable hours with Raoul? As the conversation ebbed and flowed around him, he thought for the first time about what he would do if he did not take over the management of Shorecliff House and its attendant properties.

Say, for example, Vanessa took over those duties. And Lizzie married the presumptive heir. John did not expect to have children, so he did not begrudge Marley the inheritance, especially if he was married to Lizzie and they had children of their own to continue the line.

At some point, both his parents would die, and unless he was disinherited, the title would pass to him. Would he remain in London, living off the proceeds of the estate? Take his father's seat in the House of Lords?

He doubted he would be able to keep his writing career at that point. The longer he pursued it, the greater chance that his identity would be uncovered. He might give it up, and devote his energies to lobbying his fellow lords or working for charity, doing some good there instead.

Perhaps he would travel. He had only been to a few parts of the continent, and longed to see more of it. And there was a world beyond there—Africa, Asia, the Americas. It was as if a new door had opened in front of him, one he had never even noticed before.

"John," Vanessa said, nudging him. "Mother is speaking to you."

He came to himself with a start. "Sorry, Mater. I was worlds away."

"I asked if you would be so good as to take William around the estate this afternoon," she said. "He has already met Hetherington and I am sure that William would like to see more of the property."

John could think of little he'd prefer less, but he said, "With pleasure."

Shortly afterward the post arrived, bearing a missive from Lady Tregavethan, Lady Tyne's mother and a countess in equal rank to Lady Badgely. John's mother opened it with something close to disdain. "Earl Tregavethan and Lady Tregavethan request the honour of Lady Badgely's company at a ball to be held on Saturday February the 27th instant," she read aloud.

She looked up at them. "What must they be thinking. I am surely in no good health to attend a winter ball."

"We ran into Lord and Lady Tyne on the train," John said. "Lady Tyne mentioned a ball at that time. She wanted to invite Vanessa and Lizzie but was worried that their presence would upset the balance of men and women. When she saw Monsieur Desjardins and myself, she exclaimed that we must all come."

"Of course with no concern for my health."

"Please, Mama, may we go?" Lizzie asked. "Vanessa and John and Raoul and I?"

"You have often said that we need to be more social," Vanessa said. "Especially if I am to have a debut in London next year. Our party manners must be polished."

"But what about William?" Lady Badgely said. "Surely he is included in the invitation, as a member of our party, and yet that would change her numbers to the worse."

"It is very kind of you to want to include me," William said. "But I cannot stay that long, and in any case I do not yet have party manners, or the appropriate attire."

"But you will stay through tomorrow, will you not?" Lady Badgely asked William. "I have the dancing master arranged. I thought there would be an appropriate party of four so that you and Lizzie and Vanessa could improve your skills, with John's help."

"I am still here to help," John said. "And Raoul as well."

"I am happy to remain as long as you have need of me," William said. "I have a capable assistant at the shop who can manage on his own."

"Very good." Lady Badgely frowned. "I suppose that Therkenwell and the girls may attend the ball. With John's friend there will be four, and no room in the carriage for me."

John wondered if she would suggest that Raoul ride outside, with Osbert. But instead she said, "Fine, I shall respond with my regrets, but that there will be four in your party."

She looked pointedly at Raoul. "I hope she understands that she has invited a Frenchman."

"The Tynes were introduced to Monsieur Desjardins on the train," John said. "With a specific mention of his post at the French embassy. I am sure that Lady Tregavethan would not have extended the invitation had his nationality been a problem for her."

Eventually their party broke up. His mother returned to her correspondence, including a response to the invitation, and Raoul said, "I have devised a language game, based on one that was used with me when I was learning English. I have merely flipped the rules. Perhaps your sisters would care to play with me while you are at your tour."

"That would be fun!" Lizzie said. "Please, Nessie, join us?"

Vanessa agreed, and they all walked out to the entrance hallway together.

"Would you care for your tour now?" John asked William.

"I am quite interested to learn more about the functions of Shorecliff House," William said. "On my last visit, Lady Elizabeth was kind enough to take me on a tour of the property, but there is still so much I would like to know."

John felt irritated. First, it surprised him to hear his sister spoken of so formally within the house—he couldn't remember the last time anyone had called her by her full name. She was "my lady" to the staff and Lizzie to the family.

He could not help admitting that Cousin Marley was indeed family. Neither could Lizzie apparently, because she reprimanded him gently. "William, we are cousins. You must call me Lizzie."

He blushed. "My apologies. I was not raised with these standards, you see. Again, there is a great deal I must learn."

That was the other thing that bothered John. Marley's assumption that it was incumbent on him to learn everything about Shorecliff Manor because he would inherit it someday.

Raoul and the girls retired to the sitting room for Raoul's game, and John asked Marley, "Have you fully seen the interior of the house?"

Marley shook his head. "Only the few rooms open to guests," he said. "This dining room and the sitting room, and the gallery upstairs leading to the chamber I have been given."

"Well, then, I have much to show you," John said, forcing himself to be cheerful. "Let's begin at the entrance."

He attempted to perform the duties of a guide diligently. "The double-hung sash windows are a particular feature of the homes built when Shorecliff was, as are the huge doors and high ceilings. We share a common great-grandfather, I believe, and he was the third Earl Badgely, the one who had this home built."

"His first name was Abel, and he had two sons, Benjamin and

George," Marley said. "Benjamin was your grandfather, and George was mine."

"You have researched your history," John said.

Marley looked down. "It wasn't me. Rather your father sought me out, and instructed me on our relationship. I believe he met my father once or twice when they were children. But my father did not have the estate to provide for him, so he went into trade, and they lost touch."

"Interesting," John said. "When did my father contact you?"

"About a year ago," Marley said. "He didn't confide in you?"

John shook his head. "My father and I have many differing opinions."

"He told me you were a molly and unlikely to provide him with an heir," Marley said, all in a burst.

John's heart raced, to hear his secret so blandly repeated. What else did his father say of him, and to whom? His right hand shook, and he rested it on a doorknob to still it. His father's admission to Marley surely meant that Earl Badgely knew John was unlikely to produce an heir, and that Marley had been nominated to his position.

He turned to his cousin. "Did he give you any proof of this assumption?"

Marley looked away. "He did not."

John waited a beat, worrying that Marley would ask him to confirm the earl's suspicion, but Marley looked as uncomfortable as John felt.

"Well," John said. "Let us resume our tour. As you have seen the sitting room is to the right, the dining room to the left. This corridor leads toward the kitchen. If you'll follow me."

John stopped at the door to a spacious room of cabinets and counters, where a pair of young women were at work. "This is the pantry, where all things associated with baking bread are stored, along with baked goods and other foods."

"To keep them cool and dry and away from moisture which would cause mold," Marley said.

"Indeed. The room on the other side is the still room, where essential oils, drinks, alcoholic beverages and medicines were once distilled. Now that we have greater access to the city, this room has been largely abandoned."

"To have such a large house where one can simply abandon rooms," Marley said, shaking his head.

"Ahead of us is the kitchen, the domain of Mrs. Hampden and her staff. There is a rear door through the kitchen which leads out to the kitchen garden. That door over there leads to the basement, which contains the buttery, where we store casks of beer and wine, kegs of rum and so on. It has to be underground to keep the stores cool."

He looked at Marley. "Do you know where the word butler comes from?"

Marley shrugged. "Didn't go over that kind of thing at my school. And I stopped when I was twelve, to join my father in his business."

"The butler was originally in charge of the buttery, you see. In time he took on more responsibilities to the role you see today."

"You don't have a butler here, though," Marley said.

"No, my father has a very loyal man called Samson who he keeps in London with him. Because my mother has been a recluse for some time, she does little entertaining, and we make do with Maisie as chief housekeeper. She runs the house and manages the staff. You've met her, and seen the kitchen maid when she serves. You may also have noticed the two housemaids who keep things clean, and we have two hall boys as well, who handle the heavy manual labor below stairs. Then there is my mother's lady's maid. We used to have a governess for the girls but as they got older she was dismissed."

"Quite an operation," Marley said. "It must be expensive to keep it all running."

"It is. But because my father prefers to remain in London, Shore-cliff House runs on a tight budget."

John pointed to the left. "Over there is the solarium. In fine weather we can sit there and look out at the Carrick Roads, or use the door there to explore the property."

"It is quite a large one," Marley said, as they turned back down the hallway toward the entrance. "That is how our ancestors made their money, isn't it? Charging rent on the land for farmers who wished to use it to grow crops, raise livestock, or otherwise make a living there?"

"Indeed. There is a watermill and a brick kiln on the property. And our holdings extend to the small town you passed on the way here. The landlord of the pub there pays us rent on the land as well."

"Doesn't seem fair, does it?" Marley asked. "Collecting money from these people and doing nothing to earn it?"

John was surprised at the man's audacity. "When the first earl took over this property, he provided safety for his tenants. The capital necessary to build properties, purchase farm equipment, and so on. We do the same thing today."

"Really? The accounts I went over with Lady Vanessa the last time I was here showed a great deal more income than outflow."

John was flummoxed. "I admit I haven't looked over the books in the way Vanessa has. And our father has spent most of his time in London this last year." He looked at Marley with a different attitude. The man clearly had some intelligence. "What would you have us do otherwise?"

They then engaged in a conversation, as they walked down the corridor to the entrance, about ways Marley thought the tenants on the land could be treated more ethically. Some of his ideas were quite radical, while others seemed eminently possible.

John stopped in the sitting room to get a pen and paper. "I should like to take down some of your ideas," he said, as he sat at his mother's desk. "Pray repeat those ideas for me?"

Marley's ideas could provide the heart of John's next broadside, so he wrote down as much as he could. Then he waved the paper to dry the ink, and when it was safe to do so he folded it and placed it in his pocket.

They continued to talk as John took Marley on a tour of the upstairs. "This long hallway is called an enfilade," John said. "Your chamber, as you know, is one of those along this corridor. Each of the suites includes a bedroom and a closet—that small chamber next to your bedroom. It is a private space to do personal things like pray, write, read or relax."

"I wondered about the reason for that," Marley said. "It seemed too small and personal to entertain in."

John continued, "My father, my mother, my sisters and I all have rooms along here. While I was at Eton, father had this floor renovated to include water closets in each of the major suites. Conditions at Eton were rather spartan, so it was one of the few pleasures in returning to Shorecliff House on holidays."

When they stepped outside, the weather was mild. "Do you ride?" John asked.

"I'm afraid not. Never been on a horse myself."

"Too bad. That's the best way to see the property. But we might walk down through the valley and pass some of our tenants." They walked along a well-trodden path and John noticed remnants of ice in the hedgerow. They turned a corner to see a herd of some six cows drinking from a long metal trough.

A woman in an apron over a heavy jumper and long skirt approached from the square stone farmhouse. "Good day, my lord," she said to John, and she smiled at William.

"Good day," John said. He reached back to the crevasses of his mind. "Mrs. Fields, isn't it?"

"Indeed."

"This is my cousin, William Marley." They both bowed slightly to each other.

"How are you, madam?" John asked. "And your husband and family?"

"My husband and I are fine, my lord. Our youngest boy has a touch of the croup, but he is recovering."

"You must ask Mrs. Hampden for some hot soup. I remember that being very comforting when I was a boy in my sickbed."

Mrs. Fields smiled. "She has already provided," she said. "We stick together."

"I am glad." And he was—life was difficult in the winter, especially at an isolated place like Shorecliff. It was good that the tenants and the household staff worked well with each other.

"I am just about to take some cheese up to her," Mrs. Fields said.

John turned to William. "Mrs. Fields makes the finest cheese in all of Cornwall," he said. "My father has it brought up specially to London, where he will eat no other."

"That is very kind of you to say," Mrs. Fields said. With another slight bow, she turned and went back to the house.

They continued on a circuitous route that eventually led them back to Shorecliff.

"Thank you very much for your kindness," Marley said. "I was nervous about meeting you, based on what your father had said."

John smiled thinly. "Did you worry that I would attempt to bed you?"

Marley blushed. "Not at all. But I was concerned that you might feel I was an interloper, here to take over your rightful place."

"I admit that is what I thought when I first heard of you," John said. "But now my feelings are confused. I shall have to take some time to think things through."

"Your father is not in the best of health, is he?" Marley asked. "I understand that he suffers from the gout."

"That is true. But he is a tough old bird and I believe that he has more years in him."

At least John hoped that was the case. The future was too cloudy to consider what would happen when his father died. What would happen to him?

But more importantly, how would his father react when he learned of the blackmail attempt against him? And what would that do to John's future?

Chapter 24

Other Men

Raoul very much enjoyed the language game he played with Vanessa and Lizzie, and told John so when they met in John's bedroom late in the afternoon. "How was your tour with your cousin?"

"My feelings are very confused. This interest he has taken in the rooms of the house, and the way everything functions," he said. "It's damned impertinent of him. Yet I cannot help but like him. And he gave me many ideas which I will use in my next broadside, about how lords of manors like Shorecliff can deal better with their tenants."

"You've explained the way the house is entailed," Raoul said patiently. "So unless you produce an heir it will go to him." Raoul raised an eyebrow then. "And you aren't likely to do that, are you?"

John crossed his arms over his chest. "I might. Other men in my situation have."

"But you have made it clear, by your manners and your dress, that it is not in the cards," Raoul said gently. "This is all a problem of your own making, you know. Those 'other men' you referred to probably got on with things more quickly."

"You mean marrying a young girl, impregnating her, then abandoning her to follow the attractions of men?"

"It has been done, and quite notoriously."

John turned to him. "Have you ever…"

"Been with a woman?" Raoul asked. He looked down at the floor. "Yes."

"You have?" John was stunned.

"I was much younger," Raoul said. "Before I left Souvigné for university, Father Maurice had a talk with me. He did not want me to feel that the relations we had enjoyed together were the only path before me. He worried, he said, that he had 'spoiled' me for women. So he made a clandestine arrangement with a whore in town to spend a night with me and show me the difference."

"What was it like? Were you able to… perform? I would be completely embarrassed if I was in such a situation and couldn't… you know."

"At eighteen, my cock hardened with every passing breeze," Raoul said, laughing. "Of course, I was nervous, but I had done so many things with Father Maurice that I felt I knew what I had to do. And of course I had read about sex, usually the kind of books that Father Maurice took away from other boys. I let my arrogance rule the day."

"How was it?"

"I had only Father Maurice to compare it to, and he had ever been gentle with me, and expressed emotion. The whore had none of that—it was a business to her, after all. She opened my pants, grabbed my cock and stroked it, then opened her skirt and directed me to insert it."

John gaped, open-mouthed.

"It was all over very quickly. I closed my pants, handed her the money Father Maurice had given me, and ran away. I was frightened that my parents would smell her on me, so I raced to the river and dunked myself thoroughly." He smiled. "It was not an experience I chose to continue."

"And I am glad of that," John said.

They all dined together that evening, and Raoul was interested to see that John's cousin continued to grow more comfortable around the family. He noted how Lizzie spoke to him so freely, and the way their eyes met frequently.

That evening in their room, he said, "Do you think that your sister will marry Mr. Marley?"

"It would not surprise me. But first she must have her season in London, and it is quite possible she will catch the eye of a more suitable bachelor, perhaps even one with a title and a storied home of his own."

"Where would that leave you and Vanessa?"

"Marley might still inherit Shorecliff. Perhaps he will settle for Vanessa instead. After all, in the Bible Jacob marred Leah though he preferred Rachel, because Leah was the elder."

John shrugged. "But there is still much time ahead of all of us before decisions must be made. I feel that the world is slipping away from me, that no matter what I might write as Janner nothing is truly within my control. It is frightening—and yet exhilarating at the same time."

He turned to Raoul. "A few weeks ago I heard a man talk about sexual behavior among the animals. His belief was that those males with a lower sex drive or weaker personality could not secure females, and that was why they turned to other lesser males. Do you agree with that?"

Raoul shook his head. "Not at all. I would not have a woman even if one was thrust upon me—as Father Maurice did."

He paused. The priest had directed him by his cock from an early age, instructing him what to do with it, with his mouth and his buttocks. Then he had sent Raoul away to college, where his professors had continued to mold him, which led him to Paris, the ministry and Morvan.

"Though I have let other men lead me, I do not believe that I am a weaker man because of my instincts," he said finally. "And how about you? You had the same introduction to such congress at around the same age as I did. Were you weaker than the boys you were with?"

John shrugged. "Sometimes, of course. Many of the boys were older than I was or stronger, and there was a custom of usage that was part of our lives. But eventually I realized that I wielded power as well. I could decide whether to let another boy service me, or whether I should take care of him."

"But then you were exploiting the weaker ones?"

"No, not at all. Some of the boys who wanted to play the woman's role with me were older or stronger than I was. But there was something other than power at work."

"What was that?"

John smiled. "Love," he said. "I wanted the love from other boys that I didn't get at home. And even if that love was fleeting, and rooted only in sexual congress, it moved my heart."

Raoul smiled back at him. "I hope I move you in that way."

"You do, my dearest," John said, and they came together, first lips, then arms, then bodies.

Chapter 25

Dancing Master

The following morning dawned bright and warm for February, so while Raoul continued to tutor Lizzie, Vanessa accompanied John on a stroll around the property. At the barn, they ran into Hetherington, a rotund, round-faced man with a shock of red hair. One of the stable boys was shoveling hay out for their feed.

"Good morning, my lord," Hetherington said. He bowed slightly. "My lady."

John greeted him. "I saw Mrs. Fields the other day, and a herd of only six cows. We used to have more, did we not?" John asked.

"Back in the days when the house was full," Hetherington said. "Now we just have enough to provide milk and cheese for the family and the tenants."

"I complimented her on the cheese when I saw her. There's a freshness to it, and a bit of the salt air in the taste as well. I know you ship some of it up to my father's house in London. Have you thought about increasing the herd so Mrs. Fields could make more cheese, which could be sold in London, if Mrs. Fields is willing to up her cheese production?"

"Her two little ones are old enough to help out now," Hetherington said. "That might be a good idea. I know she and her husband could use the extra income. And the estate, as well."

"Do you think you could draw up some numbers? I know you have the head for such things—the number of cows we could accommodate on our land, how much milk they would generate, and so on?"

"I can, my lord. I could have something for you tomorrow."

John thanked him, and he and Vanessa continued their perambulation. "I didn't realize that our father had cheese shipped to him in London," she said. "Or that Londoners would ever consider eating cheese from such a remote location as Shorecliff. Don't they have farms closer to the city?"

"I learned an interesting concept from Raoul," John said, as they walked through the glen toward the long-disused mill. "A French word called *terroir*, which represents a concept he learned from his father, who works in a vineyard."

"*Terroir* means land," Vanessa said. "Surely you learned that at Eton."

"There is a deeper meaning," John said. "As Raoul explains it, the quality of the soil, the weather, the proximity to a river or a body of salt water, all of those affect what is grown there. So though two vintners might grow the same grapes at two different vineyards, they will have slightly different tastes. Perhaps one set of vines is on a hillside, while the other is in a valley. One set is close to the sea, while the other is farther inland."

He frowned. "I'm not explaining it as well as he does. But I can taste the difference in the cheese we make here, because of our proximity to the English Channel. The grass the cows eat is different because our soil may have more clay than that of Essex, for example."

Vanessa nodded. "I understand. And perhaps the breed of cow makes a difference, too. Those Mrs. Fields raises are called Red Devon. I understand that the milk from the longhorn cattle is much higher in butterfat, so makes an entirely different kind of cheese."

They talked more about cows as they walked home, and John thought he had never felt so close to his sister as he did then.

In the afternoon, the dancing master whom Lady Badgely had employed arrived. The ballroom at Shorecliff was small, but it did have a serviceable pianoforte, and Mr. Newsom pronounced it acceptable. He was a trim man in his forties, with an impressive mustache curled at the edges.

He had brought with him a Miss Laybourn, a spinster in her fifties who was to play while they danced.

"We shall begin with the waltz," Mr. Newsom said. He looked over John, Raoul, William, Vanessa and Lizzie. "Which are to be the couples?"

"I am here only to watch," Raoul said. John partnered with Vanessa, leaving William with Lizzie, and Miss Laybourn began to play a piece which John recognized as the waltz from the opera "La Sonnombula."

He was fairly accomplished and able to lead Vanessa well, but Lizzie and William stumbled quite a bit, so Mr. Newsom directed them to change partners.

William was even more awkward with Vanessa than with Lizzie, but she had the advantage of more practice over her sister and was able to lead him smoothly. John did the same with Lizzie, who was a quick learner.

After some time, Mr. Newsom pronounced them capable enough, and moved on to the schottische. "You will make two side-steps to the left and right, followed by a turn in four steps," he said. He used Vanessa to demonstrate, and then they were partnered again.

John longed to be able to dance with Raoul, especially at those points when he held his sister close, or when he was directed to stare into her eyes. At one point he and Lizzie dissolved into giggles.

"You will not laugh when you are dancing with one you might wish to marry," Newsom said.

When Lizzie and William had mastered the steps, they returned to their original partners, though Raoul remained on the sidelines. During one break, Vanessa asked, "Might I have one dance with Monsieur Desjardins? To explore how it feels to dance with different partners?"

John bowed. "It would be my pleasure to allow you to dance with someone much better than I am."

"I doubt that is the case," Raoul said, but he rose from his seat and took Vanessa's hand for a round of the schottische. John was lulled by his lover's smooth movements and evident grace—though had seen all of that grace in private as well.

After Mr. Newsom and Miss Laybourn left, Hetherington and Mrs. Fields arrived to discuss the cheesemaking operation. They sat around the table in the sitting room where John, Raoul and the girls had played whist, and Hetherington laid out a plan for John and Vanessa to review.

It was quickly clear to him that because of her position, Mrs. Fields could not advocate for herself, and was used to accepting what was offered. The deal that Hetherington presented left little for Mrs. Fields and her family.

That was the estate manager's job, to maximize the revenue for the landlord. But John wanted Mrs. Fields and her family to prosper as well. "I understand that the estate will bear the initial investment, in the purchase of the cows and the extension of the fields where they may graze," he said, after reviewing the plan. "But the estate also will retain the herd, and benefit from any improvements to the land. I propose that we revise these numbers so that more of the initial profit goes to the Fields family, to reward them for their labor."

Hetherington frowned, but Vanessa nodded her head. "Yes, Mr. Fields will need to hire a boy to help with the cows," she said. "We must add something to account for that."

They went back and forth, and John noticed the surprise in Mrs. Fields' eyes as he negotiated on her behalf. But to him, it was nothing more than putting into practice the ideals he had espoused as Janner.

To fail to do so would make him a hypocrite, no matter what Hetherington, or indeed his sister or father, might believe.

"You were very fair to Mrs. Fields," Vanessa said, when they were alone in the sitting room. "She and her family would have received a much smaller percentage of the profits had you not intervened."

"Who could use that money more?" John asked. "Mr. and Mrs. Fields, who depend on the vagaries of the land and the weather, and who live in relative poverty?"

"Of course they could," Vanessa said. "It's just that I didn't expect it of you."

"There may be much you do not know about me," John said.

Chapter 26

A Ride with his Lover

The next morning Raoul overslept, and barely made it into the bath before Beller approached. After they were dressed, he joined John to descend to the breakfast room off the kitchen.

They were joined there by Vanessa, Lizzie, William and Lady Badgely. "I would like to thank you for your hospitality, my lady," William said. "I have enjoyed my visit and coming to know my cousins better. But I must return to my business. I am afraid I can only leave it in the care of my employees for a few days at a time."

"You must come back again in the spring," Lizzie said. "Shorecliff is so lovely then."

Raoul interpreted the glance between them as one of growing romantic interest. "I am sure I should enjoy a visit here in any season," William said.

The carriage arrived for Marley soon after, and John pulled Raoul aside. "I would appreciate some time to work on Janner's next broadside, if you could keep my sisters occupied until lunch."

"I would enjoy returning to our vocabulary game," Raoul said, and they enjoyed several happy hours until Maisie called them down to the dining room.

Lady Badgely sent a message with the maid that she was in ill health, and their party seemed much smaller without her and William. After lunch, Lizzie and Vanessa left to study, and Raoul asked John how he could post his letter to Morvan. "We can ride into St. Mawes if you like," John said. "It is the nearest town of any consequence. I should say about two miles."

"I would appreciate that."

John called the housemaid over and asked her to take a message to Osbert that he and Raoul would need horses ready in a few minutes.

"Do you resent your cousin's presence here?" Raoul asked, as they climbed the stairs to change into riding clothes. Beller had thoughtfully packed an extra pair of John's breeches that would fit Raoul.

"You know, I don't think so," John said. "Cousin Marley may be the solution to my worries."

"But surely if your father overlooks you and leaves the estate to him..." Raoul began.

John shook his head. "In the future I envision, upon my father's death, the estate comes to me. You saw the way Lizzie was so flirtatious with Marley, did you not?"

"I did."

"So she might marry him, and be allotted a marriage portion. Vanessa could marry or not, take over management of the estate if she wishes, while I remain in London, or travel, at my pleasure."

Raoul nodded. "And then, once you have lived your life, the title would pass to Marley or one of his and your sister's offspring."

"Exactly. Completing my responsibility to the family line."

"Of course, you must remain in your father's good graces until such time as he passes," Raoul said.

"Ah, yes, that is the problem before us."

Once in John's bedroom, Raoul and John slid into riding

breeches. "There is quite a scenic path along the hillside that shows great views of the Carrick Roads. I should like to show you the waterfront that formed so much of my life."

"I would appreciate that. And someday, perhaps, we will share the view of the Atlantic Ocean from the rocks of the *Plage du Roux*." It was comforting to Raoul to consider that if they were able to overcome their current difficulties, that he and John might have a future together.

By the time they reached the stables, Osbert had saddled two horses for them, a chestnut mare and a gray one, and John appeared to know the chestnut, called Bitty. The gray was a newer addition, but Osbert assured Raoul that she rode well.

The stables were at the rear of the manor house, so they were able to head directly toward the water, on a dirt path. That led them to another path, a few feet from where the land sloped down to the water. John assured him that path would take them down toward St. Mawes.

"And you are sure it is perfectly safe?" Raoul asked.

"I have ridden this way many times myself," John said. "I assume you finished your letter to Morvan?"

"I did. Would you like to read it?"

"If you wish me to. There is a vista point up ahead where we can stop for a few minutes. You may contemplate the wonder of this estuary, created centuries ago during the ice age, while I review what you have written."

When they stopped, Raoul handed the letter to John, and they both remained astride their mounts. Raoul looked out at the spectacular vista valley before him. A few clouds scudded slowly overhead, and the water moved relentlessly down toward the English Channel. He made out the headland across the channel, and then farther to the south a fishing port.

"I think this letter is quite good," John said, handing it back to him. "Of course, my French is not as good as yours, but it expresses the situation very well."

"Thank you," Raoul said, his voice shaking. "It may be the last letter I compose as a member of the embassy staff. Or indeed as a resident of Britain."

"You really think he would send you away?"

Raoul found it difficult to raise the reins of the gray mare. "I think it quite possible," he said. "Morvan is not a kind and generous man."

And yet Raoul had followed him, for the sake of his career, and because it seemed to be his destiny to give more powerful men control of him. He frowned, took a deep breath, and shook the reins slightly.

They continued their journey as John said, "But surely you have value to him aside from this situation."

Raoul shrugged. "No more than any other intelligent young man in government service. I have my skills, certainly, but there are others with an equal education to mine, and better breeding, who could serve just as well."

That was what he said, but did he truly believe it? Was he simply an interchangeable tool that other men could use? How could he reach for his own independence? Well, he knew one thing he could do.

The path ahead of them sloped down gently, far enough from the water's edge to be safe. Raoul smiled, shook the reins, and kicked lightly at the gray mare's side, and they took off down the hill at a canter.

"Oh, ho, is it a race you want!" John cried, and soon they were running neck and neck down the path, the wind racing past them and coloring their cheeks red. Raoul spotted a round stone castle before them, guarding the headland, and he and John both reined in as they reached the outskirts of a quaint town of stone and whitewashed houses.

John led them into the center of town, where the buildings huddled close to each other. Colorful rowboats were moored in the harbor, and they passed women carrying their shopping and a man pushing a cart of firewood.

The post office was a simple storefront with a sky-blue sign. John dismounted and walked inside, while Raoul remained on the gray mare on the cobbled street, holding the bay's reins as well. The sun had already begun its downward movement, casting deep shadows that reminded Raoul of the dark import of the letter John was posting.

When John returned and mounted the bay again, he said, "I don't wish to be out after dark, so we shall take an inland road where we can make better time."

He led the way out of the town and they climbed a dirt road. Along the way they came to a pile of entrails and bits of brown and white fur.

"A rabbit," John said. "Or once was. Looks like a fox got him."

Though he had eaten rabbit often at table, Raoul was revolted by the sight, and surprised John could be so unmoved by it. He hurried the gray mare along as the light dimmed.

Neither of them spoke. John seemed to be intent on the path, while Raoul considered the consequences of his letter. In it he had told Morvan as explicitly as he could that exposing his son's proclivities would matter little to Earl Badgely. In short, the attempt to blackmail him would only end in failure, and if there was any hint of the embassy's involvement in such a scandal, it would reflect poorly on France.

If Morvan decided to ignore Raoul's ideas, then he knew that he might end up as useless and ravaged as that poor rabbit.

The next two days passed quickly. Raoul spent time each day with Lizzie, engaged in conversation and discussion of the Dumas novels he had brought her. She was particularly rapt in her appreciation of *Les Trois Mousquetaires,* which Raoul loved as well. He tried to engage her regarding the political issues the novel raised regarding the injustices, abuses and absurdities of the *Ancien Régime,* but she was more interested in mooning after d'Artagnan. For his part, he rather favored Aramis, who decided to join the priesthood at the end of the novel, and though he worried that it was evidence of a lasting affection for Father Maurice, that was not something he could confess to Lizzie.

The next day was Saturday, and that afternoon everyone, save Lady Badgely, had to prepare for the ball at Tregavethan House. "I shall wear my pale blue tulle," Lizzie said as they were finishing lunch. "I think it complements my complexion well. And tulle is such a lovely fabric for dancing." She turned to her sister. "What will you wear, Nessie?"

Vanessa shrugged. "I'm sure I have something appropriate."

"Your green floral crepe de chine would be lovely," Lizzie said. "And I can fix your hair up for you after I do mine."

Vanessa did not seem so eager for the party as her sister, and Raoul empathized with her. He had to attend many such functions in London as a representative of the embassy, and though he danced well and had, as Marley had called them, party manners, he did not relish spending the evening with a group of strangers when the alternative was a night in their shared room with John.

Beller had tidied and pressed Raoul's formal wear, and his gloves looked as white as the day he'd purchase them. He must ask the man his secret.

Osbert had the carriage ready when they prepared to depart, and planned to stay at the stables of Tregavethan House with the other carriage men until the party ended. Lizzie created enough of a festive air for the four of them on the ride toward Truro, laughing gaily and asking her sister about this man or that, and whether he might be present.

Tregavethan House was a manor similar to Shorecliff House, though this evening all the windows on the front face were lit with candles and a line of carriages stood ahead of them waiting to drop off guests.

"I do hope they will have good food," Lizzie said. "I was too nervous to eat much at luncheon."

"The Tregavethans always have good provender," John said. "I remember one event here where I came straight from Cambridge and hadn't eaten all day, and they had the most marvelous roast pheasant and an almond and potato pudding."

"It figures you would remember the food," Vanessa said, smiling.

Eventually Osbert was able to pull the carriage up to the front door, and John and Raoul stepped out and assisted the ladies. Inside, they gave their coats to a maid in the front parlor and then proceeded to the ballroom at one end of the house. A young man already sat at the piano, with another holding a cornopean, a large sort of trumpet Raoul had often seen at such events in London.

The foursome had to greet Lady Tregavethan first, as courtesy required, and Raoul noticed that she had passed her narrow face and blonde curls to her daughter. She was somewhat younger than Lady Badgely, though her husband, who was pointed out to them in a corner of the room, seemed much older.

After they had paid their courtesies, Lizzie led them to a side room laid out as a buffet. "Oh, look, John, they have the pheasant you enjoyed," she said. A young lad and a lass in serving costumes helped them to the food, and they sat at a corner table to eat.

A steady procession of young people passed them by, greeting the Badgelys and being introduced to Raoul. This was what country life was, he thought. Days of isolation on far-flung properties interspersed with evenings such as this one. It was not a life he envied, preferring the city and its endless possibilities. And he was also resentful, as he watched the young men and women chat together, smile, share flirtatious glances.

This life was never going to be open to him. He could not see a future in which he and John could attend a ball like this together, be presented as a couple, dance together. And while the behavior of single young people were governed by a strict set of rules, this life was one that would ever be denied to him. Despite the pleasantness of those he met and spoke with, he felt a shell hardening around him. This society was just as demanding as Father Maurice had been, as Morvan was. Where was the escape for a man like him?

They heard the musicians strike up as they finished eating, and went into the ballroom for the first quadrille. John lined up across from Vanessa, and Raoul across from Lizzie.

Then John asked Lady Tyne for a dance, and Lizzie introduced Raoul to a girl she knew, so that he could dance with her, and the evening proceeded. He was rather jealous of all the attention paid to John, but he could not blame the ladies at the ball. John was handsome, had a good education and a wealthy father, and stood to inherit a substantial property. He was quite marriageable material, except in one regard.

One which Raoul was sure he was the only attendee who knew.

After he came to that understanding, Raoul found it in himself to enjoy the ball. Vanessa and Lizzie both danced quite a bit with several different young men, and appeared to enjoy themselves. He was even able to catch John's eye several times, and the two of them enjoyed a quick clandestine kiss behind the door of the house's library.

By the time the evening ended, the four of them were tired and glad to collapse into the carriage for the cold drive back to Shorecliff House. Fortunately Osbert had stocked it with heavy wool blankets for each of them, and Lizzie and Vanessa curled up beneath them and dozed.

"How did you enjoy your first country ball?" John asked Raoul in a low voice.

"More so than I expected," Raoul said. "Though I wish the world were different, and I could dance with you."

"We shall have our own little dance in my room," John whispered, with a sly grin.

The last night before they were to return, they both pleaded weariness, and retired to John's bedroom ostensibly to rest up for their journey the next day. But instead John approached him with a gleam in his eye, one that Raoul had come to recognize. "I am not tired, are you?" he asked.

"I hope I shall never grow tired of you." Raoul untied his cravat and tossed it aside with a flair.

John mirrored the gesture, then went one step further by undoing the first few buttons of his shirt, so that the top of his smooth chest was exposed.

Raoul looked at him and smiled, holding eye contact as he undid all the buttons of his shirt, then gracefully slipped it off and slung it over his shoulder, holding it there with the thumb of his right hand.

He felt the cool air on his chest. Unlike John, he had a light pelt of hair there, which John loved to run his fingers through. Raoul shivered with the anticipation of his lover's touch.

John smiled wickedly. He undid the rest of his shirt, then turned and left it lying by the wardrobe. He returned to facing Raoul, and let his fingers drift lazily down his own chest, until they reached his trousers, which he undid carefully, letting them splay open to reveal a stiffness pressing against his underdrawers.

That was a sight Raoul could not resist. He quickly crossed the floor and knelt in front of his lover. He opened his mouth and licked against the press of John's cock against the fabric.

John shuddered with pleasure, and with a quick motion, Raoul grabbed John's drawers at the waist and jerked them down.

John responded by stepping back from Raoul's eager mouth and sitting on the edge of his bed. He lifted his right leg into the air, still encumbered by his trousers and dress shoes. "Shall I valet for you, sir?" Raoul asked with a grin.

John leaned back on his elbows. "If you would, my good man."

"I must be suitably prepared." Raoul pulled off his own shoes and socks, then undid his trousers. He removed them and his silk drawers, feeling the cool air sweep across his body. His erect cock slapped against his groin as he turned away, presenting his hairy buttocks to his lover.

He carefully folded his own clothes and then John's before taking his position on the floor. His body tingled with anticipation as he slipped off John's right shoe, then held it to his nose.

"Silly man," John said, and laughed.

Raoul made quick work of both shoes and the trousers, leaving John clad in his drawers. He reached up to the waistband and gradually drew it down, making sure to ensnare John's hard cock in its folds so that it finally twanged up when John lifted his buttocks from the bed so that the drawers could be taken away.

Raoul returned to kneeling on the floor. He lifted John's right foot again, and this time licked his tongue across the sole. John wiggled with pleasure.

He began massaging John's lower leg as he kissed and licked his way north. But then, just before he reached the dark thatch that surrounded his lover's bollocks, he stopped and returned to the sole of the left foot.

John groaned. "Oh, how you torture me."

It was torture to Raoul, too, as his cock dripped pearls and ached for release. But he wanted to make the most of their remaining time together. Once he'd finished with the left leg, though, he forced himself to switch to the fingers of John's right hand, sucking them each in turn as John moaned with pleasure.

He lifted John's arm and nestled his mouth in his lover's armpit, inhaling the scent that was so uniquely John's, a combination of human sweat, lavender, and citrus. Then he licked his way along John's collarbone, as John curled his fingers through Raoul's hair.

He gave up on the left hand, so eager was he to sample John's lips. They kissed passionately, pressing against each other, and Raoul climbed on the bed, his knees on either side of John's thighs, so they could be closer together. He grabbed John's cock in a hand with his own and rubbed them together, lubricated by their fluids, until John gasped and pulled back. "I do not wish to spend so quickly on our last night together."

"Now who is the torturer," Raoul said, but he backed away and stood by the edge of the bed. He extended his hands forward and

John grasped them, and he pulled John to his feet. By then Raoul's bollocks had begun to ache in their desperation to empty.

He reached behind John to grasp his lover's smooth buttocks, and then they bucked and frotted together until he felt his passion rising and could no longer stop, even if he wanted to.

John gasped and muttered muffled cries into Raoul's throat, and then he spent, followed a moment later by Raoul.

They stood there in a lazy embrace, swaying to a rhythm they shared, until Raoul pulled away and wetted a cloth from the basin on the dresser. He cleaned them both up and they settled on the bed, facing each other.

"We will continue to see each other in London, won't we?" John asked.

"As long as I remain in the city."

"What if Morvan sends you back to Paris. Must you go?"

"What will I do in London if I have no income?"

"You could lodge with me," John said.

"And be your kept man? I don't think I could. And what would people say?"

"There are men who live together, you know. Lord Dawson and Toby Marsh, for example."

"Dawson has a private income, and Marsh earns his keep through tutoring and translating," Raoul said. "Neither is beholden to his family, as you would be. And my skills are political and diplomatic. Not something a casual consumer would need."

Raoul had come to understand that Dawson and Marsh had power of their own—both in Marsh's skills and Dawson's connections. They had been kind enough to encompass him, Silas, and John in their circle, which seemed to operate much as a family might. Yet he did not see that they could be models for him and John. He was a foreigner, and a Frenchman at that, so he would never be accepted unless he were to become a powerful man himself. And given the way that Morvan could crush him at will, that seemed unlikely.

"Come, come," John said. "This is our last night together before we return to, as the Americans say, face the music. For tonight, we call our own tune. And we must be sure to grasp passion from every moment we have." John reached down to caress Raoul's cock, which reacted by stiffening. "Shall we see how many rounds we can go for in one evening?"

Chapter 27

Dinner at White's

John stared out of the carriage window as Osbert returned him and Raoul to the train station in Truro. The day was moderately warm, and Beller rode up at the top of carriage with Osbert.

"I'm sure that my father will want to see me as soon as I return to London." He turned to Raoul. "What should I say to him?"

"How about hello?"

John elbowed him. "You know what I mean. Should I confront him about cousin Marley and his interest in the estate?"

"That depends on what you want. Obviously your mother likes the man."

"More than she likes me," John said morosely. He looked out of the window again. He was a good enough fellow, wasn't he? His sisters loved him. Why couldn't his parents feel the same way?

"You spent some time with the estate manager and Vanessa, didn't you?" Raoul asked. "Focus on that. Find a way to express some enthusiasm about what goes on there, if only to protect your own interests."

"That won't be easy to do. I don't have the head for mathematics that Vanessa does, so I can't talk about how many sheep can graze on a parcel of land. I find most of the tenants rude and unlettered and can't imagine how I could talk to them regularly. And I'm only interested in vegetables when they show up on my table."

"All those are reasons why you should not inherit," Raoul said. "Is there any reason why you should?"

"Heredity? Breeding?"

"You forget, I come from a country that overthrew its hereditary rulers in 1789. We have little sympathy for fops who are out of contact with the people they govern."

John turned to him. "Is that how you see me? A fop?"

Raoul fingered the lace cuffs on John's shirt, then stroked the several gold rings on his fingers, including the massive signet he usually only wore around his family.

"Bah!" John said, snatching his hand back.

"You are very dear to me," Raoul said in a consoling tone. "Do not think I despise you because I make a little fun."

"I know, and that is the image I want others to see. But you better than any other know that I am passionate about social issues. Which would not endear me to my father."

Raoul pursed his lips in thought. "What about that conversation you had with Hetherington about cheese? You could mention that to your father."

"I believe that the contract we put together with Mrs. Fields will benefit both parties," John said. "I suppose I could mention that to my father."

"Imply to your father that if you put your mind to it, you might come up with other small improvements. You might even mention some of Mr. Marley's ideas, which with some careful considerations could be presented as a joint effort between the two of you."

John sat back against the carriage seat as they approached Truro. It wouldn't be much, in his father's eyes, but at least he might show that he was trying. And that might forestall any immediate efforts to supplant him with William Marley.

Indeed, when he returned to Russell Square, a note awaited him, summoning him to dinner that evening with his father at White's. It took most of the afternoon for Beller to unpack and organize and John used that time to write up for himself a report of his visit to Shorecliff House. Then he chose some points he could raise with his father, including the contract for Mrs. Field's cheeses.

As his father loved to remind him, White's was the oldest gentlemen's club in London, founded in 1693, and the place where the best of the peerage met to socialize. His father had told him many stories of White's when he was a boy, about conspiracies hatched to topple governments, broker huge financial deals, change the course of politics, and plot espionage.

For his part, John preferred his own club, which was much lighter and friendlier in tone, though he imagined that once he took his father's title he would have to take on his father's membership in White's as well.

That thought did not cheer him as he stepped up to the Portland stone entrance on St. James Street, beneath the elegant Palladian façade. A liveried footman opened the door for him and took his coat. The maître d' of course recognized him, and welcomed him. "Your father is in the reading room," he said. "Would you like me to have a boy escort you there?"

"I can find my way, thank you." As John climbed the marble stairs to the reading room, he wondered how well the boys were treated there. Wouldn't it be marvelous if he could compose an exposé about this beating heart of the London establishment?

Then he reminded himself that to do so would mean that the boys at the club were mistreated, and he sincerely hoped that was not the case.

He found his father perusing a copy of *Fraser's Magazine for Town and Country*. Earl Badgely put the magazine down and said, "Good, you are here. We can go into dinner."

The walls of the dining room were the color of green baize, lined with an eclectic collection of formal portraits of past members. They sat at spindle-backed chairs and his father ordered for both of them, as was his wont. Fortunately he and John shared the same taste in food, thick steaks and boiled potatoes.

"Tell me about your visit to Shorecliff House," his father said, after the server had walked away.

John was glad that he had written up his thoughts, and he launched into a few observations about the upkeep of the property. His father nodded appreciatively. "Did you mention these issues to Hetherington?"

"Only in passing," John said. "I did not feel it was my place to reprove him for such things, only to point them out."

"Good. You don't want to aggravate the man. He does a good enough job with what he's given."

"We did discuss some of the accounts," John said, and he mentioned his idea about increasing the dairy herd and directing the milk to Mrs. Fields and her cheese-making operation.

His father's eyebrows raised. "I didn't realize you took such an interest in financial matters."

"I believed that you sent me to Cornwall specifically for such ideas," John said. "After all, at some point I may be responsible not only for the living of my mother and sisters, but of all the tenant farmers and their families as well."

"You are sharpening up, my boy," Earl Badgely said as their dinners were delivered. "It has been a long time coming."

John did not respond, and for the rest of the meal his father led the conversation with talk of his committee's work to advance efforts in British West Africa.

"It's a tricky thing," he said. "The French are constantly advancing their own interests, and if Britain does not step up quickly we may find that they have colonized the whole interior of the continent."

"There are the Portuguese and the Belgians also?" John asked.

"Indeed. I feel it is up to Britain to carve the map so that no one power ascends, which could be very dangerous for all the rest. We depend so much these days on the riches to be exploited there for the continued prosperity of our own empire."

They carried on that way for a while, his father pontificating while John listened politely, though his mind kept straying to thoughts of Raoul Desjardins and questions about what he had found that day on his return to his office. Was he, as he feared, to be dismissed from his post and remanded back to France?

The idea made his stomach drop and his mouth go dry. The world was so unfair, no matter how much he wrote as Janner. He couldn't even keep the man he loved from harm.

Or could he? What if he went along with Morvan's scheme, and caused him to lose his position with the committee? Would that save Raoul's job? Or would there be another request or threat, another problem? Even if John agreed to Morvan's plan, how would that protect Raoul? He could easily be sent back to France on some other pretext.

Perhaps it was up to John to do something to save them both, though it might break his heart to do so.

Chapter 28

Morvan's Decision

Raoul was not surprised to be called into Morvan's office on his first day back from the trip to Cornwall. He had already prepared his speech, which he launched into as soon as Morvan motioned him to close the door, and he did.

"As I wrote to you in my letter, the earl does not love his son, nor does he care if Lord Therkenwell goes to jail and destroys his own reputation," he said. "I witnessed firsthand the lord's relationship with his family. His mother favors her two daughters, and his behavior is only tolerated by his father because he is destined to inherit. I met the son of the earl's cousin, who would accede to the title if Lord Therkenwell does not. He is much better favored than the earl's own son, more interested in the maintenance of the estate, and desperate to do anything to ingratiate himself to the Badgely family."

"So what do you propose we do?"

Raoul shrugged. "You can expose the lord to his father, but that will not change the earl's position on the exploration of West Africa."

"What do you believe would?"

Raoul hesitated. If he was correct, he might cause irreversible harm to the family he had come to care for. And if he did nothing, he was likely to lose his position and be sent back to Souvigné in disgrace. Finally he said, "I believe that the earl is lonely. That finding a woman for him might result in more effective blackmail."

To his surprise, Morvan laughed. "I did not expect you to be able to carry out this assignment. You *pédéraste*s are all alike. Unreliable. So I had to take matters into my own hands."

For a moment, Raoul thought that Morvan meant that he was going to seduce John himself, to gain the proof he needed. Instead Morvan said, "Do you know a woman called Louise Wickes?"

Raoul shook his head. "Well, you will meet her soon enough. She is a dressmaker's model, and very pretty. I have recruited her to seduce the earl. If we can't get to him through his son, we will get to him through his cock. He is notorious in his disdain for our country, and planting a Frenchwoman in his bed will cause him no end of trouble. Every aspect of his behavior will come under scrutiny. He will be forced to end his committee leadership and slink off to his country home."

Morvan was positively gleeful. "Another enemy of France vanquished!"

Raoul was having trouble understanding everything. Did this mean that John was off the hook? That Morvan had found another worm to use as his bait? And what did that mean for him?

"You may return to your desk. A great deal of correspondence has accumulated during your holiday which you will need to attend to. And you will need to meet Madame Wickes this evening to tell her everything you have learned about Earl Badgely's relationship with his family."

Thus dismissed, Raoul returned to his desk, still in shock. So he was to keep his job? At least for as long as it took him to manage this Madame Wickes, and see if she could accomplish what Raoul himself had not been able to.

Shortly before it was time to close the office, Morvan passed by his desk. "Here is her address," he said. "She has been told that you will call on her this evening at six o'clock and take her to dinner."

The address was on Bonhill Street, near Finsbury Square. "There is a chophouse on Worship Street, near to her lodgings," Morvan said. "I suggest you take her there." He laid a one-pound coin on the desk. "This should cover your carriage to her residence, and your meals. Be sure to treat her gracefully because even though she may be a harlot, she is a useful one to us."

Once again, Raoul was at a loss for words. Even though he still had piles of correspondence to go through, much of it needing translation, he left as soon as Morvan was gone. He hailed a carriage outside the embassy and gave the driver the address on Bonhill Street.

They drove through Kensington and along the edge of Hyde Park, past the monument erected the year before in memory of the queen's late husband, Prince Albert. The ornate gothic building with its tall spire, surmounted by a simple cross, was a testament to enduring love—the kind he hoped to continue building with John Seales. He couldn't help seeing that spire as an erect penis, which embarrassed him—but fortunately there was no one with him to notice.

Though it was evening, a ragged man stood at Hyde Park Corner hectoring anyone who passed about some political topic Raoul couldn't grasp. They passed the Wellington Arch, which always made his French heart quiver at the British monument to Napoleon's defeat at Waterloo.

Then the carriage turned onto Piccadilly, buzzing with pedestrians and other traffic, and he got a brief glimpse of the glorious dome of St. Paul's Cathedral before they turned inland to Finsbury Square. He paid the driver and then stood outside Madame Wickes's address, surveying it.

The house was older and showed a lack of upkeep. A discreet sign in the front window advertised rooms for twenty shillings per week, breakfast included. He rapped on the door and an elderly woman in an off-white dressing gown answered.

Raoul bowed low and asked, layering on his French accent, for Madame Wickes. The old harridan looked him up and down and then called back into the house, "Louise, another fancy man is here for you."

He waited in the cold, on the house's stoop, for Madame Wickes to appear. When she did, he was pleasantly surprised. He knew from Morvan that she was a widow in her mid-thirties, yet she looked nearly ten years younger, close to his own age. She wore a long black dress of surprisingly good quality, a sprightly gray bonnet with purple flowers, and a black woolen overcoat.

"My name is Raoul Desjardins," he said in French. "My supervisor at the French embassy, Georges Morvan, has asked me to escort you to dinner."

He saw the old crone hovering in the background, and hoped that she didn't speak French. "It would be my pleasure." Louise stepped down to the sidewalk and Raoul offered her his arm.

They walked easily together and he said, "I hear in your voice an echo of my childhood in Charente-Maritime," he said. "Do you come from that area as well?"

She looked at him in surprise, and answered in the affirmative in the Bourguignon dialect. They chatted about geography, and discovered that they had grown up only twenty miles or so apart, and that both their fathers had worked in the vineyards.

By then they had arrived at the chophouse suggested by Morvan. "I suppose you would like to know how I got myself into this situation," she said, when they were settled at a table.

He nodded slightly. "If you wish."

"I was only eighteen when I met my husband, Desmond Wickes. He was a British wine importer, a man of great charm and good humor, and very quickly I fell in love with him. On his next trip to Nantes, we were married, and I came to London with him."

The server approached, and Louise deferred to Raoul to order for both of them. Since he was paying with Morvan's money, Raoul ordered the Filet de Boeuf with olives, and a gratin Dauphinois as a side dish.

"Sadly, Desmond died only a few years later, before we were able to start a family," Louise continued. "I was left nearly penniless."

"I am sorry for your loss," Raoul said.

Louise smiled. "A friend introduced me to Madame Swaebe, a couturier dressmaker who specializes in attire for wealthy Americans. She appreciated my proportions and hired me as a model for her designs. She uses me as a canvas to create, and often I model the dresses in the salon. She then modifies each pattern for the customer."

"Is it satisfying work?" Raoul asked.

Louise laughed. "I am little more than a dummy. I am not to talk to Madame or any of the clients. Not even when she sticks me with pins." She leaned forward. "When Monsieur Morvan approached me, I did not feel I had any choice but to accept his suggestion."

"How did he know to reach you?"

"I belong to a loose circle of Frenchwomen here in London," Louise said. "Some are better fixed than I am, while others are in my situation. One of them is married to a prominent French businessman here in the city, an importer of textiles. Her husband and Morvan often met at functions, and Morvan approached him to ask if he knew a woman of great beauty but poor circumstances."

She blushed. "I say that not to promote myself, but merely to provide you with the context of his request."

"Understood," Raoul said. "And you need not apologize for your beauty."

"This man spoke with his wife, who suggested me, and she arranged for me to meet Morvan at a French café near the embassy, where apparently he is quite well-known. He took pains to impress on me his devotion to La France, and asked me about my patriotism."

She looked down at her plate, but when she looked up again her face had hardened. "When he was satisfied, he offered me a large amount of money to seduce Earl Badgely and then present evidence of the lord's infidelity to him. At first I was resistant, but the money... well, it would be a great help in my current circumstances."

"How did he effect the meeting?"

"He introduced me to a man he knew who also knew Badgely, and that man invited both of us to a dinner party. Then it was up to me to charm him."

She sat back and touched a handkerchief to her lips. "I managed to do that quite easily. He was lonely and in need of female companionship. Apparently his wife has been ill and abandoned their marital bed. He has called for me in his carriage and taken me to dinner three times, and to bed once."

Raoul did not know what to say.

She stared at him defiantly. "I know what that makes me. But I prefer to live rather than merely exist."

"And you do not wish to wait for love?"

She laughed. "I had love once, with Desmond. And see where it got me."

The server brought their meals and they ate, forestalling future chatter, commenting only on the quality of the filet and the savoriness of the potatoes. When she finally finished, Louise lay her cutlery by the side of the plate. "What is it you wish me to do now?"

He had to wait to speak until a loud pair of men had passed them by. "Morvan requires you to supply proof of your liaison, which can be presented to Earl Badgely in order to pressure his political leanings."

"And once that is provided? What happens to me?"

"That will be at Morvan's discretion."

"You are young, so perhaps you do not understand the full import of my situation," Louise said. "I have found a wealthy man who admires me and wishes to treat me well. If you use our liaison to blackmail him, I will lose all possibility with him. I must be compensated for that."

In the light of the chophouse, Raoul finally saw the faint lines etched on Louise Wickes' face, the price she had paid for years of penury. She would not have her looks for much longer, particularly if the malice he saw in her eyes continued to rise to the surface. He could not blame her for seeking to secure her future.

"You know that Earl Badgely is married," he said. "I have met his wife, and though she is not in the best of health she could linger for many years."

"Years in which he will continue to take me to expensive dinners, buy me jewels, and treat me as a lady should be."

He paid the check and was pleased to see that he had plenty left over. He'd treat himself to a carriage ride home, after he returned Madame Wickes to her residence. He stood and offered his hand to the lady, to help her rise. "I will speak with Morvan and address these issues with him."

Chapter 29

Many Resources

John went directly from White's to Raoul's lodgings in Bryanston Mews West. But Raoul was not there. Had he already left London? Was it possible that his boss, being so angry at Raoul's letter, had dismissed him that morning and sent him home to pack and then depart? Would he have sent a letter to John at Russell Square?

Should he go home and look for it? Find a bar to pass the time and return to Raoul's lodgings later?

His decision was forestalled the arrival of a carriage, which stopped at the door to Raoul's lodgings. He waited, his breath forming white clouds in the night cold, as Raoul stepped out of the carriage and bid the driver good night.

Only then did John call out to him.

Raoul turned swiftly. "John! What brings you here?"

"I had to know what happened to you today."

"It is an interesting story. Come upstairs with me and I will tell you."

His room was chilly, but Raoul poured them both glasses of brandy, and they began to warm up. Raoul relayed Morvan's surprising act, and the introduction of Madame Louise Wickes to the mix. John then told him about his dinner with Earl Badgely.

"So there we are," John said, when he was finished. "What do we do next?"

"It seems to be out of our hands at the moment," Raoul said. "Morvan has passed the direction of Madame Wickes to me. She is to induce your father to buy her some expensive trinket, which we can then use to blackmail him about the affair."

"I do think he cares more for my mother's feelings than for my own," John said. "So it is entirely possible that Morvan's scheme will work. And my father's known antipathy to the French will contribute to snide comments behind his back. But will he resign his position?"

"Morvan believes that once his liaison with a Frenchwoman is disclosed, your father's loyalty to the crown will become suspect. Though our two countries are not currently at war, there is a long-standing anger between Britain and France, and anyone who crosses lines, especially surreptitiously, will be suspect. Morvan believes that your father will be forced to resign the chairmanship of his committee."

John shrugged. "So? Someone else will take over."

"Most likely. But you know how slowly governments move in this regard. Your father's resignation may leave his committee in confusion, and a delay of a few months or a year in the establishment of their goals could be quite helpful to France."

"I understand. We are talking about the movement of governments. But why must you and I be involved? Let this Frenchwoman confront your father on her own, and make her demands."

"You cannot be so naïve," Raoul said. His face darkened.

John crossed his arms over his chest. "What do you mean?"

"A man like your father has many resources at his command. Compare those to what an impoverished Frenchwoman, an alien in your land, has at her disposal. What kind of threat could she pose? And imagine how easily your father could have her neutralized, if he holds you, his son and heir, in so little regard?"

"Are you suggesting he would have her killed?" John protested. "He would not do such a thing."

"But would he have her bundled off to France? Perhaps with a cash payment?"

John frowned. "Quite possible."

"If the blackmail comes from you, however, that makes it more dangerous for him," Raoul said. "You have connections. You have credibility with your mother, with the press. It would be much harder for him to dismiss a threat if it comes through you."

"And your Morvan holds a threat over me, to compel my compliance," John said miserably. "Exposing our relationship, and my deviance. Not to mention what he could do to you if I do not comply."

"It is a very difficult situation." Raoul took a deep breath. "Perhaps we should sever our alliance, at least at present. Then Morvan will have less leverage over you."

John felt his stomach cramp. "Do you wish that?" he said, his voice cracking.

"Not at all, my dearest," Raoul said. "It would probably mean that Morvan would dismiss me immediately, if I am of no further use for him. I would go back to France. Perhaps to Paris, where I have friends and past colleagues. Or eventually back to Souvigné."

"But what would you do there?"

Raoul shrugged. "My political career would certainly be over," he said. "I might be able to get a post as a teacher or administrator at a school. It depends on what Morvan spreads about me, and how damaged my reputation becomes. I may have to follow my father into the vineyards."

"That cannot happen," John said. "You and I have linked our fortunes together. I will not see you destroyed on my account, or in some futile effort to protect me."

"We must let time take its course," Raoul said.

John shook his head. "I cannot let you suffer on my account. If life as a member of the landed class has taught me anything, it is that we are responsible for those beneath us."

Raoul stared at him open-mouthed. "You think me beneath you?"

"No, no, that is not what I meant. I have a title, a status in society, family money. You have none of that. I cannot take advantage of you."

"You seem to believe that you are in control of my life," Raoul said. "You are not Father Maurice, using my body for your own pleasure. I give that willingly to you. And you are not Georges Morvan, forcing me to act against my will. Do you not understand that I have been under the direction of powerful men my entire life?"

He glared at John. "Morvan can do with me what he will, and I will survive. I do not need your title, your status, or your money."

John wilted under Raoul's onslaught. "I wish that I could scratch out all that I have said, as I might in writing one of my essays, and begin again. My only desire is to love you."

Raoul's shoulders fell. "I know, *mon cher*. But we are at the mercy of larger forces. We must bend but not allow ourselves to be broken."

Chapter 30

Louise's Assignment

During the following week, Raoul met twice with Louise Wickes, each time during a break from her duties at Madame Swaebe's. They met at a coffee shop on New Burlington Street on the Wednesday after their first dinner.

"I have requested a trinket from Earl Badgely as a token of his affection," she said. "He has promised to bring one to me the next time we meet. Thursday evening."

Raoul felt dirty, and he wasn't sure if it was because of the smoke in the coffee shop or the transaction he was participating in. But he said, "That's very good."

"And what of an arrangement for me?" Louise asked.

"I spoke of that with Monsieur Morvan. He spoke with the man who effected your introduction, who is an importer of wine from France, like your late husband. He has need of an assistant who is fluent in French and English, and has a knowledge of wine. After you have completed your assignment, Morvan assures me that this man will hire you, at a salary much greater than you achieve from Madame Swaebe. And he will also see you clear to a payment of one hundred pounds. That combination should adequately compensate you for the risks you are taking, and the loss of Earl Badgely's companionship."

One hundred pounds was more than Raoul's annual salary, so he was sure she would accept the offer, and she did, though reluctantly. "I do like the man," she said. "Above and beyond his generosity to me. I find his loneliness affecting."

"Well, let him cure that feeling by returning to his wife," Raoul said.

Louise's countenance hardened then. "How will I pass you the bauble, once I receive it?" she asked.

"Morvan will send you instructions. I may receive it from you, or the earl's son may be given that task. He has yet to make a decision, but he will arrange to have a message sent to you with specific details."

He met with her once more, mid-morning on Friday, to confirm that she had been given a pair of earrings. "Morvan told me that he will send you a coded message telling you where and when to meet Lord Therkenwell. There will be a naval term, a reference to history, and a connection to birds."

He leaned close. "I can tell you the substance, but in absolute confidence. I have been given a copy of the message to pass on to Lord Therkenwell." Then he told her what to look for in the message.

"This is a difficult time for us both," he said. "I hope that everything works out so that all involved can move on safely."

Then he left her to return to his office.

Chapter 31

Rendezvous

The message from the Foreign Office arrived at eleven-fifteen on a Monday morning, as Toby Marsh and Magnus Dawson were sitting down to a late breakfast.

"I say, the boys have cleaned up sharply," Magnus said. "And to prepare a solid English breakfast after we were all up so late last night. Quite commendable."

The party the night before had been filled with much banter, and the guests had drunk copious bottles of wine.

"A letter for Master Toby," Will said, returning to the dining table, where both men were drinking cups of hot tea in the hope of awakening their dulled senses.

"Oh, dear," Toby said, as he took the letter from Will. "What do they want now?"

"Your help in deciphering some obscure message, I would think," Magnus said.

For some time, the Marsh-Dawson household had been engaged in a delicate relationship with the Foreign Office. Their louche arrangement—two men living together, in a home only a short distance from two women who were their close friends—proved occasionally useful in understanding the gossip of the time.

And Toby's skill at languages—he was fluent in French, German and Russian, and conversant in Spanish and Italian—had been useful as well, particularly in interpreting coded messages.

The missive that midmorning contained another.

"This is odd," Toby said, after a moment's perusal. "Not just in French, but encoded in some way."

Magnus shifted his chair around so he could see the paper in front of his lover. "Not the original, certainly," Magnus said.

"No, this must be one of several copies circulated. I can't see their regular translators being able to make heads or tails of it."

"Read it out," Magnus said. "Perhaps there is something in the rhythm of the language."

« *Rencontre moi a la fin de César, quand le soleil est au-dessus du bras de la vergue et que l'hirondelle rencontre la vigne,* » Toby read. "It sounds like a rendezvous of some type, but it makes no sense. When the sun is above the arm of the yard?"

"Ah, but you do not have a nautical bent, my dear," Magnus said. "We have an expression in the Navy, 'when the sun is above the yardarm.' The yardarm is a horizontal bar on the mast of a ship. The sailors were not allowed to drink until the sun had passed over it—about noon."

"Interesting," Toby said. "But what about the other business, of the *hirondelle* meeting the vine?"

"That makes no sense to me," Magnus said. "But a hirondelle—what's that in English?"

"A swallow," Toby said.

"So where does the swallow meet the vine?" Magnus asked.

Will came in to clear the teacups. "You're looking for directions?" he asked. "The intersection of Swallow Street and Vine Street. It's just off Piccadilly, across from St. James' Church."

"And Caesar's end," Magnus said. "The death of Caesar, the Ides of March."

"Today," Toby said. "Well, there's not enough time to get a return message to the Foreign Office and have them arrange a surveillance of this meeting."

"Then we shall have to do it ourselves, and report back afterward." Magnus pushed back from the table. "But we must hurry. Noon approaches."

"What's the weather like, Will?" Toby asked.

"Unaccountably sunny," Will said. "But there's a chill. What will you both be wanting to wear?"

"I shall handle the valeting for both of us, as we are in a hurry," Toby said. He followed Magnus out of the dining room and up the stairs to their room on the second floor. It was a narrow house in a mews off Piccadilly, once intended for servants. Two bedrooms on the first floor, public rooms on the ground level, and accommodations for Will and Carlo in the basement. Carlo, being of a Mediterranean background, particularly liked being close to the oil burner there, while Will was grateful they were both off the street.

"I think your fawn lounge suit and a white shirt," Toby said as they reached the bedroom. "We shan't be calling on anyone." The lounge suit was among Magnus's most casual yet still formal clothing. It had a cutaway jacket over a vest with four bone buttons, the bottom one always unbuttoned, and striped trousers – a daring look. A member of the aristocracy without Magnus's louche connections would always wear a matching pair of trousers.

"And we will want to be relatively anonymous," Magnus said. "Especially if we must follow someone."

Toby began taking clothes from their wardrobe as Magnus stripped off his morning robe. Toby took a clandestine moment to view his lover's naked body in the warm sunlight. Years of service in Her Majesty's Navy had honed his musculature, and Magnus took regular exercise to keep it thus. He had a broad, nearly hairless chest, with a single line that ran down to the furry patch surrounding his ample penis.

Magnus caught him looking. "Now, now, none of that, my dear.

Perhaps when we return from this brief bit of surveillance we shall have chance to enjoy ourselves."

"You were certainly enjoying yourself with that German last night," Toby said. "Had you flirted anymore with the man he'd have had your trousers down in front of the company."

"You know that you are the only one allowed to remove my trousers," Magnus said. "Though I must admit he had such a sweet mouth on him, I did imagine it once or twice wrapped around my cock."

"Take these," Toby said, tossing a pair of underdrawers at him. "Cover yourself before I do something untoward."

They dressed quickly, Magnus keeping an eye on his pocket watch. "How do you think we shall recognize these men?"

"Who says they are men?" Toby said. "We must watch for any encounter that appears suspicious."

They finished dressing quickly and headed out toward Piccadilly. The street was bustling with fashionable ladies enjoying the unexpected sunshine, tradesmen going about their ways, and a shabby old man with a monkey on his shoulder. "How will we ever recognize our mysterious rendezvous?" Toby muttered.

"Instinct and insight," Magnus said. They moved quickly down Piccadilly, passing the corner of Sackville Street, until they were across from St. James-in-the-Fields, designed by the noted architect Sir Christopher Wren. The square brick edifice, with its white pointings where the exterior walls met, seemed to Toby to symbolize all that was Britain. Reassuringly simple and solid. The very image of what he and Magnus had to fight for, in their occasional work for the Foreign Office.

They turned into a narrow street of brick and marble buildings clustered close together, and as they approached the intersection of Swallow and Vine, they saw a well-dressed man of about their own age, late twenties, looking nervously ahead of them.

"Isn't that Lord Therkenwell?" Magnus asked. "How very odd to find him exactly where we are supposed to be."

Magnus was about to hail him when Toby stayed his arm. "Magnus," he muttered. "He may be our prey, not just our acquaintance." He steered Magnus toward a break in the buildings, where they could loiter unseen, and watch.

Lord Therkenwell wore a dove-gray single-breasted morning coat with a swallow tail, and his black trousers had a fine cut, with a barely visible gray pinstripe. Atop his head was a crowned bowler hat of black felt, with a black silk ribbon above the brim. He was the very picture of a Victorian dandy of great wealth, down to his shiny black shoes.

Therkenwell pulled a pocket watch from his vest and checked it, then looked up at the sky as if for agreement. Then suddenly he put the watch back, and his posture straightened.

Toby looked back toward Piccadilly and noticed an elegant woman approaching, wearing a maroon silk dress in the latest Parisian fashion. She carried a small reticule and a furled parasol, both in matching maroon.

"Well, we know this is not a romantic assignation," Magnus said. "Unless Therkenwell has been hiding more than a long, skinny cock from us."

"Which you have only spied through his trouser," Toby said. "And I hope he continues to hide that from you. Or he might find himself losing it."

Magnus smiled broadly. "My dear, do I detect a bit of jealousy on your part?"

"Therkenwell is handsome, if a bit foppish for my taste. But he is of the aristocracy like you, whereas I am not."

"You have no need to be jealous, Mr. Marsh," Magnus said. "My eyes, lips, tongue, cock, ass—indeed my entire being—is all owed to you, and no one else."

Toby gulped, thinking of Magnus's naked body for a moment, then returned his gaze to Therkenwell. The woman moved smoothly toward him, and then, almost unseen had they not been watching closely, slipped something from her reticule into his hand.

The light caught it for a moment, and it glowed a bright blue. Then it was inside Therkenwell's vest pocket, and the woman had moved on, continuing down Vine Street toward the Man in Moon Passage, which led to Regent Street.

"Shall we split up?" Magnus said. "I will take Therkenwell, and you follow our new female acquaintance."

"Be careful," Toby said, and then Magnus was gone, his aristocratic gait more a saunter as he kept the lordling in front of him.

Chapter 32

The Man in the Moon

Magnus remained far enough behind Therkenwell so that he could not sense he was being followed, even as they approached the Man in the Moon passage.

He recalled learning the story of the Biblical connection to the passage when he was a boy. A man had been caught gathering sticks for a fire on the Sabbath day, and was brought before Moses and Aaron and the people of Israel. He was found guilty and sentenced to be stoned to death. Magnus's nanny had told him that the man in the moon he saw on clear nights was that unnamed man who had been punished by God.

She had shown him a book with a picture of a man in a crescent moon carrying a bundle of sticks, with a lantern and a dog. At the time, he'd only registered the figure of the dog, because he loved the hounds that his father kept for hunting, and longed for a dog of his own. But the Duke of Hereford had dictated that dogs were working animals, not pets, and Magnus was chastised whenever he was caught petting them or feeding them treats.

He wondered, as he followed Therkenwell, if he and Toby could get a dog. It would be lovely to have one who would sprawl on his lap, lick his face and provide him with unconditional love.

But then, he had Toby for all that.

The alley was short, lined with back doors for the shops and cafés on either side. There was enough traffic that he could keep an eye on Therkenwell without getting too close. The younger man moved quickly, darting past slower pedestrians, until they emerged in sunlight again at Regent Street.

The light struck Magnus's eyes after the dimness of the passage, and he bumped right into his target before he realized that Therkenwell had stopped. So much for his tracking talents.

"Terribly sorry," he said. Then his prey turned around. "Therkenwell! My! Out for a morning stroll?"

Unexpectedly, Therkenwell turned to confront him. "Do you know a man called Raoul Desjardins? I met him at a salon at your home."

Magnus cocked his head. "Last night?"

"No, several weeks ago."

Magnus pursed his lips together, trying to recall. Their salon guests came and went, often foreigners whom Toby knew through his translation and tutoring work. "I can't say I recall him."

"About your height—tall enough that he had to lower his head to..." He stopped himself. "Um. Handsome, in a very French way of course. Wavy black hair with pomade, green eyes with flecks of gold, eyelashes like a girl's..." He stopped again. "Blast! I'm not doing this very well, am I?"

"There's a café across the road," Magnus said. "Would you like to talk about this more privately?"

Therkenwell nodded eagerly. "I would."

They crossed Regent Street, avoiding a carriage whose driver was going altogether too fast for the busy roadway. Then they ducked into a café called The Round Cheese, and Magnus, seeking to put Therkenwell at ease, said, "Did you hear that story, when you were a boy? That the moon was made of cheese?"

For the first time Therkenwell smiled. "Yes, my nanny used to tell us that, when we'd see the full moon reflected in a puddle of water. You know, I never connected it to the Man in the Moon passage."

Magnus requested a table in the back corner where they could talk privately, and after they had both ordered cups of Earl Grey, Magnus said, "So, you met this Raoul fellow at one of our soirées and you'd like to get to know him better."

Therkenwell shook his head. "I already know him quite well enough, thank you."

"Then why ask me about him?"

Therkenwell's body seemed to collapse in on itself. "Therkenwell, whatever is the matter? Can I help?"

"May I tell you a secret, Dawson? And have you pledge to tell no one else?"

"I do not keep secrets from Mr. Marsh," Magnus said. "But between the two of us we are very skilled at holding our cards close to our chests, as you may have already intuited."

"He took me to bed!" Therkenwell blurted, fortunately before the server arrived with their tea.

Once the old dear was gone, Magnus said gently, "You may already know that Toby and I share more than accommodations. So your revelation is not upsetting to me."

Therkenwell's hands were shaking, and Magnus put his right on the other man's left and held it there for a moment. "It's a frightening thing to admit to someone else, isn't it?" he said in a low voice. "I know, because I have had to do it myself. But trust me, it becomes easier once you have acknowledged it to yourself. That is the first step toward making a full life."

"It's not like you and Marsh." Therkenwell extricated his hand and then raised the teacup to his mouth. Then he put the cup down again. "I am worried, despite his protestations, that he doesn't love me. That perhaps is only using me for his own purposes."

"Sometimes men are like that," Magnus said, between sips of his own tea. It was lemony, due to the aroma of bergamot, and reminded him of breakfasts at Martindale House, his family seat. "Some men take their pleasure without concern for the other man. Particularly in school years, as sometimes what a stronger boy wants is taken from us. Sadly that occurs among grown men, as well."

He leaned forward. "If you are ill, there are potions and treatments."

"For a broken heart?" Therkenwell said bitterly.

"Perhaps it would help you to tell your story," Magnus said.

Outside the café's broad windows, he saw a young ragamuffin running down Regent Street, chased by a bobby. Against the beliefs of his class, he hoped the young man got away.

"As I said, we met at one of your salons. He caught my eye, and we spoke covertly, though his intentions were clear from the very beginning."

"And this was not your first such encounter?" Magnus asked.

Therkenwell laughed. "No, I fagged for several older boys at Eton, often with pleasure. So I knew what I was in for."

He picked up his teacup with one shaky hand and sipped again. "We went back to his room after the soirée," he said. "And that's when it started. Our relationship."

"What happened?"

"We have been intimate for several weeks," Therkenwell said. "At his rooms and once or twice in mine, but never in public. Until recently this was a secret I kept even from my valet." He looked up at Magnus. "My father has no direct knowledge of my... proclivities, though he has often expressed suspicion. If he were to learn, I would be disinherited."

"You could make your way in the world on your own," Magnus said gently. "Many men of my acquaintance do."

"It is not myself I worry about. I have two younger sisters, and my father's estate is entailed. It must go to a male member of the family, and the nearest one has already been nosing around my family as if he was already entitled. Despite his statements, I do not know that I can trust him. I fear that if he inherits the title he will have no obligation to look after my sisters or enter them into profitable marriages."

"How old are they?"

"Fifteen and seventeen."

"So your oldest sister has a year until her debut."

"She is quite the scholar, our Vanessa. She would like to study at the Bedford College for Women. She would prefer not to marry until she has gained her education. Lizzie is a girl of a lighter temperament, and cannot wait for her debut, though of course it would be a scandal if she were to marry before Vanessa."

He shook his head. "So you see, I cannot abandon them."

"Would your father not look after them himself and see them educated, and married?"

"He would, but though he is in otherwise good health, he has gout and I worry for his survival long enough."

"So," Magnus said. "Your father must not learn of your proclivities. If you are careful, then you may keep them hidden until his passing. Then you inherit the title and the estate and see to your sisters."

"But there is Raoul," Therkenwell said, his voice strangling. "He is an assistant secretary at the French embassy here in London. His boss has discovered not only his inclination, but his relationship with me, and has concocted a blackmail scheme against me and my father."

Magnus cocked his head. "A blackmail scheme?"

"At first, he threatened that Raoul must tell my father about me. But then Raoul convinced him, after meeting my family, that my parents care little about me and my reputation. That even if such demands were made to him, that he would ignore them and let me flap in the wind like a disconnected sail."

"You say at first. What has happened since then?"

Therkenwell reached into the pocket of his vest and withdrew the sparkling amethyst Magnus had caught sight of as the woman passed it to him. "What is this?" Magnus asked. "A token between you and Raoul?"

Therkenwell shook his head miserably. "No, a token from my father to his mistress. A Frenchwoman."

Magnus examined the earring. The central amethyst was quite fine, surrounded by a ring of tiny diamonds. Then, in the girandole style, three amethysts in declining sizes hung by gold chains. He turned it over and peered at it closely. He saw the distinctive *A* with a tail that curved under it. Asprey's, one of London's finest jewelers. Such a bauble must have cost a pretty penny.

Therkenwell smiled grimly. "It seems father and son have at least one romantic tendency in common. An affinity for the French."

"Your father has a mistress," Magnus said, nodding. "Sadly, not uncommon of men of his age, wealth, and station. Your mother still lives?"

"She prefers to stay at our county seat in Cornwall."

"And she knows nothing of your father's doings in town?"

"No. But it would destroy her. She has always had a delicate constitution, and almost lost her life delivering Lizzie. Since then, she has kept herself to her rooms. Even as children, we were not allowed to yell or cry out in play, for fear that she would be overcome with fright that one of us had been harmed."

"I am not sure I see the full picture yet," Magnus said.

Therkenwell took a deep breath. "My father sits on the Committee for British West Africa," he said. "He is its chair, and a very influential vote on any policies concerning exploration and commerce with the African colonies. As far as I understand, there is a crucial vote coming that would devote considerable resources to bringing African territories under the Queen's rule."

Magnus realized with a start that Therkenwell's problems were of a part with the letters Toby had been translating. If the Foreign Office was already involved, then young Therkenwell was in greater trouble than he realized.

"And where does this love token come in?"

"I am to show it to my father and convince him that if he does not change his vote, his paramour will reveal herself. His reputation will be destroyed, as will my mother's."

"Was that your father's mistress, the woman who handed you the stone?" Magnus asked.

Therkenwell looked up in alarm. "You saw the exchange?"

"I did."

"I didn't recognize the woman, but she knew me. So she is probably the one, a Louise Wickes. But how did you happen to be there to witness the exchange?"

"I'm afraid your problems are bigger than you believe." Magnus pulled coins from his wallet, left them by the saucer, and stood. "You should come to our home immediately so we can discuss this further."

Chapter 33

Louise Wickes

Toby followed the elegant woman as she retraced her steps to Piccadilly. She did not appear frightened, or in a hurry. Indeed, when she reached Piccadilly she strolled slowly down the avenue, looking into shop windows.

Toby hung back, looking at his reflection in a window and smoothing his hair. After two blocks, she motioned to a carriage outside the Burlington Arcade. After a brief discussion with the driver, she stepped inside and the carriage made off down the street.

Toby spotted an urchin lingering outside the Arcade and approached him. "Did you hear the address that lady gave?"

The boy stuck his hands in his pockets and glared at Toby. "What if I did?"

"There's a penny in it for you. But I have to know you're telling the truth."

"How can you know that?"

"What kind of accent did the woman have?"

"French, of course," the boy said.

Toby was satisfied and fished out a coin from his pocket. He held it up to the boy. "The address?"

"Number nine, New Burlington Street," the boy said, and Toby handed him the coin. "She your lady friend?"

"Not quite." He tousled the boy's light brown hair. "Good lad."

Then he hurried back to Ormond Yard, where he looked up the address on an ordnance survey map. It was a business, and when he checked a directory of London business addresses, he discovered it was a dressmaker's shop. The proprietor was a Madame Swaebe. He wasn't sure if that was useful information or not; he'd have to see if one of their lady friends, the Honorable Sylvia Cooke or her companion, Miss Parker, knew anything about it. Did it cater to Frenchwomen? How could they learn more about the identity of this mysterious woman in maroon silk?

He was tempted to walk over there and survey the area himself, but he knew he had to wait for Magnus to return home with whatever he had learned about Lord Therkenwell.

He was in the front room he used as an office when meeting with students or translation clients, looking out the window for Magnus. He was surprised, though, to find that Magnus had brought the young lord himself to their home.

Magnus looked serious, while Therkenwell resembled a dog who had been chastised for chewing a shoe. He faced the ground, moving one foot slowly after the other, his shoulders slumped in desolation.

This was not the young fop who had graced their salon in the past, but rather a ghostly shadow of him. Toby rose and went into the front hallway, and opened the door to them, bringing in a gust of chilly air. The sun had gone behind clouds and none of the morning's bright promise remained.

"My lord," he said to Therkenwell.

"Please, can we dispense with the formality? My name is John, John Seales."

"And I am Toby."

He held his hand out and John took it in his clammy one. "Magnus seems to think you can help me."

"We will do whatever we can," Toby said. "Please, come into the front room. Would you like some tea?"

"We've just had," Magnus said. "Perhaps something a bit stronger for John here. Brandy? Or we have some good Scotch whisky."

"A whisky would help," John said.

Toby went to the kitchen to fetch it, and found Carlo there. "Whisky all around, please. And perhaps some crackers if we have them."

"In a moment, sir," Carlo said.

Toby returned to the front room where he found Magnus on the sofa, and John in an armchair across from him.

"To spare John the ordeal of repeating what he has told me, I'll summarize for you." Magnus sketched out the problem John faced. "Did you have any success in following the woman?"

"She picked up a carriage in front of the Burlington Arcade, but an urchin overheard the address and revealed it to me. A dressmaker called Madame Swaebe, with a location in New Burlington Street. Does that mean anything to you?"

"Raoul told me that she is a dressmaker's model. I presume that is where she is employed."

"The damnable problem is what we tell the Foreign Office," Magnus said. "And when."

"The Foreign Office!" John startled, but could not say more until Carlo had delivered the refreshments and left the room. "But why would you tell them?"

Magnus looked to Toby, who said, "On occasion, I do some translating work for them, when their own staff is too busy or the work too complicated. I have recently been engaged in translating some documents which relate to your father's committee. And somehow they got a copy of the message sent to you, which they forwarded to me for translation."

He leaned forward. "How good is your French?"

"I spent a year in Paris after college and I would say I am reasonably fluent."

"Enough to understand words like *hirondelle*? And a reference to Julius Caesar?"

"You've read the note," John said with resignation. "Raoul brought it to me three days ago. Apparently a separate copy was sent to Madame Wickes to arrange our meeting today. But how did the Foreign Office intercept it? Raoul swore to me that he concocted it himself, and made only one copy, which someone in his office was to deliver to Madame Wickes."

"There are two possibilities," Magnus said. "One is that your lover is a double agent, working for the British as well as the French."

John shook his head. "I have worried that might be the case. But my judgment is that it is not possible. He is as likely as I am to be destroyed if our secret comes out."

"You said that Raoul's boss at the embassy had discovered your affair, and confronted Raoul with evidence of it," Magnus said. "Is it possible that to save his own hide, Raoul made a contact with the Foreign Office?"

"I suppose. But we are in this together. I am sure that he would have discussed the option with me."

"Then there is one other choice. The messenger who delivered the epistle to Madame Wickes. We will have to speak with Raoul about him."

Toby stepped in. "Be assured the Foreign Office was baffled by the message. That's why they sent it to me. And when we figured out the rendezvous mentioned in the message was to take place at noon today, we did not have time to notify anyone. That's why we were there."

"So the Foreign Office doesn't know?"

"Not yet," Magnus said. "Though at some point we need to involve them. You have been entreated to enter into an act of espionage against her Majesty's government."

"But I haven't done anything yet," John pleaded. "Only receive the blasted earring from the woman who claims to be my father's mistress."

"Though you are a member of the upper class, you could be implicated in the act of sodomy," Magnus said. "Which leads to imprisonment, if convicted."

"Do you recognize Raoul's name?" Magnus asked Toby. "I feel it is familiar but I wonder how he got himself invited to our home."

"Let me think for a moment." Toby rose and pulled an appointment book from the shelf. He paged through it. "Here it is. Monsieur Desjardins came to me for a work of translation."

"But why?" John asked. "He spoke fluent English and French."

"Ah, but I can translate German as well," Toby said. "Let me see if I made any notes."

He put the appointment book down and turned back to the bookshelf, where he paged through a stack of manila folders. "Here it is. A German explorer's journal of his expedition through a part of Africa. Monsieur Desjardins understood the general gist of the material, but he wanted help with certain words and phrases in the East Prussian dialect."

"Do you remember him personally?" Magnus asked.

Toby frowned. "Young, handsome, but a bit slick for my tastes. Now that I recall, he nosed around about our salons and asked how one could gain an invitation."

"When was this?" Magnus asked.

Toby looked back at the folder. "He was here in mid-January."

"That's about when I met him," John said.

Magnus sat back against the sofa with his glass of whisky. "Interesting. So he came to Toby for a bit of translation work, which he might have managed on his own with a good dictionary, and asked for an invitation to a salon."

"He told me that his friend Silas put him up to it. Silas Thorne, a barrister's clerk."

Magnus smiled. "I believe I met Mr. Thorne that same evening. He was most eager to make the acquaintance of Richard Pemberton, that fat barrister at Gray's Inn."

Toby looked at John curiously. "And did he, do you know?"

John nodded. "Though not in the way you might imagine. He merely wanted to insinuate himself with the man to get a better job. Which he achieved, apparently without exposing either his ass or his cock to the man."

Toby concentrated for a moment. "Let's put Silas Thorne and Richard Pemberton aside, until we see a further connection. I think we must take the long view," he said. "Someone in the French government wants to influence British decisions in West Africa. They target Earl Badgely because of his position on the committee that makes these decisions."

Magnus picked up his thread. "They look for ways to influence him. Perhaps they learned of John first, and thought that by confronting the Earl with evidence of his son's sexual activities with other men that they could sway him to their way of thinking."

"My father would never agree to that," John said. "He'd just as soon see me committed to gaol for life." He put his head in his hands. "When I was a child he cautioned me repeatedly against becoming an invert. When I stepped too delicately, or refrained from manly pursuits such as shooting, he very nearly accused me of buggery. When I would come home from Eton and he'd ask about my time, he refused to hear anything about the boys I fagged for."

"Were you having sex even then?" Magnus asked.

Both Toby and John looked at him. "Magnus was sent to sea as a young boy," Toby said. "He doesn't know what goes on behind those ivied walls."

"Really?" Magnus asked. He looked at Toby, who shot him a warning glare. Now was not the time to discuss Toby's school days, in front of a visitor.

"Raoul came to my family home at Shorecliff House for two weeks," John said. "A trip from which we have just returned. My father had been pressuring me to go, and Raoul felt that the sojourn would give us time to figure out how to respond to his boss. He inscribed a letter, indicating that based on his observation of me and my family, he believed that I would not be a pressure point for my father. He posted the letter from St. Mawes. Apparently his boss received it and moved forward with a secondary scheme involving Madame Wickes."

"You mentioned your mother's frailty," Magnus said.

John nodded. "My father would protect her. At least, he would protect himself from scandal. If it were to come out he was consorting with the enemy, as he might say, then he would certainly lose his place on the committee."

"So somehow your adversaries brought Madame Wickes into his orbit. She did appear to be quite an attractive woman, if you are interested in such," Toby said. "They have waited until they have evidence of the affair, this earring. Now their plan is in motion."

"You say you have connections within the Foreign Office," John said. "Can you present them with this evidence and have them arrest this Wickes woman?"

"And then the whole sordid business would come out," Magnus said. "Leading perhaps to your father losing his position, your mother losing her health, and you losing your inheritance. Not to mention what such a revelation would do to your sisters' marriage potential."

John sunk down into the armchair and began to sob. "I've been such a failure. This is all my fault."

"Now, now," Magnus said. "Not all your fault, surely. Neither you nor Monsieur Desjardins are to blame in this situation. Your father is the one having an affair that could compromise his position, and spending quite a bit of your potential inheritance at Asprey's."

"Why is this all so important?" John said, when he had dried his eyes. "I mean, who cares about a cluster of natives in some godforsaken land?"

"Speaking as a former naval officer, I can tell you that governments see colonies as assets in 'balance of power' negotiations. There have been numerous occasions when overseas territories have been exchanged between rulers."

He sipped his whisky. "And colonies with large native populations are also a source of military power. For example, some of our strongest soldiers have come from India."

"So there is quite a lot at stake, for both your family and our government," Toby said. "This will require a good bit of consideration."

Chapter 34

An Old Shipmate

"We need several pieces of information," Magnus said. "Toby, if you please, could you take notes for us? Your handwriting is so much better than my own."

"Which is not saying much," Toby said to John. "His hand is abysmal. Comes from so much time at sea, scribbling anything while the waves rock the boat."

"It could also be that Mr. Marsh has had a great deal more education than I have." Magnus smiled. "Or perhaps that I am the one accustomed to giving the orders around this house."

"Humph," Toby snorted, but he retrieved a pen and an empty journal from the desk. "Please, sir, may I take your dick—tation?" Toby smiled, as if butter wouldn't melt in his mouth, and for the first time that afternoon they saw John Seales laugh.

"First, we need to know more about this committee that the earl directs," Magnus said. "I have read about it occasionally in the papers, but what exactly is its purpose? When does it meet, and when must it make decisions? That will give us an idea of what the French timetable is."

Toby wrote all that down.

"We must also be careful that in any of our actions, we do not harm her majesty's government," Magnus said. "Despite our eagerness to help our young friend we must remember our loyalties."

"I agree," Toby said.

"Next, I would like to know more about Madame Wickes," Magnus continued. "We must see if we have any acquaintances in common who could tell us about her origin, her connections to the French government, and so on."

"You must speak with Raoul as soon as possible," Toby said to John. "Establish if his superiors have a timetable for him. And what he knows of Madame Wickes."

"His boss directed him to take her to dinner soon after we returned from Cornwall," John said. "She seems to him a decent enough sort of person, trapped in the same web Raoul and I are, though in her case due to economic necessity."

Toby wrote more in the notebook. "I will speak with Gervase Quinn at the Foreign Office. I can provide him with our translation—but sadly, it will be too late for them to engage in surveillance. I'll try to determine how Quinn came across this message and what else we can do to help him, without revealing that we already know the parties involved."

They chatted for a while longer, and then the grandfather clock in the hallway chimed two o'clock in the afternoon. "I'd better get over to the Foreign Office," Toby said. "John, how shall we communicate with you? Send you a summons to come back here? I'd rather not put anything sensitive in writing. You don't know if anyone in your household has been spying on you."

"On me! But why?"

Magnus gave him a pitying look. "Someone got hold of that coded message and got it into the hands of the Foreign Office," he said. "The leak could have come on your end, or on Raoul's. Until we know further it's best to be careful."

John shook his head. "It is not possible. I have one manservant,

Beller, who is devoted to me. And a girl comes in to clean a few days a week."

"And when you go out?" Magnus asked. "Do you know for certain that no one tracks you? Not to a bar or molly house?"

"But that's ridiculous. I am no one."

"You are a man of title," Toby said. "And your father is a member of the House of Lords. And as we have seen, the French have taken an interest in your father."

By the time Toby ushered him out of the front door, John looked as shattered as he had when he had entered it. "Poor chap," he said to Magnus when he returned to the sitting room. "In way over his head."

"We could be in a similar situation someday. It is only your connection to the Foreign Office, as well as my father's name and my place in society, that protects us from the effects of the Offences Against the Person Act."

Toby had been a mere boy when the death penalty for acts of sodomy had been lifted, but he knew that if he and Magnus were ever caught in flagrante, that because he was not part of the gentry, he'd be the one punished by a minimum of ten years' imprisonment. Magnus might escape that, but his name would be ruined and he would be shunned by society.

"I know, my dearest," Toby said. "And I know that our protection by the Foreign Office only goes so far, as long as we prove useful to them."

Their arrangement, such as it was, had begun after both of them had completed a dangerous assignment. At the time, they were told that establishing a somewhat louche household, including the regular sponsorship of soirées, could prove useful to her majesty's government.

Between the income that work generated, and certain investments undertaken on Magnus's behalf by his elder brother, who upon their father's death had acceded to the title, they managed well. They kept Will and Carlo to maintain the house, entertained and dined out, and were looking forward to some travel on the continent when the weather warmed.

After John left, Toby said, "You spent some time on the West Coast of Africa station when you were in the Navy. Do you know anyone who could provide us information on the status of British colonization there?"

"I was there only briefly, under the command of Commodore Hornby," Magnus said. "I do have some friends from that time. Let me think."

He stood and walked over to Toby's desk, where he accumulated a pile of periodicals. "Do you have the Sunday *Lloyd's*?" he asked.

"On the bottom," Toby said. "Is there something you're looking for?"

"I remember a notice that a former shipmate was in town," Magnus said. He paged through the paper. "Here it is. Humphrey Westmacott has recently returned from a tour of duty on the African coast. His new assignment is with the Board of Admiralty in London."

Magnus inscribed a note to Westmacott at Admiralty House and sent Will with it, asking if they might meet for a cocktail soon. Will was instructed to wait for a reply, if Westmacott was available to provide one.

He went upstairs and found the seaman's trunk his father had commissioned for him when he joined the Navy. It was teak and mahogany, with brass-strapped corner fittings and his initials carved in the front. When he lifted the cover he was overwhelmed with the scent of salt water and a particular memory of opening the trunk on the HMS Bristol and finding one of his fellow officers had stuck an African puff adder in it, as a prank.

It was blessedly dead, but it still startled Magnus so much he had nearly soiled his drawers. He'd had one of the ordinary seamen who was good with a knife carve the skin off, and dried it out on the foredeck. It was a straw yellow color, scattered with dark blotches, and he'd kept it hanging on a wall in his cabin for some time. He couldn't remember what had happened to it.

He flipped through the contents until he found a map they had used at the West Coast of Africa Station. Senegal, a French colony, took up a good bit of land. Next to it was Sierra Leone, in a pale yellow. Liberia, in orange, was next to it. A note in the same folder as the map indicated that Liberia had been founded in 1822 as an outpost for returning freed slaves from the Americas. It had grown into a colony and then a commonwealth, and achieved independence in 1847.

Beyond it was the Ivory Coast, already claimed by France, and then a bunch of mixed colors indicating various tribal groups. If the French were able to either conquer them, or negotiate treaties with them, it could very well isolate the British presence in West Africa, and secure French access to the interior of the continent and whatever riches it held.

By the time he had finished with the map, Will had returned with a note from Westmacott that he would be at the East India Club commencing at three that afternoon. Magnus was welcome to call on him any time until he left.

It had begun to rain by then, so Magnus had Will fetch him an oiled silk cape and matching umbrella, then set out for the East India Club. It was a quick walk, down Duke of York Street to St. James Square, where the club occupied a three-story Georgian style building of relatively recent construction. It had originally been founded for the East India Company's servants, as well as those who had been commissioned officers of Her Majesty's Army and Navy. By virtue of several years' service at that command, Magnus had been eligible for membership, and had joined soon after leaving the Navy and returning to the city. He and Toby had chosen the premises at Ormond Yard in part because of its closeness to the club as well as to the home that their lady friends shared.

He was only a bit damp by the time he entered the club and left his cape and umbrella at the cloak room. He found Westmacott in the library, sitting in a leather armchair by the fireplace. "Hello, old chap," Westmacott said, rising to shake Magnus's hand. "Pleasure to hear from you. What have you been up to since you took your leave?"

"I spent some time with my father as he was ailing," Magnus said, as he settled in an armchair catty-cornered to his old shipmate.

"Ah, yes, I heard he had passed," Westmacott said. "My sympathies."

"Thank you. Since then, I have been rather a man of leisure, managing a few investments and taking on the odd task from a friend." He leaned forward. "Which brings me to you, today. What do you know about the Committee for British West Africa?"

Westmacott steepled his fingers. "Interesting you should ask. It is a pet project of Earl Badgely, as I suppose you already know."

Magnus nodded. "Its purpose?"

"As far as I have heard, it is to lay out a plan for the exploration and conquest of the parts of West Africa that remain under the control of local warlords and chieftains. With the not-so-veiled plan of keeping the French from expanding their dominion in the area."

"Yes, that's what I've heard, too," Magnus said. "Any idea how far those plans have progressed?"

"If I may ask, why are you inquiring?"

"It is a delicate matter," Magnus said. "Be assured, my inquiries are in service to the queen and her majesty's government."

Westmacott nodded. "Very good. Though I can't tell you much more. They have been taking testimony from various personnel with experience in the area. I understand our old captain, Commander Hornsby, has spoken in front of the group about conditions on the ground and his knowledge of the various tribes which inhabit the area."

"Are they close to making a plan, do you know?"

Westmacott shrugged. "How can one know, with politicians? Was it not Aristotle who said something about politicians aiming at something beyond politics itself, power or glory?"

"I shall take your word for it."

Westmacott leaned close. "I did see Hornsby here in this room a few weeks ago, just as I took up my position at the Admiralty. He was afraid the committee was going to start a new war with France if it persisted in its direction. Which would imply to me that they were close to some sort of plan."

"And with our governments' animosity toward the French, it must be quite important to control their spread through the Dark Continent," Magnus said.

"Indeed. It would prove catastrophic to our aims of empire should the French gain access to so much land."

His friend had little else to contribute, so Magnus sat with him for a while longer, swapping stories about former shipmates over brandy, until Magnus took his leave. The rain had stopped though he still wore his cape, and carried his umbrella.

He had a much clearer impression of the Earl's committee and his purpose, but he was no closer to an idea of how to solve the problem Lord Therkenwell had found himself in.

Chapter 35

A Bed of Roses

Soon after John's departure, Toby left for the Foreign Office. As he approached the area of Whitehall, he wasn't sure what his reception would be with Gervase Quinn. Their relationship had so far been very informal, Quinn calling on Toby for the occasional bit of translation.

He and Magnus were both uncertain what they would say if they were asked if a specific man or woman had attended one of their soirées. Some of their guests were in positions of power, or married to someone of the opposite sex, and news of their unnatural attraction might greatly damage their lives.

In this situation, however, Quinn already knew about Lord Therkenwell and Raoul Desjardins, because of the missive that had been intercepted, and perhaps the office's own surveillance. As long as he wasn't required to provide any other names, Toby felt on secure ground there.

But would Quinn accept their willingness to intercede in this affair, to protect both John and Raoul? From what Magnus had told him, governments tended to tread heavily on the rights of individuals when national security was at stake.

As always, he felt a thrill of connection to his country in the white stone building with its arched and pilastered balconies and Greek statues on the roof. He had been told that the use of rich decoration was intended to impress foreign visitors, and it worked for him, too.

He entered the main quadrangle, under the ornately carved ceiling of classical Greek figures, with its interlocking circular skylights. He gave his name to a porter and was despatched to Gervase Quinn's office, a small room with a window overlooking the street.

He rapped lightly on the door frame and Quinn looked up. "Oh, good, Marsh. Have you deciphered that message? Dashed complicated." He waved Toby to a chair across from him.

"Lord Dawson and I worked together on it." He pulled a folded paper from his pocket and passed it across to Quinn.

"But this is today," Quinn said, after he had read the translation.

"Indeed. We had no time to notify you before the rendezvous, so Lord Dawson and I went to the intersection of Swallow Street and Vine Street." He leaned forward. "Before I tell you what we witnessed, may I ask how you intercepted this message? I don't want to waste your time duplicating what you already know."

"We have had a certain group of Frenchmen under surveillance for some time," Quinn said. "One of our operatives has been able to monitor various pieces of correspondence."

"Would that involve a Frenchwoman called Louise Wickes?"

Quinn looked at him closely. "You have been clever."

"You are aware, of course, of the soirées that Lord Dawson and I host. One of our guests has been Lord Therkenwell, whose father is Earl Badgely."

"We intercepted the message on its way to Wickes, and had it copied before it was passed on to her. You're saying that Therkenwell was the other recipient? And that he was the one who met with Wickes?"

Toby nodded. "Wickes handed him a bauble, an earring in the

girandole form. Then I followed Wickes to Piccadilly, where she hailed a carriage. I was able to discover the address she gave to the driver. Number nine New Burlington Street. We are given to understand that she works for a dressmaker there called Madame Swaebe."

Quinn nodded. "We've uncovered that. Do you know any more about her?"

"Lord Dawson followed Lord Therkenwell from the rendezvous, and met up with him as they both exited the Man in the Moon Passage." He relayed what Therkenwell had told Magnus as well as what Raoul had told John. That Georges Morvan of the French embassy had identified her as a good prospect to seduce Earl Badgely, and that she had been successful.

"You see, it is a very delicate situation," Toby said. "A double case of blackmail. With your permission, Lord Dawson and I would like to pursue some inquiries before involving your office."

Quinn sat back in his chair. "What kind of inquiries?"

"What can you tell me about the Earl's involvement with the Committee for British West Africa?"

"Are you familiar with the explorer David Livingstone?" Quinn asked in return.

"In passing," Toby said. "I don't see what that has to do with the current situation, though."

"Livingstone described his work using three C's: commerce, Christianity, and civilization. There is a fourth, however, and that connects us to the group behind Madame Wickes. And that C stands for conquest. Ultimately, who will conquer the dark continent, and control the riches we know hide within?"

Toby nodded. "So the Committee for British West Africa is a veiled attempt at such?"

"Not so veiled," Quinn said. "However their work has gone largely sub rosa. It is our belief that the French would like to know more about their operation, and seek to dissuade the powers that be—in the person of Earl Badgely—to abandon hopes of colonization and conquest, and leave the bulk of the territory to French control."

"Hence the attempt to blackmail the Earl through first his son, and now his mistress."

"Exactly." Quinn steepled his hands. "The question is how the Foreign Office should proceed. The earl is a powerful man, and not one we would like to have as an enemy. Nor are we willing to expose his all too human frailties to the public."

"All the more reason to allow Lord Dawson and me to dig around before you take any official action."

"I can give you a very brief dossier on what we have already learned about this group," Quinn said. "Though I don't know what you will be able to do with it."

Toby smiled. "As you have noted in the past, Lord Dawson and I have some connections outside polite society. It is possible we will be able to come up with a solution that would preserve reputations, while still acting in the best efforts of her majesty's government."

Even as he spoke those words, Toby worried that they might get in trouble protecting John when he had made himself so vulnerable to foreign efforts. Their relationship with the Foreign Office was a tentative one, and their reputations and their livelihoods rested on staying in the Office's good graces.

There was also the question of John himself. Was he smarter than he appeared? Could he be playing himself and Magnus in support of a greater, more personal game?

He walked out, wondering how on earth he and Magnus could manage to find a solution to a problem with more thorns than a bed of roses.

Chapter 36

Dossier

As Magnus turned onto Ormond Yard from Duke of York Street, he spotted Toby ahead of him. Stepping carefully over the cobblestones to muffle his footsteps, he hurried up behind his lover unnoticed. Then he leaned close to Toby's ear, and effecting a low-class accent, said, "Oy, mate, fancy a good rogering?"

Toby shook with surprise as he turned to face Magnus. "You are an evil man," he said, as he caught his breath. "To suggest such a thing out here in the street, rather than inside in our bedroom."

Magnus grinned. "I can suggest it there, if you prefer."

"Right now we have work to do," Toby said, resuming his walk to their front door. "I have a dossier from Gervase Quinn we need to read."

"And I have some news to share as well," Magnus said. Once they were ensconced in their sitting room, with tea and scones on the way, he told Toby what Humphrey Westmacott had said.

"A new war with France?" Toby asked. "That doesn't sound good, for either country."

"Tensions are already high, especially over Egypt and Africa, though thus far diplomatic solutions have kept us from having at each other."

As Will entered with their tea, Toby said, "But a British declaration of intent to colonize West Africa could bring things to a head again."

"Indeed," Magnus said. "Shall I be mother and pour the tea?"

"You tease me once again," Toby said with a grin. "If you are mother, that makes me father and puts me in the dominant position."

Magnus felt his cock rise. "Perhaps we should dispense with the tea and conversation and shift to the bedroom?"

Magnus poured a cup of tea for his lover and added two sugar cubes, as he knew Toby liked. "Work before pleasure, old chap," Toby said, lifting the cup to his mouth.

The dossier they had before them was skimpy, but it did indicate that a group of Frenchmen had been under surveillance for potential activities against her majesty's reign.

"There," Magnus said pointing. "Georges Morvan, of the French embassy. Isn't he Raoul's boss? The one who has been pushing forward this blackmail?"

"So Raoul has said, to John." There were a half-dozen other names, and both were glad to see that Raoul Desjardins was not among them. "Is this something we should share with Raoul and John?" Toby asked.

"I think we'd have to speak with Raoul ourselves before giving him access to what is presumably classified information," Magnus said. "He is, after all, an employee of the French embassy, and it's possible that he has been part of this effort to first frame John Seales and then blackmail his father."

"You're right. And as far as I can tell from reading this dossier, Morvan hasn't done anything that he could be charged with yet. He could argue that he's simply a French diplomat acting in the best interests of his country."

Magnus said, "We must catch him doing something that the Foreign Office could prosecute him for. And if they already have operatives shadowing him—witness their ability to intercept the message we read earlier—then we must make sure we're not getting in their way."

Toby leaned back. "I am curious about this Frenchwoman. Is she really a patriot? Or simply Morvan's pawn? I wonder how we could learn more about her than Raoul has conveyed to John."

"We should have both John Seales and his lover here for a meeting," Magnus said. "Dinner? Perhaps tomorrow?"

"That is a capital plan."

They continued to review the dossier, which began when an unidentified informant notified the Foreign Office of a plot to influence the British colonization of west Africa. This informant, apparently a Briton fluent in French, had overheard two men in a café in South Kensington, not far from the embassy.

The informant recognized one of the men, an undersecretary named Georges Morvan. He had written down several phrases he'd overheard, including *the British must be stopped* and the name of Earl Badgely, the head of the Committee for British West Africa. He understood the general import of the conversation was to influence the earl's vote through persuasion of the strongest kind.

"This conversation took place in November of last year," Toby noted. "So this has been an ongoing project since then."

"Clearly the French are playing the long game," Magnus said.

The Foreign Office had begun an investigation into Monsieur Morvan subsequent to that. He had traveled to Paris twice during the winter—not unusual for a diplomat.

They continued down the list. "This man," Magnus said. "Hugo Malherbe. I recognize that name. It means weed, doesn't it?"

"It does. Do you know him?"

"I think he was here once, over Christmas. I recall he cornered me after I'd had a few glasses of champagne, and placed his hand over my cock."

"Magnus!"

"Through my pants, dearest," Magnus said with a smile. "I

pushed him away, despite the reaction he aroused. He slipped his card into my pocket and told me that he could show me delights I had never encountered before."

"Do you have that card?"

Magnus shook his head. "I made a point of tearing it up in front of him. But it was only a calling card, nothing that indicated his place of work."

Magnus closed his eyes and concentrated. He'd been a bit tipsy, certainly, or he never would have allowed Malherbe close enough to touch him there. Malherbe was in his late twenties, and wore a gold signet ring and elegant watch.

At the time he'd thought the young man a molly, using favors he had gained from other lovers to get into his good graces—or his pants—in case there could be money involved for him.

"Who do you think brought him?" Toby asked.

"I am thinking. He was quite comely. Could it have been Leighton?"

"I am not surprised. Leighton often brings young men whom he has painted, or bedded. Though Greville does not seem to mind. Perhaps they are all together in bed."

"An interesting situation," Magnus said. "Though at present I am quite satisfied with you in my bed, without any others."

Toby smiled. "Speaking of which, perhaps it is time for us to head upstairs."

They both stood, and quickly Toby walked over to Magnus and placed his hand over Magnus's cock. It was stiff, as he expected. He leaned in close, and kissed his lover's neck. "So what arouses you?" he murmured. "Leighton and Greville? The young man who palmed you?"

Magnus took Toby's head in his hands and kissed him, hard. "You, always," he said. "You, and you, and you alone."

"That is quite the appropriate answer," Toby said, and took him by the hand to lead him upstairs.

Chapter 37

Proof

Raoul was called into Morvan's office the day after John received the girandole earring from Louise Wickes. "Your lover, he has the proof of his father's infidelity?" Morvan asked.

It was odd to hear John so casually mentioned as his lover in Morvan's office. He said, "Yes, I met with him last night and he showed it to me."

"I am sure he showed you something else," Morvan said with a sneer. "What does he intend to do with the earring?"

"He is very nervous. It will take him time to calm down enough to face his father. Once he is ready, he will arrange to meet his father at the earl's club. A public setting will protect him from some of his father's wrath."

"There is a crucial meeting on the first of April," Morvan said. "The earl must know about the earring and have time to consider his situation before that vote."

"I will make sure that Lord Therkenwell knows that."

And then he was dismissed, and returned to his desk, where he had more German work to translate, additional journals of exploration in west Africa. But he was unable to concentrate, as he kept thinking about the trouble he and John were in.

It was made even worse now that John had told him the British Foreign Office was involved. If his role was revealed, he could be prosecuted, or deported from the country. John was at risk, too. He might end up in gaol, his name ruined.

That night when he returned home, he found an invitation had been left for him, for a dinner the following evening at the home of Lord Dawson and Toby Marsh. The invitation included a request that he bring Silas Warner with him. He walked down the hall to Silas's rooms and knocked, worried that he might be interrupting a tryst.

Silas opened the door, wearing a loose dressing gown of purple silk, open at the neckline to reveal his hairless chest. "Well, this is a nice surprise," Silas said. "I was just pleasuring myself, but perhaps you could take over for me?"

"I am in difficult circumstances, Silas," Raoul said, as he followed his friend into Silas's boudoir, decorated with hanging silks in bright colors. The bed was unmade, and Raoul noticed an open bottle of oil beside it. "I need your help."

"I am here for you, my friend." Silas sat on the bed and crossed his legs, adjusting the silk gown to cover himself. Raoul sat on the overstuffed chair across from him and explained the situation.

"You have trouble, that is certain," Silas said. "How can I help you?"

"I have been invited to dinner tomorrow evening at the home of Lord Dawson and Mr. Marsh. The invitation included a request to bring you."

"Interesting," Silas said. "Why, do you think?"

"I have no idea. Perhaps they will need your legal assistance."

"I certainly owe them a favor," Silas said. "My new position with barrister Pembroke is proving very rewarding, both in a financial sense and in all that I am learning. He has a great variety of cases and is most willing to instruct me in their characteristics."

"Then you'll come?"

"Of course. And I will be able to meet your lover, as well, and see how he has managed to cast his spell over you." He leaned forward. "Tell me, does he fuck you?"

Raoul blushed. "That is between John and me."

"He does!" Silas crowed. "I knew it. If only I had a taste for topping, you and I might have become more than friends."

"Your friendship is very important to me, even if it does not involve fucking."

"Might I be rewarded with a kiss?" Silas asked coquettishly.

Raoul did not feel he could refuse. He moved over to the bed beside Silas, and leaned in toward him. Their lips touched, and he felt his cock swell. And yet kissing Silas was different from his kisses with John. With Silas, it was a mere physical reaction, without the emotion that accompanied his embraces with John.

Silas took hold of Raoul's hand and moved it inside his silk robe, to press against his right bosom.

Carefully, Raoul backed away. "I have given my heart," he said. "And my cock, despite what it might feel, must follow."

Silas shook his head ruefully. "You are in love, my friend."

Though it was dangerous to love someone who could be taken from him so easily, Raoul had to admit that was the case. He stood up. "Shall we meet at Ormond Yard? Tomorrow at six?"

"I will be there," Silas said.

The next day, Morvan and Hugo were mysteriously absent from the office, and no one knew where they had gone or for what purpose. Raoul could not help looking frequently in the direction of Morvan's office, and imagining what kind of treachery he could be up to. He had an uncomfortable feeling in his stomach that could not be soothed by tea, and he found his hands shook as he tried to turn the pages of his dictionary.

Raoul worked off and on at his translation, and found there were several passages that he could not understand. That was the answer to his nerves. He was already scheduled to dine with Toby Marsh and Magnus Dawson that evening. He could go to Ormond Yard earlier, get help with his translation, and at the same time be reassured that there might be a way out of his problems.

He sent a message to Marsh, asking if he might arrive earlier than expected for dinner to go over them, and the messenger returned an hour later with an acceptance.

He gathered his materials and set out for Ormond Yard. When he arrived, the young houseboy let him in and led him to the study, where he found Toby, who stood to shake his hand. "So you have more problems with German?" he asked.

"I do. It is the same sort of material as we discussed last time, travel journals in west Africa. Some of the East Prussian dialect is beyond my comprehension." He hesitated. But Marsh had become a friend, someone he trusted.

"It has been a bad day for me. Morvan has disappeared and I fear that he may be making more trouble for John and me. And I worry that the deadline for John's conversation with his father approaches rapidly, and that whatever happens will not be good."

Toby smiled and put a hand on Raoul's arm. "Your troubles are large enough that they do not need magnifying by your imagination. I have found that when I focus on something else, I am able to push my problems aside for a while. Let us see if we can do that with some East Prussian."

Raoul sighed with relief. He was right to come to Marsh.

They worked through the translation for an hour or so. "Your embassy is very concerned with this kind of exploration," Toby said, when they had finished. "It is clearly connected to the attempt to blackmail Earl Badgely."

"I agree. Do you think I should manipulate this translation to attempt to sway Morvan, and whoever he reports to?"

Toby sat back in his chair. "An interesting idea. A few words here and there could change the tenor of this explorer's interactions with the local tribes. Make them seem more warlike and less inclined to be conquered, or to engage in treaties."

"Morvan has some German," Raoul said. "So our changes must be subtle."

"Let us give it a try, then," Toby said, and they continued to work until they heard the doorbell.

A moment later, Will appeared at the door to the study. "Lord Therkenwell," he said, and ushered John into the room.

The stress of his situation had clearly taken a toll on him. He appeared tired and sad, quite unlike the cheerful, foppish young man Raoul had fallen in love with. He could not resist jumping up and embracing John, kissing him on the lips.

At least that served to brighten John's countenance. Raoul felt his cock swell, as it had with Silas the night before, only this time the rising was accompanied by a feeling deep in his chest. Love, indeed.

Toby closed the folder they had been working on and rose, offering his hand to John once he and Raoul had parted. "Good evening, my lord," Toby said.

John smiled. "We did discuss this, Toby. I am John to you."

Toby sketched a quick bow. "Force of habit. John it is then. How are you holding up?"

John's shoulders sagged. "I cannot eat, I cannot drink, I cannot sleep. I sit at my desk and try to write but no words come. I do not know how much longer I can continue this way."

"You are among friends now," Toby said. "Magnus and I have spoken of this. We are both fatherless, and neither of our mothers are nearby. Magnus has two brothers, one of them far off in Ceylon, the other at their country seat with his wife and children. So we have begun to construct a family of our choosing here in London. You will meet our friends, The Honorable Sylvia Cooke, and her companion, Miss Cleaver. The four of us form the circle, the parents if you wish. We have taken in Will and Carlo, and begun to gather other friends who share similar proclivities."

"A family," Raoul said. "Though I never felt comfortable with my own parents, I would relish the opportunity to belong to a family here in London."

"A family that accepts us as we are, and supports us," John said. His smile brightened. "I do feel better."

Marsh walked to the door of the study. "Will, can you fetch Magnus for us?" he called.

"Silas Warner will be joining us directly from Gray's Inn," Raoul said.

"Good," Toby said. "I am surprised that someone so louche would find himself a place at Gray's Inn."

"My friend Silas has two sides," Raoul said. "One for the public, and one in private."

"As do so many of us," Toby said.

Magnus entered then.

"I have been working some translations with Raoul," Toby said, when everyone had been greeted. "We have an interesting idea."

He explained to John and Magnus what he and Raoul had come up with.

"But how does that help us resolve our situation?" John asked.

"Small steps, my friend," Toby said. "It is often best to tackle a large problem by breaking it down into smaller ones. The large problem here is how we can thwart France's interests in west Africa. Though the way Morvan is forcing you to confront your father is the biggest issue for you personally, perhaps we can also approach it from a side angle."

They chatted for a few minutes, and then the houseboy announced Silas. Raoul was surprised at how conservatively his friend was dressed, in a somber gray suit and white shirt. Not even a colored pocket handkerchief.

Toby let the houseboy know that they were ready for dinner, and they moved into the dining room. "First, some wine, to lubricate our conversation," Toby said, and poured them all glasses of a burgundy that was as good as any Raoul had tasted back in France.

Magnus lifted his glass in a toast. "To problems solved," he said, and they all clinked glasses.

Their first course was a vichyssoise which Raoul found quite flavorful. "Your cook has an excellent hand," Raoul said.

"He does," Toby said. "We are quite lucky Will introduced us to him."

"Your houseboy and your cook, they are..." John said.

"A couple," Magnus said. "Will worked at my father's house, and agreed to come to Toby and me if he could bring Carlo. Once Carlo cooked a meal for us, we were sold."

"Though we would have taken him on for Will's sake," Toby said. "It is rare enough for two men to find each other."

"I find them easily," Silas said. "It is getting them to stay which is the hard part."

"That is because your part is so often hard," Raoul said, and everyone laughed.

Silas had removed his cravat and opened his shirt at the collar, and retrieved a bright red handkerchief, which he put in his pocket. That was the Silas Raoul knew.

The soup bowls were cleared and slices of beef were provided, with a savory jus and a side of sauteed onions and slivers of tender broccoli. They made casual conversation while they ate.

"So let us discuss the situation," Magnus said, when the dinner plates had been cleared. "We will have pudding later, after we have exercised our brains."

"I have only the barest idea of what is going on," Silas said. "Perhaps one of you could explain it to me."

Raoul began, aided by John and then Toby and Magnus, until the whole plot was laid bare.

"I am not completely familiar with the crime of sedition," Silas said. "The definition, as I understand it, is conduct or speech inciting people to rebel against the authority of a state or monarch. That does not seem to apply here."

"You are correct," Magnus said. "It is more about the machination of a foreign power against the interests of her majesty's kingdom."

Silas nodded. "But you would need the same information to prosecute. Is that the direction you intend to take?"

"We are unclear at present." Toby turned to Raoul. "Has Morvan established a time by which John must act?"

"He has. There is apparently a crucial vote on the first of April, so he would like the earl to be pressured by then."

"I can't even think about having such a conversation with my father," John said. To Raoul, his face seemed to grow even paler, and Raoul reached next to him to grasp his lover's hand.

"Then we must find a way to forestall that," Toby said. "My contact at the Foreign Office has given me a dossier about Morvan and his associates." He stood. "I will return with it momentarily."

Everyone at the table was quiet until Toby returned. He read out a list of names, and Raoul answered that three of them worked at the embassy, in some connection. "Hugo Malherbe works with me, under Morvan's direction, though I can't tell you exactly what he does."

"Malherbe," Magnus said. "Is he one of us, do you know?"

"It has never been obvious to me, but he disdains the scent of women and has so far not chosen one as a companion. Why do you ask?"

"A man of that name attended a soirée some time ago, and attempted to push himself on me," Magnus said.

Raoul shuddered. What if he had come with Silas on the same night that Hugo had attended? He might have been able to bluster himself with an interest in the artists who were there that evening, but Hugo would have had a card against him.

Then his mouth opened wide. "What is it?" John asked.

"Morvan knew about you and me," he said. "Hugo must have been his informant. Perhaps he saw the two of us together, or learned that we had met here."

Raoul struggled to regain control of himself, and looked at the list from the Foreign Office again. "Jacques Blanc is our messenger boy," he said. "He is the one who was dispatched to carry the invitation to the rendezvous to both John and Madame Wickes."

"Then we may assume for the moment that Blanc is the one who conveyed the message to the Foreign Office as well," Toby said.

Raoul said, "He is a simple boy, paid very little. I can see that he could be swayed by money."

"Well, that explains how the Foreign Office learned of your meeting," Magnus said. "And it provides us with a weak link in the chain. What do you know of him?"

"Only that he is in very poor circumstances. I have heard him mention a girl he wishes to woo, if only he can set enough money aside to pursue her."

"Excellent," Magnus said. "If we need to we may appeal to his pocketbook."

"What do you want of him?" Raoul asked.

Toby answered. "Again, we are merely at the stage of gathering information now. Once we have more pieces of the puzzle, we will see how they fit together." He turned to Raoul. "You have met with Madame Wickes?"

"We dined together last Monday evening."

"Do you know how she was drawn into this circle?"

"She said that she was approached by Morvan through a Frenchwoman who knew her and knew of her circumstances."

"He is quite the schemer, your boss," Magnus said to Raoul.

"Indeed. He is determined to rise to the level of *Secrétaire des affaires étrangères*," Raoul said. "The right hand of the ambassador."

"And perhaps we will be able to catch that hand in dark deeds," Magnus said.

Toby notified Will, who brought out a very rich almond pudding, and they all indulged. When they were finished, Magnus said, "And now for your assignments."

They all looked to him. "John, you are to arrange a meeting with your father, at the very end of March. Raoul, you will convey that information to Morvan."

"What am I to tell my father?" John asked.

"I'm sure you will come up with an idea, John," Toby said.

"Remember, the purpose of setting this date is to have something to show Morvan."

"And me?" Silas asked.

"You are to sound out barrister Pemberton about how one goes about prosecuting a foreign national. Do not reveal any specific details, but we will need information about how we can entrap Monsieur Morvan and his associates."

"And what will you be doing?" Raoul asked Toby and Magnus.

"I will return to the Foreign Office to consult with our contact there," Toby said.

"And I am going to see if there are any rumors about Earl Badgely going around," If Magnus said. "If he does need to be confronted, then knowledge that others are aware of his dalliance will help."

They all rose at that time. Raoul, Silas and John returned to Bryanston Mews, where John and Raoul politely refused Silas's invitation to come to his rooms, and instead went to Raoul's.

"He is nothing if not persistent, your friend Silas," John said, when they were behind closed doors. "Did you and he…"

"When we met," Raoul said. "He is something of a satyr, not content unless he is pursuing cock, or engaged in intercourse with one."

"Sounds like an interesting friend to have, if one is single," John said, and looked at Raoul. "You don't consider yourself single, do you?"

Raoul smiled. "Well, I am not married. However there is a young man I have my eye on. I am reserving myself for him."

John put one hand on his hip and posed. "And this young man, how would you describe him?"

"Quite handsome," Raoul said. "And altogether irresistible."

Chapter 38

The Taste of Salt

John reached for Raoul. It seemed like it had been ages since they had last touched each other, though it had only been a few days.

Raoul's scent hadn't changed, though. It was still lavender, with a hint of orange, and John inhaled it as he nestled his lips against Raoul's neck. When he licked the skin he tasted salt, and it reminded him of oysters they had eaten at Shorecliff House, and how they had made love immediately after, the taste of the bivalves still on their tongues as they kissed.

John was so enraptured by that memory that he hardly noticed Raoul hurriedly undressing. When he opened his eyes it was to find his lover naked before him, his cock hard and dripping. Faced with such an opportunity, he sunk immediately to his knees and took the tip in his mouth.

He licked it with the edge of his tongue, then grabbed Raoul's meaty buttocks in both hands and pulled him forward, so that his lover's cock impaled him like a stake to his heart. Raoul moaned, and then began bucking back and forth, fucking John's mouth like a piston engine, relentless in its onset against his tonsils.

Raoul's passioned cries spurred John on, licking and sucking and then fingering the hallway between his lover's bollocks and buttocks. Raoul shuddered deeply and then erupted in John's mouth, so much that some of the precious fluid dripped down his chin. He gasped and swallowed, then threw his head back and looked up.

"You are a marvel, *mon cher*." Raoul reached down to John's shoulders, and then John stood and they kissed, the creamy fluid still in his cheeks.

"Better than Silas?" John asked with an impish grin.

Raoul pretended to consider. "Well, he does have inimitable technique," he said. And then the warmth of his smile dove deep into John's chest. "But he is not you, and I would have things no other way."

By then John's cock was hard as the cliffs overlooking the Carrick Roads, still trapped in the fabric of his trousers, and he pressed it into Raoul's leg and rutted there.

"I know a better place for that shaft of delight of yours." Raoul pulled away from John and lay back on his bed, his legs open. "There is oil on the counter."

"I must undress," John said.

"No. I want you to take me that way, as if I am your whore."

John opened his trousers and withdrew his cock from them, then greased it up. Raoul lay back on the bed and grasped his lower legs, pulling them toward him and opening his hole to John like a rare flower.

John knew the way Raoul wanted him, fast and hard, and he knelt on the bed and lifted Raoul's ass, placing a pillow beneath it. Then he aimed his missile and rammed it home, and Raoul yelped.

"Too much?" John said, pulling back.

"Not enough! Onward!"

John resumed his thrusts. Raoul's ass clenched him as he pushed forward, the rubbing and the feeling of enclosure mounting the ecstasy within him. Though he wanted to stay like that forever, his cock could not hold out for long, and he spasmed and shot, then rested there for a moment, catching his breath.

Then he staggered back, standing over Raoul's body. He was the very essence of wantonness, and John wanted nothing more than to have a go again. But his worm had already turned, resuming its curled state. Raoul pulled the pillow out and relaxed his legs as John stripped off his clothing. He feared that his drawers and his trousers would smell of spend, but Beller would take care of them without comment.

"You are the only man for me, *mon cher*," Raoul said, and John lay beside him, so that their legs were entwined, their faces close enough to feel breath.

And thus they slept.

John crept out of Raoul's bed at first light, pausing for a moment to see his lover asleep, the dark curls against his forehead, his lips pursed as if ready for a kiss.

He dressed with little care, and then hurried home through the streets of London, already busy at dawn with deliveries and servants and shopkeepers on their way to work.

Beller was already awake, and ready to begin a bath for John. John handed him his clothes, donned a robe, and then went into the bathroom.

It was so lovely, he thought, to have someone to wait on you. As he luxuriated in the warm bath, scented with neroli oil, he thought of Magnus Dawson and Toby Marsh. Did they bathe together, waited on by that young houseboy? Could he imagine such a future for himself and Raoul?

But then reality intruded. He doubted that Raoul's superiors at the embassy would condone him living with another man. And it was possible that John would have to sacrifice these luxuries if his father disowned him.

What could the two of them do? Steal away to France? He could not imagine laboring, and his broadside work brought in no money at all. Despite his university education, he had no particular skills. He was not clever like Toby Marsh, nor did he have the military bearing of Magnus Dawson. He could command a household staff, pen elegant missives. He had all the right manners for visits to friends and relatives and country houses. He could dance with the best of them.

He laughed. He could become a dancing master, perhaps. He and Raoul would find themselves a hidey hole deep in the country, and Raoul could work the farm as his father had done, and John would travel to parties and teach dancing.

It was a lovely fantasy, but then the bathwater chilled and he had to rise. Chances were great that Raoul would be sent back to Paris in disgrace, no matter what happened to the earl and his committee. John's father would devise new ways of imprisoning him in the countryside, where his fate would be sealed.

But he remembered Raoul's impassioned statement that he would no longer be content to be under the domination of more powerful men. John had to follow his example. He would never have his father's love, but he might exert what little power he had.

He sat down to write the letter to his father that he had been delaying, requesting to meet with him before the first of April. He was about to seal it up when Beller announced the morning post.

"A letter from Shorecliff House, my lord," Beller said, presenting it to him.

"Nothing good ever comes from that address," John grumbled. "Blast. I suppose I shall have to open and read it, and then post a response of some kind."

As he opened the envelope he was struck by the faintest scent of salt once more, which reminded him of the taste of Raoul's skin.

The letter was in his mother's hand, easily recognizable by the loops in her G's and Y's. It did not begin with an endearment—just his title.

Therkenwell, I write to tell you of some news which shall interest you. Vanessa has been admitted for study at Bedford College for Women in London, and has petitioned your father to cover her expenses there and allow her to stay at Briar House while she studies.

She has expressed a willingness to take part in the London season in addition, which as you know pleases me.

John put the letter down. That was capital news. Vanessa could get the education she desired while satisfying her mother's wish that she be presented to society and introduced to potential mates. Most women in the season were in the city only for rounds of parties and dressmaking, leaving them plenty of time at home. John was sure Vanessa could manage to squeeze everything in. She was clearly the smartest of the three of them.

There was more to his mother's letter, and John was loath to read it, preferring to linger on the happy news, but he continued to read nonetheless.

As you know, the dower house at Shorecliff has been empty since your grandmother's passing. Lizzie has suggested that we let it to Cousin Marley, so that he gains an appreciation of country life, should he be in a position to inherit the estate at some point in the future. He shall sell his property in Bristol, and your father will settle some portion of the estate proceeds on him for his living expenses in Cornwall.

Especially since you appear unlikely to marry and produce an heir, this is a satisfactory solution to the problem of entailment.

Well. The nerve of that rascal, insinuating himself in the family before the earl was even dead. And what of this assumption that he would not marry and produce an heir! He was barely twenty-six.

The earl, however, had already been married at that point in his life. He had come down to London from Cambridge after his own graduation, joined the merry round of parties that season, and set his eye on the woman who would become John's mother. She was very pretty, and came with a good-sized dowry. He had a title to offer, and the prospect of a country manor with a significant income.

They had married and lived in London, with regular visits to John's grandparents in Cornwall. John's grandfather passed when John was fourteen, and his father took on the title of Earl Badgely. Vanessa was five then, and Lizzie three. Their mother was still sickly from her third pregnancy, and the family relocated to Cornwall in the hope that the sea air would heal her.

His grandmother had relocated to the dower house, and she had lived there through his childhood. She had taken a chill while he was at Cambridge and passed away, and since then the dower house had been empty.

It was little more than a cottage, however. A few rooms for the dowager duchess to live in and entertain, an adequate kitchen and small staff quarters. It was reasonable for a single man, though John recalled that Marley owned a small haberdashery shop in Bristol.

Given that he had taken a mistress in London, it was increasingly less likely that the earl would return to Cornwall regularly, and had already planned to turn over the management of the properties to Marley. Though it was not unexpected, and not altogether a bad proposition, it was all too much for John to consider, and he put aside the letter to his father. He would show his mother's note to Raoul and ask his advice before communicating further with either parent.

Chapter 39

The Badger

Once his father passed away and his brother took on the title of Duke of Hereford, many things had changed for Magnus Dawson. His father's will had effectively closed his hereditary sources of funding to him, but through some cleverness on his part, and that of Toby, he had managed to steer a lucrative investment scheme to his brother, the new duke, with the condition that he receive part of the funds.

Thus he was able to pay his tailoring bills, support his household, and pay his dues at the East India Club and the London Thames Fencing Club. The afternoon after the dinner with Raoul, John and Silas, he had Will gather his fencing kit and he traveled to the club in search of a match and some useful conversation.

Many of the men who belonged there traveled in the same social circles as Earl Badgely, and he hoped to engage in some banter regarding that gentleman that might illuminate whether polite society knew of his relationship with Louise Wickes.

He was pleased to find his friend Sir Arthur Sullivan, the noted composer, lounging by the side of a playing watching a match. They greeted each other, and very quickly took to a neighboring strip to engage. It was great fun and good exercise, and Magnus felt the cares of the Therkenwell affair lifting from him for a while.

When they finished, both men had worked up a good sweat, and retired to the bar for refreshments. Sullivan replaced his monocle and said, "So what brings you down here today, Magnus? I have not seen you in an age."

"Settling into new lodgings in Ormond Yard. The tedious bit of furnishings and training household staff."

"And furthering your acquaintance with your housemate, I presume." Sullivan's eyebrow lifted.

"Ah, we were well acquainted before joining our households," Magnus said. "But living with someone is somewhat different from merely seeing them on occasion."

"I can't verify that," Sullivan said. "I have been lucky to avoid the matrimonial noose thus far."

Since Sullivan had carried on love affairs with both Rachel Scott Russell and her sister Louise, that clearly hadn't been an option. "And Mrs. Ronalds?" Magnus asked.

"She has already been married, as you know, and has two children from it, and is loath to engage herself again. Which suits me well. I am not the type to have a wife in the country and a lover in the city."

"As many men do," Magnus said. "I have heard rumors that a friend's father has done so."

Sullivan looked at him appraisingly. "Let me think for a moment and see if I can identify your friend, and his father."

Sullivan had many connections in music and the arts, including numerous men who preferred men, so it was not unlikely that he might make the connection between Magnus and Lord Therkenwell.

Eventually Sullivan said, "I believe I might know your friend, and his father as well. Does the father have something of the aspect of his namesake animal?"

Magnus laughed, realizing that Sullivan had conflated "Badgely" with "badger."

"I have not been introduced to the father, though I have seen him on occasion. He does have a stripe of white hair at his forehead."

"Indeed," Sullivan said. "The lady in question is quite lovely, if her tastes do go toward the Mustelidae."

Magnus recognized the Latin family name, which encompassed a number of different mammals. "Well, at least she has forsworn polecats and ferrets."

Sullivan laughed heartily. "Though it is odd that he should take a French mistress when he is so publicly against her countrymen."

"Ah, but love is blind to nationality, isn't it? One may not like Americans in general, and yet favor a certain New Yorker."

"I am heartily in favor of Americans in general, particularly those who are generous in their support of the arts," Sullivan said.

They bantered thus for a while, and then Sullivan excused himself, and Magnus returned to Ormond Yard.

"Sir Arthur Sullivan confirmed that he knows of the affair between Earl Badgely and Madame Wickes," he said, when he found Toby in his study, working on a translation.

He had a dictionary and thesaurus at either side of his pad, as was his wont. He looked up. "Did he confirm by name?"

"Rather by appearance," Magnus said. "I never recognized that the white stripe in Earl Badgely's hair resembled that of a badger."

Toby laughed. "Well, that is something off our list, at least. And it adds to the ammunition Therkenwell can bring to bear when he confronts his father, to have evidence that other men in the earl's circle already know of the affair."

"Wouldn't that make it easier for the earl to shake off any censure?" Magnus asked.

"There are two things at work here. First there is a personal reason. Your friend's awareness of the earl's dalliance would not make it easier for his wife. We know that she is in poor health, and such news might push her closer to death."

He ticked off a second finger. "And then there is the political fallout. The earl is a professed hater of the French. To reveal he has a French mistress might call into question his judgment, and the possibility that she is influencing the committee he chairs."

Chapter 40

Quinn's Solution

Gervase Quinn was in conversation with another man when Toby appeared at his open door. Toby knocked lightly on the frame, and Quinn looked up. "Oh, Marsh, good. Give me just a moment."

He finished his conversation with the other man, who walked past Toby as he left.

"That was Shoemaker, from the French desk. We were sharing a chinwag about something related to your interests, as it happens. Come, sit down."

Toby sat.

"Tell me what's been happening on your end," Quinn said, and he listened attentively as Toby described what they had all done.

"Very good. This whole affair is going to require some delicate handling. A peer of the realm has put himself in a situation that could potentially compromise the queen's interests, and we don't want that to become public knowledge."

"What happens next?" Toby asked.

"Well, I think the simplest solution is a word in Earl Badgely's ear. If others in his circle are already aware of his affair with the

Frenchwoman, then he will not wish to risk a conflict of interest between that and his work on the Committee for British West Africa."

He looked at Toby. "The only question is who should plant that word."

"Do you mean Lord Therkenwell?"

"He seems the logical candidate. We don't want this situation to spread to any more people than necessary."

"But Lord Therkenwell's relationship with his father is fraught, to say the least."

Quinn steepled his hands, then entwined his fingers. "Monsieur Desjardins is a diplomat, and Silas Warner understands the legal implications of such a situation. I am sure between the three of them they can find a way to convey the information such that it does not imply blackmail, but rather a word of caution."

"Easier said than done," Toby said. "But as you said, Monsieur Desjardins is a diplomat."

They were both silent for a moment, until Toby asked, "And what of the implications for Georges Morvan and his group?"

"That matter you can leave up to us. It needs to be carried out at the highest levels, to ensure that we do not aggravate the relationship between our two countries unnecessarily."

Toby agreed to that and left the hallowed halls behind him. The March day held the promise of spring, so he ducked behind the Foreign Office to stroll along St. James's Park. A few daffodils agreed with his belief, and had tentatively poked their heads out along Horse Guards Road. Many of those he encountered had shed their heavy winter overcoats for lighter wear. Even the Queen's Life Guard seemed to have some spring in their step.

When he turned onto Waterloo Place, he was struck by the fact that history continued to repeat itself. London was filled, it seemed, with monuments to its wartime victories, and yet no one seemed to have learned from the past. The British were still squabbling with the

French, though now it was over jungles and sand in west Africa rather than national sovereignty.

By the time he reached home, the salubrious effect of the warmer weather had worn off, replaced by a darker worry over the future of the world. If nations couldn't get along, how could individuals?

He and Magnus decided to call another meeting of their group that evening, and sent communiques to the French embassy, Gray's Inn, and Russell Square, in a kind of code of their own devising that they hoped Raoul, Silas and John would easily understand but might baffle anyone who intercepted the messages.

They sent Will out for provisions, at Carlo's direction, and then spent some time considering their plan and its many ramifications. "This is all contingent on Quinn doing his part, you realize," Magnus said, finally sitting back from the desk where he and Toby had been confabulating.

By seven that evening they were all at dinner, and after an excellent roast, Magnus raised the reason why they were assembled. "The Foreign Office believes that the best course of action is two-fold. First, they will deal with Morvan and his cabal in their own time, with gentle regard to relations between the two nations. It is up to us, however, to convince Earl Badgely that his position on the Committee for British West Africa has been compromised by his affair with Madame Wickes."

"Easier said than done," John said. "Who is to convince him?"

All faces were toward him. "Me? But we have already established that my father cares little for me or my regard. That he would sooner see me roasted on the spit of public opinion than do anything to protect me."

"This is not about you, or revealing anything about your private life to the public eye," Toby said. "It is about him, full stop."

"But he will twist it to be about me."

"Twist he may, but it is up to Raoul and Silas to coach you in the right words to use to show him that it is in his best interests to resign."

"And the best interests of your mother," Raoul said. "I saw how fragile she was when I was at Shorecliff House with you. Such a public scandal would be quite harmful to her health. At least he must care that much about her."

John shook his head. "I have spent my life bowing to my father's ill words and ill will. I do not have it in me to stand up to him now, especially when my own life is at risk. You will have to find someone else to deliver your message."

"I had a difficult relationship with my own father," Magnus said. "He sent me to the Navy when I was little more than a child and though he never said so I believe that he hoped the Navy would beat the molly out of me."

He looked lovingly at Toby, who felt himself blush. "As you can see, that did not work. And even though our relations were somewhat repaired toward the end of his life, that did not stop him from disinheriting me. And yet I survived, with the help of those around me."

John shook his head. "I do not believe that would be my fate."

"Look around you, John. Here you have assembled men who care about your fate. A new and better family, perhaps, than the one you were born into. We shall support you."

John stood up abruptly. "While I appreciate your words, what you ask is simply beyond me." He turned and departed the dining room. Moments later they heard the front door slam.

"I should go after him," Raoul said. "He is upset. I will calm him."

"Please do," Toby said, and the remaining three of them watched Raoul rush after his lover.

Chapter 41

A Grasp of Geography

John had made it only as far as the corner of Ormond Yard and the Duke of York Street before Raoul caught up with him.

"You are acting like a child, John." Raoul grabbed John's sleeve. "Please, wait, and let us discuss this."

"I can't do it, Raoul. It's as simple as that. You are asking me to walk naked and exposed into the lion's den, to be gored to pieces by his deadly jaws and claws."

"Don't you see, this is the only way we can be together," Raoul said, hurrying to keep up with John, who would not stop. "To remove the threat against your father."

"How does my exposing myself to him help me?"

"We can figure something out."

"I won't do it. If the word is already on the street about his affair, then he will come a cropper himself. Surely that benefits me more, if he is reduced and forced to return to Shorecliff House in ignominy."

"I don't see it that way. If this becomes public, and Morvan goes down, he is likely to drag me down with him. I will be exiled back to France, either to a low-level role in Paris or one of the provinces, or lose my career entirely."

John stopped and confronted him. "So it is up to my sacrifice or yours?"

"John, please. I don't see it that way."

"Well, I do. I thought I was making a new life for myself, with my writing and my circle of friends, and you. Now I see it was all a house of cards, ready to tumble at the slightest disruption."

A world of emotions passed over Raoul's face. But where in the past he would have reached for Raoul, to make things better with words and gestures, he could not find the courage to do so once more.

"It destroys my heart to say this, but I must distance myself from you. I may already have to suffer slings and arrows because of my father, and I cannot bear to have our relationship, which has been so precious to me, consumed in the oncoming flames."

He realized that his hands were freezing, and pulled his gloves from his topcoat pocket. Sliding them on, he said, "Let me go, and face this disaster. Should we both emerge in the future, I shall be willing to consider resuming with you. But for now you must consider our affair over."

With that, John turned once again and continued to walk forward. At least Raoul had stopped following him, and he strode down Piccadilly until he reached Leicester Square. There he paused for a memory of visiting Wyld's Great Globe as a child, on one of his few trips to the city with his parents before heading to Eton.

He remembered marveling at the hollow globe in the center of the hall, which contained a staircase and elevated platforms. He had only the dimmest grasp of geography then, thinking England, and Cornwall in particular, at the center of the world, and the globe had been a revelation, showing him the surface of the earth and a display of maps, globes, and surveying equipment.

It was now part of a squalid, poverty-stricken area, and John hurried forward, his head down, rejecting the importuning of beggars and prostitutes. How naïve he had been then, he thought. Thinking that the world revolved around him and his family. Now he knew they were all pawns in a larger struggle, one that threatened to destroy him.

And Raoul. He, too, was bound to be brought down by this debacle. Though John could not think about him anymore. He had to focus on how he could keep his own head above water.

Could he retreat to Shorecliff House until whatever fuss was generated over the revelation about his father had died down? No, because his father was sure to go to ground in Cornwall if London became too hot for him to bear. He could not imagine being stuck in the same remote house, however large, with his father, baited like a bear in a trap.

He had some money in his accounts. He could give up the rooms in Russell Square and take to the continent. He had a few contacts in Paris and Nice, and perhaps he could hide with one of them for a while. But where would that lead? Would he be doomed to wander the earth on some perilous odyssey in search of home?

Chapter 42

Butterfly

"John simply walked away from me, Silas." Raoul slumped on his bed, his back to the wall. Unfortunately, that raised John's scent from the bedclothes and he inhaled it miserably. "He said he did not wish to see me anymore. He abandoned me to Morvan's wrath, and the mercy of the British authorities."

"Without John's testimony the police will have little to charge you with." Silas sat on the wooden chair across from the bed. "Unless... you have been indiscreet with other men?"

"I was indiscreet before I met John. But if I don't know their names I doubt that the police will, either. I don't know how long Hugo has been observing me, though. He may have witnessed and documented an indiscretion I have long forgotten."

He looked toward the window, where a spring rain had begun, spattering the glass.

"Hugo is in Morvan's pocket. Whatever he knows, Morvan already does. You must stall Morvan now. Don't tell him of John's refusal. Rather that John is waiting for the right time to broach the subject."

"But there is a deadline," Raoul said. "The committee's vote on April 1."

"These committees never do anything all at once," Silas said, waving his hand. "There will be a vote, and then more discussion, and then another vote, and another, before any real action is taken."

"Morvan doesn't think that way."

"Then you must convince him. I will gather some evidence for you, based on past meetings of similar committees. Barrister Pembroke has all kinds of records."

Silas got up and sat next to Raoul on the bed. "This is not the end of your life, Raoul. Perhaps the end of one segment, but there will be more." He raised his arm and the sleeve of his dressing gown slid down, revealing his pale, hairless skin, and the ink at his elbow. "You have never asked me about my tattoo."

"The butterfly?" Raoul asked.

"When I was sixteen, in Sheffield," Silas continued. His voice caught for a moment, and then he went on. "My father caught me in flagrante with an older man. The father of one of my friends. I was bent over, with my shirt up and my pants down, and the man was thrusting his cock into me."

"That must have been awful," Raoul said.

"It was. My father punched me in the face while I was still engaged, blackening my eye. He told me I had no place in his home ever again."

He wiped a tear from his eye. "I had only the clothes I was wearing. Fortunately, my friend's father was kind. He made me promise never to speak of the incident, and in exchange he let me stay in his home for a few days, until he arranged for me to apprentice with a barrister he knew in Manchester."

"That is how you came to the law?"

Silas nodded. "I impressed the barrister quickly with my handwriting, which you know has been ever elegant, and my ability to read and summarize complicated texts quickly. But I did not want to stay in Manchester forever. As soon as I had the opportunity, I made my connection here in London and relocated."

"I appreciate your story, Silas, and I certainly comprehend your pain. But what does that have to do with me, or with tattoos?"

"I had this butterfly tattooed on my skin to remind me that I was in a cocoon, and then after some pain a butterfly emerged. It will be the same with you."

Raoul nodded. "It is hard to see that while one is engaged in the struggle."

"But you already have a life behind you, my dear. Your childhood, your education, your time in Paris. That history will feed you as you push forward."

"None of them meant as much to me as my romance with John Seales," Raoul said. "What if he is the one great love of my life, and I have lost him only months after finding him?"

"I cannot believe we have only one great love ahead of us." Silas tossed his head. "What if I fell in love with a man with a small cock? How could I spend the rest of my life with that?"

Raoul smiled, for the first time that evening. "Or with a man who preferred that you penetrate him?"

Silas pushed his shoulder lightly. "Exactly! There are so many men, my dear. If John is truly your destiny, he will return to you. And if he is not, then the man for you is still out there, when you are ready to look for him again."

Silas went back to his own room shortly after that, but Raoul remained sitting upright on the bed, lost in thought. When he was a boy and met Father Maurice, he was unformed, though he held no illusion that the good father and his impressive cock had made him what he was. Those desires had been inside him, waiting for the right man to bring them out.

He had been the priest's tool for years, as the man used his body and simultaneously formed his mind. He thought he had finally become his own man when he went to the university in Nantes, but really, he had been another lump of clay for his professors to craft into an educated individual.

Even when he went to Paris and joined the government, he still had much to learn, and his mentors there, even down to Georges Morvan, had had a hand in directing him. He had met men along the way, formed transitory alliances, but no one had ever made him feel like the master of his own fate until John Seales.

And now, even that mastery had been taken away from him. He was once again at the mercy of more powerful men. He had merely traded Father Maurice and his cock for Morvan and his pen. A few strokes of that pen, and his fate would be sealed. Sent back to France, his job and career lost.

He was at John's mercy, too. If only the obstinate prig could see what was best for both of them! But he did not believe there was malice in John's refusal. He was governed by fear—of his father, of his class, of his government. Of what might happen to him if his desires became public.

Raoul could not blame him for that. If only John had been willing to let down his walls and allow Raoul to support him and allay his fears. If only the blasted fool had listened to reason.

He felt himself beginning to cry. He took a deep breath, and once again inhaled John's scent from the bedclothes. And then he flung himself down, absorbing himself in his sorrow.

Chapter 43

Inconvenient Arrival

John did not sleep well that night and was slow to wake on Friday morning. He realized that the only way to get over his despair over the way he had left things with Raoul was to return to work. He had accumulated a list of ideas for Janner's broadsides, and he worked on them intermittently through the weekend.

Whenever he stopped, though, he thought of Raoul. He wondered what the Frenchman was doing, whether he missed John at all. Was there any hope of them continuing? But each time he came up against the brick wall of his father's situation.

He was up late Sunday putting the finishing touches on a follow-up essay to the role that impoverished children played in supporting the titled world. He slept late on Monday morning, and was still in his dressing gown when he heard a rap on his front door, and Beller answering it. He was so sure that it was Raoul that he burrowed down in his bed and pretended to be asleep, so that Beller would send him away.

Instead Beller opened his door and said quietly, "My lord? There is a message from your mother."

He sat upright. "What is it?"

"I have not opened it, sir."

"Give it here." John extended his hand. The letter had come via the post, and been sent from St. Mawes four days before. He recognized his mother's elegant handwriting on the front, though it looked like she'd had trouble writing it, the letters more wobbly than usual.

"This is odd," John said. "This should have arrived yesterday at the latest, or the day before."

He opened it and scanned it. "My sister Vanessa wishes to visit Bedford College for Women, where she is to begin her studies, and my sister Lizzie is to accompany her to the city, chaperoned by Cousin Marley."

He read further. "Oh, dear. They are to arrive this afternoon at Waterloo. If this message was delayed to me, then a similar one sent to my father may have been delayed as well." He looked up at Beller. "There's a good chap. Can you send a message over to Briar House to see if the ladies are expected? Otherwise I shall have to meet their train myself."

Beller disappeared to dispatch a boy to Earl Badgely's house, and John rose and washed himself. By the time Beller returned he was ready to be dressed. He spent the next hour in consternation. Why had Vanessa chosen to come to London now, when he was in the middle of a personal crisis? He paced back and forth across the living room, refusing Beller's offer of tea, until the boy returned from Eaton Square.

Beller spoke with him and gave him a coin, and then returned to John. "Apparently your father's house is in some state," he said. "Mr. Samson has taken ill and gone to hospital, and many of the house staff released," Beller said. "Only one housemaid remained to receive the message, and she said that Earl Badgely had already gone out to the House of Lords."

The only staff John had in his employ was Beller, and a girl called Ruth who came in to clean daily. "You shall have to get Ruth, and go to Briar House to prepare the house for company. The maid there should be able to help. I will take a carriage to Waterloo Station and meet my sisters and my cousin."

Beller and Ruth left soon after, and John spent what was left of the morning and the early afternoon worrying. He finally hailed a carriage to Waterloo, instructing the driver to wait for him to return with his party.

Fortunately, Vanessa and Lizzie had brought only a bag apiece, and Marley the same case he had carried to Shorecliff House. "This is a pleasant surprise," John said, kissing each of his sisters' cheeks in turn, then shaking hands with Marley. "I must admit, however, that you have caught us all on the wrong foot."

He hailed a porter to manage the bags, and led them to where he had left the carriage. He explained about the late receipt of Lady Badgely's letter, and the state of the household at Eaton Square.

"Perhaps we should stay at a hotel instead," Vanessa said. "Do you know of a respectable establishment nearby?"

"Nonsense. I've sent my man and my maid ahead to ready the house. I'm sure father will be delighted to see you."

"I should find my own lodging," Marley said. "I don't want to trouble your father."

"Of course not," Lizzie said, putting her arm in his. "You are always welcome with us."

The porter loaded the bags into the carriage, and the driver assisted the ladies inside. John and Marley assumed the seats across from them.

"Is this your first visit to the city?" John asked him.

Marley shook his head. "I have been to Briar House twice to meet with your father. He is a most gracious man."

Not the words John would have used, but perhaps his father's attitude was different because he had already assumed Marley was his heir.

As the city shambled past, John worried again what his future would hold. How much longer would his father live? With luck and good doctoring, many years might pass before John had to face any consequences. Then again, if Lord Dawson was correct and others in his circle already knew about his affair with Madame Wickes, then things could come to a head much more quickly. He knew of peers who had been forced to give up their titles after scandal. What then?

The carriage pulled up at Briar House, and John and Marley got out, then helped Vanessa and Lizzie down. The front door opened as the coachman was unloading their bags, but instead of seeing Beller, or one of his father's maids, the woman who exited the fan-topped doorway was the same one who had handed him the girandole earring.

Chapter 44

Jacob's Ladder

Raoul was disconsolate after leaving John on Thursday evening. He trudged through work on Friday, paying little attention to anything going on around him. When Alexandre tried to speak of his date that Saturday night with Betty, Raoul waved him away, then felt bad about it. But not bad enough to make amends.

It snowed in the city on Saturday morning, which gave him the excuse to remain indoors, and he spent most of the weekend in his bed, under covers, rereading his frayed copy of Flaubert's Madame Bovary. The demise of Emma's romantic fantasy hit him particularly hard, and he cried rather more than he ever had before.

The weather cleared by Monday and he slogged along the icy pavement to reach the embassy. He was at his desk that afternoon, a set of pages on his desk he was supposed to be reviewing, but he'd had no appetite for the work all day.

He looked up to notice a procession of three gentlemen walk into Morvan's office. One of those was the *chargé d'affaires*, whom Raoul had never seen in his area before. Despite his short stature and his plumpness, he exuded an air of authority, even without the medals he had worn at the ball at the Austrian embassy.

Raoul looked over to Alexandre at the next desk, who shrugged in equal puzzlement.

They did not have to wait long. Morvan emerged from his office with those three men, and one of them escorted him toward the staircase. Then the remaining two approached Hugo's desk.

From across the room, Raoul could near nothing, but he could see the way that Hugo's mouth opened wide, yet was unable to speak. He was not allowed to take anything from his desk other than a silver-framed *carte de visite* of his parents, which was his prized possession. He left the room accompanied by the second unknown man.

The *chargé* then approached Gabriel, who sat at the farthest of the four desks from Raoul, and spoke in a low voice to him. After only a few moments, Gabriel rose, took his jacket and bag, and walked out. The two men repeated the performance with Alexandre.

Finally the *chargé* and his associate approached Raoul's desk. "Please gather your personal belongings and leave the office," the *chargé* said. "You are to remain at your lodgings until you are contacted with further instructions."

"What's going on?" Raoul asked, though he had a very good idea.

"Official embassy business. Please say nothing of this until you are further counseled."

Well, he had been expecting something like this, Raoul thought, as the man turned on his heel and strode away. Though he'd expected it to be Morvan who made the announcement, and there to be no ambiguity in Raoul's dismissal. It was an odd turn of events, though he had heard of something similar in the past, when there'd been a leak of information from someone on the second floor.

He left the papers he'd been reviewing on his desk and gathered his coat and his case. He heard a buzz of conversation as he descended the broad marble stairs, though no one looked his way, and Hugo, Alexandre and Gabriel were all gone.

At least Morvan had been found out, though it was likely Raoul had been tarred by the same brush. He walked slowly toward his lodgings, wondering what would happen to him.

Surely he would be let go, and his diplomatic career ruined. Would he have to return to France? Perhaps he could stay in London, get a job with some company that handled exports or imports. He had the language skills and the understanding of how embassy paperwork was carried out.

That was, if he wasn't arrested for a crime. He didn't think he had done anything wrong, or at least anything he could be charged with. As he walked down along the edge of Hyde Park, he decided that rather than go home and brood, he'd pass by Gray's Inn and let Silas know what was happening, and see if he could take a break for a cup of tea.

He detoured through Green Park, and stopped for a moment to watch the pageantry around Buckingham Palace. He had never been a tourist in London—he had started to work almost immediately after his arrival in the city, and he'd spent his time off in search of bars and male company, rather than historical locations.

He watched the guards in their bearskin caps for a few moments, idly wondering what it would be like to bed one of them. He chastised himself, then remembered that John Seales had broken things off with him. He was a free man, albeit one with a broken heart.

He continued his walk through the park, heading toward the Thames. When he reached the Embankment, he stopped once again to watch the traffic along the river. Fishing boats, barges, and sailboats tacked in both directions. He admired the Cleopatra's Needle obelisk, and realized he was dallying.

Well, why not, he thought? He had nowhere to go, nothing to do other than find Silas, and the later he arrived at Gray's Inn the easier it might be for Silas to leave. Feeling like a man of leisure, he strolled along the bank, watching children play in the park. Then he continued along the river until the grand Portland stone arch came into view.

Raoul only knew that Gray's Inn was near Chancery Lane, and

when he reached that street he asked for directions and was sent several blocks inland.

It was a part of London he had never visited, and he was more than a little confused. He hadn't realized the buildings of Gray's Inn were so large, and he stopped short when he arrived there. Everyone passing seemed like they were about very important business, from the men carrying cases to those in white wigs and black gowns, who appeared to be on their way to court, or on their way back.

Finally Raoul stopped a man of about his age and asked if he knew the way to Barrister Pembroke's offices. The man pointed to an entrance and as Raoul walked there, he spotted Silas leaving, and hurried toward him.

"Has something happened at the embassy?" Silas asked. "Why are you not at work?"

Raoul explained what had happened at his office as they walked toward Bryanston Mews.

"Curious," Silas said. "It is odd to be in the midst of such a large operation and yet unsure of one's part in it."

"I am worried about the way our department was dismissed," Raoul said. "Could I be arrested for anything?

"That depends. Did you do anything against British law?"

"No. I only did what Morvan directed me to do."

Silas leaned in close. "And how about with your friend John? Anything that could be documented or proved?"

Raoul shook his head. "Though I don't know what he would say to save his skin."

"Anything he says that would incriminate you would have equal ramifications for him. So unless your boss fabricates something, you are all right." Silas looked at him. "You're in love with him, aren't you?"

"He doesn't want me. He made that clear."

"Silly boy. We poofs are temperamental, you know. Often say things in the heat of the moment that we don't mean."

"That's all men, not just poofs," Raoul said.

"Yes, but we poofs say things like 'don't worry, I won't spend in your mouth' when we mean nothing of the kind."

Raoul laughed. "Silas, you are terrible. Surely you don't talk like this at Gray's Inn."

Silas leaned in close once more. "Only with my intimates," he said.

They dined together at a café near their rooms. Raoul had little appetite, and went through nearly the whole bottle of wine himself. "You must cheer up, old man," Silas said. "You told me how Morvan and Hugo were escorted away, while you and the other fellows were allowed to leave on your own. Surely that means less trouble for you."

"With Morvan under suspicion, what will happen to our section?" Raoul asked. "Even if we are not to be charged with any crimes, the ambassador or the *chargé* may decide to close our unit, or staff it with new men direct from France."

"And you may be tarred with the same brush," Silas said. "That is another expression for you, which comes from treating the sores of sheep with tar. All sheep in the flock are treated the same way."

"Thank you for comparing me to a sheep," Raoul said. "Though it is an apt comparison. Alexandre, Gabriel and I may all be seen as sheep following Morvan."

"In which case you will make your argument that you have done nothing illicit," Silas said. "Well, aside from sucking your lover's cock. Do not mention that."

"But what if my inquisitor already knows? Am I to deny it? I could be fired for lying as easily for sodomy."

"I have watched Solicitor Pemberton in trials," Silas said. "He is very careful with his wording, as I know you can be. Never admit, never deny. Put the burden of proof on the other party."

Keeping their voices low, they talked through several questions that Raoul might be asked, and Silas coached him on his answers. "Of course you shall have to translate this all into French, if you are questioned by one of your countrymen," Silas said eventually. "With that I cannot help you."

"I do feel somewhat better," Raoul said. "More prepared for whatever may happen tomorrow."

Silas insisted on paying the bill. "Since you may be unemployed soon."

That thought haunted Raoul all that night, and he slept restlessly, with dreams of public humiliation and being sent back to France in chains. His forehead was sweaty and his sinuses congested.

Somehow he must have dozed, because he woke at his usual time and realized he was not to report to work. He didn't know what he should do, but he'd been told to stay at home and wait for word from his superiors, so he paced around his room for a while, then dressed and went outside, changing his pacing location to Bryanston Mews.

But that did him no good either. He kept imagining London police coming to take him away. So he went back upstairs, and he was sitting on his bed, his head nodding, when he heard a sharp rap on his door.

Could it be John, come to apologize? He jumped up and then realized it might be the police. He took a deep breath and opened the door.

He was surprised to see an errand boy he recognized who worked at the embassy. He'd had cause to use the boy's services once or twice in the past. "Message for you, sir," the boy said in French, and handed a cream-colored envelope to him.

Raoul tore the envelope open, his fingers shaking. It was a request to return to the office at three that afternoon to meet with the *chargé d'affaires*. "You may tell them I will be there," Raoul said in French, and the boy left.

Fortunately there wasn't much time for him to worry. He dressed and began his walk, not knowing what awaited him on Cromwell Road. All the long way there, he saw other people hurrying about their business. Surely some of them had suffered defeat, loss, or despair. He noticed a man of his own age with a single arm, the sleeve of his jacket pinned up. Several urchins in ragged clothes, an old woman who struggled to walk with the help of a cane.

All of them moved forward with their lives. Did they accept their lot? Fight against it? Shiver in the cold, wonder where their next meal would come from? At least he was not that bad off, not yet. And Marsh and Dawson had said he might be part of their family.

He wondered if the British authorities had summoned John in the same way he had been. Was his name to be blackened like his father's? Perhaps he would be exiled to Cornwall with Earl Badgely. Raoul allowed himself a small smile as to how that would not please either man.

He was directed to wait in the embassy's marble lobby until he was fetched. He watched businessmen enter and be directed to one floor, travelers to another. The affairs of the embassy continued even while some of its staff were under investigation. Soon after three o'clock he was led into the *chargé's* office. "We are investigating a plan to undermine the British government," the *chargé* said in French. "What do you know of this?"

It was such a broad question that he wasn't sure how to begin. Did he start with Morvan's knowledge of his love for men? Would that open him to other problems?

He drew on his years in diplomatic service, and Silas's advice, as he spoke. "In January Monsieur Morvan became aware of my acquaintance with Lord Therkenwell, son of Earl Badgely."

When the *chargé* did not press about the nature of their acquaintance, Raoul continued. "He wished to recruit Lord Therkenwell to convince the earl to resign his position as the head of the Committee for British West Africa."

"Before we continue, you must understand that your government does not engage in blackmail or condone such behavior," the *chargé* said. "Nor do we seek to punish you or anyone else for what is done in private and has no bearing on France."

Raoul sighed with relief. "Morvan sought to blackmail Lord Therkenwell into this act on threat of revealing the intimate relationship John and I shared." He took a deep breath. "I was able to convince him that John had no leverage over his father's behavior."

The *chargé* listened carefully. "And then?"

Raoul recited everything else that had happened.

"Who is in possession of this earring?"

"I believe that Lord Therkenwell has it."

In further conversation, Raoul was able to plead innocence to the larger part of Morvan's plan, for indeed he did not know how or why Morvan had decided to sabotage the earl.

"You know nothing of anyone above Morvan who might be directing him?" The *chargé* asked.

"No, sir."

"And what about the involvement of Hugo Malherbe?"

"I could not say. It was never clear to me what Hugo's job was, and he often engaged in clandestine conversations with Morvan."

When the chargé was finally finished with him, he was dismissed. Raoul rose, and hesitated. "What about my job?" he asked.

The chargé looked up from his desk. "Report for work again tomorrow morning. But say nothing of what we have discussed to anyone."

He felt like his heart had been set free—yet one chain still held it down. "And what of Lord Therkenwell?" he asked. "He had only a minor role to play in this drama."

"His situation is not of our concern," the chargé said. "Oh, and by the way, you will be moving into Morvan's office tomorrow. We will have new cards printed for you as undersecretary for British affairs."

With that, it was clear he was finally dismissed. He stumbled out of the office in a daze. No penalty? A promotion?

He could think of no one he wanted to celebrate with more than John Seales. But would John have him? Should he go directly to Russell Square, or would he be refused there?

The evening had begun to darken by then, but the sun managed to thrust a few rays through a break in the clouds. Father Maurice had called that phenomenon *l'échelle de Jacob*, Jacob's ladder, after the Biblical story. The father had said it identified Jacob with the obligations and inheritance of the Jews, a way for the patriarch to climb to heaven.

Raoul had found his own kind of heaven in John's arms. Could a ladder like this be a sign that he was to resume his climb?

Chapter 45

Revelations

John didn't know what to say, but Vanessa, trained in grace by her mother, took a step forward. "I am Lady Vanessa Badgely," she said. "You have been visiting my father's house?"

Madame Wickes looked as if she had dressed quickly, without the help of a maid. Her lipstick had worn away in places, the shoulder of her gown was bunched up, and her bonnet was askew. She appeared to John as if she had just leapt from his father's bed.

John moved up to Vanessa's side. "Yes, we have met before," he said. "You are a neighbor, are you not? Madame..." he hesitated, pretending to remember. "Madame Wickes! You have come to check on my father's household in the absence of his butler. Very kind of you."

She sketched a quick curtsey, obviously relieved that John had given her an excuse. "Yes, that's true, my lord." She nodded to Vanessa and Lizzie. "My ladies. I am sorry but I must hurry."

She descended the steps carefully, and John noticed one lace on her shoe was undone. "If I might," he asked, then lowered himself to the ground and tied it.

"You are very kind," Madame Wickes said, as he rose. "Much like your father."

Then she hurried off down the street.

"Well, it is good to have pleasant neighbors," Marley said, as she walked away.

John looked up to see Beller at the doorway, a curious expression on his face. "Beller, thank you so much," John said. "If you could help with the bags."

"Most certainly."

John led his sisters and his cousin up the steps as Beller passed them.

As they entered the house, he spotted his father, in a state of deshabille similar to Madame Wickes, halfway down the massive staircase that led to the second floor. "This is most irregular," he said to John. Then he noticed his daughters behind his son.

"My dears," he said, and opened his arms to them, Vanessa first, then Lizzie. "Welcome. I did not know you were coming. I was most surprised to hear Therkenwell's man bumbling around downstairs." He glared at John, as if the whole matter was his fault.

"You did not get mother's letter, then?" Vanessa asked.

"I did not."

Lizzie sniffed the air. "Are you wearing perfume, father? Because there is a very curious floral scent in the air."

Earl Badgely waved his hand. "Must be cleaning fluid," he said.

Beller entered behind them with the bags. "Shall I take these to your sisters' regular rooms?" he asked John.

John turned to his father. "Vanessa has come to see Bedford College, and Lizzie as her accompaniment. Cousin Marley was kind enough to chaperone them here. I presume you will have all of them to stay?"

"I do not have the staff at present," Earl Badgely said. "Only a single kitchen maid."

"Ruth and I prepared the rooms," Beller said to John.

"I am happy to find a hotel," Marley said.

"Father, we had hoped to see you," Vanessa said.

Badgely looked from his offspring to his intended heir. "I suppose you shall all stay. But we will have to dine out this evening, and I will have the maid call back the rest of the staff. Excepting Samson, who is in hospital." He snorted. "Dratted inconvenient time for him to be ill, though he is as old as Christ's knickers."

Marley took his bag, and Beller took Vanessa's and Lizzie's, and the two of them climbed to the second floor.

"I suppose you will want a glass of sherry," Badgely grumbled. "Though I can call for tea if you prefer."

Vanessa looked at Lizzie and John and then said, "Sherry will be fine."

Badgely led them into the study. "Shall I pour the sherry?" John asked, and his father nodded and then sat down heavily on an overstuffed chair.

Vanessa and Lizzie sat demurely across from him, and accepted their glasses. When they were all seated, Lizzie said, "Who was that woman we met as we arrived?"

His father clearly had not expected them to have run across Madame Wickes, and he stared at them. Finally he said, "Oh, a woman of no import. Bringing a message from the House of Lords."

"She said she was a neighbor, checking in on you," Lizzie said.

"No, John said that," Vanessa said. "And she agreed. She did not look like any kind of messenger to me."

"She looked like a fancy woman," Lizzie said. "And she had a French accent. Father, you deplore the French. What was she doing here?"

"This is altogether an inappropriate conversation." Badgely stood up abruptly. "Therkenwell, will your man help me dress for dinner? The footman who assisted me this morning did a deplorable job."

He stalked out the door, and they heard his heavy footsteps on the stairway.

Vanessa looked at her brother. "John, what is going on here?"

He pursed his lips. Better to have reinforcements than to lie, he presumed. "Her name is Madame Louise Wickes," he said. "She is a model for a dressmaker called Madame Swaebe, whose premises are in New Burlington Street."

His sisters both leaned forward. "And?" Vanessa asked.

"And she is our father's mistress."

Both sisters opened their eyes wide and sat back. "To have her in our mother's home," Lizzie finally said. "How impertinent."

"It is his home as well," John said. "And our mother prefers to stay in Cornwall." He shrugged. "I believe he has been lonely for some time."

"And you condone this?" Lizzie shook her head and her loose brown curls bounced.

"It is not for me to approve or disapprove," he said. "Or you either. He is a grown man, and our father."

"The source of our income," Vanessa said drily.

John shrugged.

"Surely we can't allow this to continue," Lizzie said. "Something must be done."

In for a penny, in for a pound, John thought. "There is more to the situation." He explained, in the simplest terms, about his father's position on the Committee for British West Africa, and how his opinions might sway the government in its position against France on that dark continent.

"How does this Madame Wickes play into the situation?" Vanessa asked.

"It appears that she was put in father's way by agents of the French government," John said.

"To sway his opinion toward France?" Lizzie asked.

Vanessa took her sister's hand. "I believe there might be blackmail involved."

"Vanessa is correct. Through acquaintances, I have been in contact with the Foreign Office. I have been requested to persuade our father to step down voluntarily from his role on the committee." He paused and took a breath. "Or else his affair with Madame

Wickes will be made public, his name blackened, and our mother's already frail health made worse."

Neither of his sisters spoke. Then Beller knocked discreetly on the door. "Mr. Marley wishes to know if he may join you."

John looked at his pocket watch. "I believe we should all prepare for our dinner," he said, and rose. "My father has asked that you help dress him. I can go as I am."

"Lizzie and I will freshen up," Vanessa said. "We can continue this conversation later."

"I am sure we will," Lizzie said.

Of that, John had no doubt. The girls preceded him to the staircase. He met Marley hovering there. "We are all preparing for dinner," John said. "Have you seen the footman?"

"I believe he is in the kitchen."

John walked over to an ormolu table by the front door, where his father kept visiting cards. He wrote a restaurant name and address on the back and then handed it to Marley. "If you would be so kind as to ask the footman to run over to the restaurant and notify them to expect our party within the hour," he said. "I ..."

"I understand." Marley took the paper and disappeared toward the back of the house.

John remained in the entry hall for some time, lost in thought. It was not to be a pleasant evening, he was sure.

Chapter 46

An Awkward Affair

Dinner was quite an awkward affair. John sat at the foot of the table, with Earl Badgely at the head. Lizzie and Vanessa sat to one side, Marley to the other. His sisters made their best effort at leading light conversation, with Lizzie mentioning neighbors and friends in Cornwall. Vanessa spoke about her appointment the next day at Bedford College, where she was to meet the director of admissions and a woman who would be her tutor.

John and Marley were both quiet, speaking only when spoken to, and their father was almost mute. He grunted or nodded occasionally, but that was it.

Dinner was never easy with his family, John thought. For years he had been hiding so much from them that he hardly had anything to say. His sisters had been instructed in the art of dinner chatter, but even their attempts eventually fell short.

He recalled the way that Magnus Dawson had referred to their group of friends as a kind of family. One he had found in London, and which he realized with a deep longing that he was loath to lose.

John was quite glad when his father rose. "The bill will be put on my account," he said. "I shall walk home from here. You may call for a carriage if you prefer."

There was a clear implication he wanted to be alone. "If you would permit, perhaps Vanessa and Lizzie would appreciate a glass of chilled champagne," John said. "To allow their dinners to settle."

Badgely grunted in approval and walked out. John called for the champagne, and then moved to the chair beside Marley, to face his sisters.

"I could barely keep a civil tongue in my head," Lizzie said.

"Our mother has taught you well," John said.

"There is something afoot, clearly not my business." Marley made to rise. "I will leave you to it."

"No, William, you are a part of this family," Lizzie said. "Please, stay."

They shared a glance that John was sure was more than cousinly regard, but he had bigger problems to face. "Shall I take our cousin into our confidence?" he asked his sisters.

Vanessa nodded. "I think it appropriate."

Quickly, in a low voice so that they could not be overheard by other diners, John sketched out the situation for Marley. He looked quite surprised.

"I had for quite some time believed your father to be a man of good repute," he said. "Sadly, I have seen many men fall in like manner. It is not to be considered his fault."

"You mean it is our mother's?" Vanessa demanded.

"I know many married couples," Marley said. "And when there are problems, they are on both sides, the result of human frailties. We are none of us perfect." He raised his hand when Lizzie wanted to object. "I do not seek to place blame on either side. Your parents married young, did they not?"

"They did," John said.

"And people change as they grow older. Your father developed an interest in politics and London life, and your mother's illness caused her to prefer to remain in Cornwall."

"I should hope that I choose a husband who will stay true to me," Lizzie said.

John and Vanessa shared a glance. "That is the hope of many young women," Vanessa said.

"And many young men," Marley added, once again sharing a glance with Lizzie.

"But that does not solve our problem," John said. "Something must be done." He looked at Marley. "You appear to be in all respects the heir apparent, despite the issue of my birth. You should be the one to broach the matter to our father."

Marley shook his head. "I am but a minor relation. And as to your birth, that supersedes any claim I have to title or estate. You must be the one."

Vanessa and Lizzie shared a look, and then Vanessa said, "We agree. It must be you, John. Otherwise it will be a common tabloid that unveils the secret, and that will be damaging to all of us."

John felt besieged on all sides. First Magnus, Toby, Silas and Raoul had put the burden on him, and now his family had joined in. How was he to find the nerve to carry out this mission, which he knew would be damnably awkward. Would his father raise doubts about his own suitability to take on the title? Accuse him of being a fop, or a molly, as he had alluded in the past?

How would he survive such an onslaught?

Vanessa stood up. "It is time for us to return to Briar House. Whether or not you are prepared to beard the lion in his den, John, the hour is late and I, for one, have an important appointment tomorrow I must prepare myself for."

The four of them left the restaurant, and John could not help but notice that Marley and Lizzie held back a bit and shared whispers. If only he hadn't been such a fool as to walk out on Raoul, he could go to him tonight for a shot of confidence. But he had closed that door firmly behind him.

When they arrived at Briar House, Beller opened the front door for them, as if he had been watching from the window. Beller directed him aside. "Your father requested that you join him in his study as soon as you returned," he said.

"I don't want to talk to him. I just want to go home."

"My apologies, my lord. It was not framed as a request. Rather a demand."

John stared miserably at his valet.

"If I may be so bold, sir," Beller said. "Buck up, my lord."

John looked at him and laughed. "Thank you, Beller. It is a great comfort to me knowing that I have you behind me."

He looked at Vanessa. "The old man demands an audience. Good night." He sketched his sisters a brief bow.

"We are here for you, John," Lizzie said. She looked at Vanessa, and then Marley. "All three of us."

Marley nodded, while Vanessa smiled. John set out down the hallway to his father's study, where he hesitated at the door, his hand on the knob.

Though his heart beat a rapid tattoo, he felt stronger than he ever had before. He had ever been thought silly, by his airs and his manner of dress. But he was, under the frippery and the gay mannerisms, a man. It was time for him to act like one.

He knocked lightly on the door and then entered. His father sat in a big leather armchair beside a lamp, which was the only illumination on the room. A table beside him bore a bottle of brandy, half-empty.

"Just in time, Therkenwell," his father said, gesturing with his empty brandy snifter. "Pour me another. And one for yourself, while you're at it."

He obeyed his father's request, and once they both had glasses in hand, he sat across from the older man.

"I've certainly cocked this up." Badgely laughed ruefully. "In a word."

"Do you recall, when I was about to go up to Cambridge, you called me into this very room for a conversation?"

His father turned his head. "Brain's a bit fuzzy right now. What did I say?"

"I think you had had some brandy then, too," John said, smiling. "You told me that having a cock meant having responsibilities. That you did not want to become a grandfather before you were a father-in-law."

Badgely laughed harshly. "Didn't have to worry about that, now, did I?"

"You counseled me to always have on hand a little something for the weekend," John said. "And you handed me a sheepskin, with a ribbon to tie at the end, and counseled me to use it."

"Do you have it still?" Badgely asked.

"I do. I have used it, on occasion. For the prevention of disease rather than pregnancy, though."

"Well, at least you've done that. I may not have shown you much when you were a boy, but I do love you, son, and I don't wish you any harm." He shuddered. "To think you in the grip of a terrible disease."

"And you, father?" John asked gently. "Have you been as careful?"

"I have. Madame Wickes is still of a child-bearing age, and I have no interest in creating a by-blow. My current offspring are complicated enough."

"You know, your affair is not as secret as you might believe," John said carefully. "I heard of it before today. And I know the Foreign Office is aware of it as well as the French embassy."

"The devil you say! How in the world would you know that?"

"There is an effort afoot to blackmail you, sir. A plot concocted by the French to discredit you or force you from your place on the Committee for British West Africa."

Badgely's face flushed and he resembled nothing so much as Punch, from the pantomimes. But John was too nervous and upset to find it humorous.

It took Badgely several minutes to regain control of himself. Finally, he deflated, as if someone had let all the air out of him.

"I always believed myself to be the master of my own desires," he said at last. "I wanted to live up to my title, to have a home and a family, to make an impact on the world I inhabit. And I have done all that, only to be brought low by my own base longings."

He looked at John. "You must think me a terrible hypocrite, chastising you for chasing after your own pleasure, when I have brought ruin on the family by doing just the same."

"I do not blame you," John said. "Understanding my own desires and how to master them has given me knowledge of how difficult such a practice can be." He wanted to offer some reassurance that he had found pleasure in a safe haven, but he had left that port completely.

"You surprised me the other day when you spoke of cheese-making," Badgely said. "That was the first time I recognized that you might have a working brain underneath your frippery. And now you surprise me again, with an ability to channel your desires that I somehow lack."

"I have only met Madame Wickes briefly, but I appreciate her beauty, and I have heard testimony of her character. I do not believe you have been completely unwise."

He leaned forward. "Even as you have always mouthed a great distaste for the French."

"Sometimes that which we loathe is also that which we desire," Badgely said.

"I understand that," John said, and an image of Raoul's face flitted before him. "However, you must see that there is a way forward from this dangerous situation."

"And what is that?"

"That you step down from your position on the committee," John said. "I know you believe that you would only act in her majesty's best interests, even if it means voting in a way that might be harmful to your mistress's countrymen. But others will not see you that way. You have been quite vocal in your distrust of the French, and yet you welcome a Frenchwoman to your bed."

"You do not mince words, do you, John?"

"Neither do you, father. Beyond the issue of your performance with the committee, there are those who wish to topple you. And they will make public your affair, which will harm everything you have worked for your whole life. Your reputation, your family, all the good you have done for the government."

He gripped the stem of his glass so hard he was afraid it might break, but he had to speak. "And think of the harm you would do to my mother, whose health is already parlous. Not to mention the reputation of my sisters, who must still enter society and find good husbands."

"I have been backed into a corner," Badgely said. "I do not appreciate that."

"And yet you have backed yourself in there." John forced himself to place the brandy glass on the table, and stood up. "It is time for me to return home. If I can do anything to help you through the difficult times ahead, please do not hesitate to ask."

Then he turned and walked out, closing the door softly behind him.

Beller was waiting in the hallway. "Ruth has gone home, and the household staff have been summoned to return. Will we be staying here tonight, my lord?"

"No, it is time for us to go back to Russell Square. I do not know what the future holds, but I have set the cat among the pigeons, so to speak, and we must wait for the result."

Chapter 47

Quinn's Office

Tuesday evening Magnus sat at the dinner table and opened the issue of the *Standard,* the evening paper which Will had brought in. He was browsing through the articles when one caught his eye. "Toby, there is a mention of Earl Badgely," he said.

Toby looked up. "Don't tell me he has been exposed."

"No, rather the contrary. He has chosen to resign from the Committee on British West Africa, citing his own health and the pressures of drafting legislation. The committee is to be halted, and reformed at a later date."

"Well, certain people will be happy at that news," Toby said.

"I cannot think this was an easy decision for Earl Badgely."

"On the contrary, I think it the only logical one. Imagine if one of us was in a similar position, and our relationship were to be exposed, and perhaps even ruined, if it were to come to light. I would do whatever I could to protect you."

"But that is because you love me, my dear," Magnus said.

"And you don't believe that Badgely loves his wife, and his children?"

"Not from what has been demonstrated to us. Rather he values his position in society and his good name. I think it a wholly self-serving decision."

Toby reached for his glass of wine. "And yet one that has positive implications for John and Raoul."

"I would like to hear that from them," Magnus said. "Shall we host a dinner?"

"I think that would be a capital idea. I have developed a fondness for those three, including Silas Warner. They have become a part of our family, and I am eager to see how they will proceed."

They sent Will out that evening to the lodgings of all three men, with an invitation to a dinner Friday evening. Wednesday morning, they received responses from Raoul and Silas, but nothing from John.

"I wonder what will happen to our two young lovers," Magnus said, as they surveyed the two acceptances. "Will Raoul be sent back to France, do you think? John exiled to Cornwall?"

"We need to call on Gervase Quinn again," Toby said. "I have a client coming in this morning for a translation from the Russian, which you know is my weakest language. So I might be tied up for some time."

"Would you prefer that I go?"

"That might be necessary. I must spend some time before my client arrives familiarizing myself once again with the Cyrillic alphabet, and get those verb tenses in my brain so that I do not waste my client's time."

Magnus agreed, and Toby spent a few minutes outfitting him for the visit to the Foreign Office. "You are spoiled, you know," Toby said. "Just because you have had a personal valet in the past does not mean that I must perform those duties for the rest of our time together. You are perfectly capable of dressing yourself."

"But no one ties a cravat like you do, my love," Magnus said. "And you know that you enjoy intimate contact with my body." He quickly reached out and palmed his lover's cock, which strained against his trousers.

Toby laughed and batted his hand away. "None of that. I cannot have you reaching the Foreign Office smelling of spend."

Magnus left a short while later, strolling through the crisp spring air. A house down the street had a window box of green daffodil shoots breaking through the dirt in search of sun.

Magnus was in a cheerful mood until he reached the Foreign Office. He was informed that Gervase Quinn was in a meeting and might be some time. He chose to wait, and asked that his name be passed to Quinn if there was an opportunity.

About a half-hour later, as he was considering whether he ought to return to Ormond Yard and try Quinn at another time, Quinn popped out of an office down the hall. "Good afternoon, Dawson," he said, and they shook hands. "You might as well come in."

"I read the piece in the *Standard* yesterday," Magnus said, as he settled down across from his old schoolmate. "And there was no hint of accompanying scandal. Am I to assume that Earl Badgely succumbed to the persuasion of his son?"

"Haven't you had a part in that?"

"We did facilitate a conversation with Lord Therkenwell in which the positives of the situation were pointed out to him. However when last we saw him he was opposed to participating."

"I don't know any specifics. We have been busy instead with the fallout from his decision. Should the committee be disbanded? Choose a new chair? What is her majesty's position on further exploration in west Africa?"

He frowned. "As you can see, it's a much larger issue than whom Earl Badgely chose to bed."

"Any negative implications for Lord Therkenwell?" Magnus asked.

"Not from our end, certainly. Though I imagine his father might be displeased with him."

"And what about Raoul Desjardins, of the French Embassy?"

"His name is not on the list of co-conspirators, though his supervisor, Georges Morvan, is prominent there. We will be conducting a full investigation shortly. Should Monsieur Desjardins' name come up… well, I cannot promise anything at this point."

"Marsh and I remain available to you, as you need," Magnus said, and he rose.

When he returned home, Toby had still received nothing in return from John regarding the dinner invitation. As the hour for dinner approached Friday, Toby was uncertain of what to tell Carlo. "Do not worry, my love," Magnus said. "If only Silas and Raoul arrive, we will go to a restaurant."

"I am worried for John and Raoul. Their love is so tenuous. A bad move by either of them, or against either of them, could destroy everything."

Magnus took his hand. "If their love is anything like ours, it will survive." Then he smiled. "And if it does not, then I am sure each of them will move on."

"Easier said than done."

They heard a rap on the door, and Will went to answer it. He appeared in the door of the study a moment later. "Mr. Warner and Monsieur Desjardins," he said.

They all embraced heartily. "Have you heard from John?" Raoul asked.

"I am afraid not," Toby said.

The four of them stood uncertainly in the study, and Magnus noticed Raoul looking periodically out the window at Ormond Yard. "Well, I think we must congratulate ourselves on a successful resolution to the problem that faced us earlier this year," he said. "Who would like a whisky?"

There was general consent, and Magnus led them into the sitting room, which was better appointed for a group. He poured them all glasses of his favorite Scotch whisky and handed them around.

He was pleased to have the threesome arrayed in front of him. Toby, of course, was first in his heart. And Raoul and Silas had both come to be friends, a connection he hoped would continue no matter what happened after that evening.

After a toast, they settled down into chairs, and Magnus saw that Raoul had picked one that faced the street window. Oh, well, he thought. If John is to arrive, he will. If he does not, and Raoul's heart breaks, then at some point in the future it will mend.

Of course, he could believe that because he was secure in Toby's love. They had gone through some difficult moments. Magnus recognized that he was a son of privilege, and Toby was not, and that there would always be some barriers between them. But he believed in the Latin phrase *amor vincit omnia*—love conquers all.

If only John believed that, too.

Chapter 48

An Empty Jar

John Seales cursed himself for being late. But there was no getting around it. He and his father had many things to consider, and their conversation over the last three days had gone on much longer than he had expected.

Now he hurried down Piccadilly, his head full of the plans he and Earl Badgely had begun. But for him, it all hung on one thing. Would Raoul still accept him after his temper tantrum? Would he even be at Magnus and Toby's home when John got there?

He stumbled on a loose cobble and then righted himself by grabbing onto the wall of a building. Anyone looking at him would probably think him a drunkard, but he no longer cared what other people thought of him—excepting Raoul.

He turned the corner into Ormond Yard and began to run, holding his hat to his head. The crisp wind stung his cheeks and brought tears to his eyes—or so he told himself.

He'd almost reached his destination when the front door opened, and Raoul Desjardins stepped onto the stoop. He looked as haunted as John felt—his curly hair rumpled, his eyes dark. But John smiled at him, and Raoul smiled back, and suddenly the world was wonderful.

Raoul half dragged him into the doorway and pushed the door shut behind them. Then he took John in his arms and kissed him, long and hard. In the background John heard a wolf whistle, probably that rascal Silas, and he kicked out his leg behind Raoul.

Finally Raoul let him go. "I was so worried you would not appear tonight."

"My apologies. My appointment with my father ran much longer than I expected, and given the delicacy of our discussions I could not pull myself away."

Raoul took his hand. "Come into the sitting room and tell us what has transpired between you and your father."

Will the houseboy appeared behind them and took John's coat and hat, and John followed Raoul into the sitting room, where he was welcomed and handed a glass of whisky.

He sat beside Raoul, and with his free hand grasped Raoul's. His hand was warm inside John's and John felt his whole being subside into a froth of happiness.

"You all probably know that my father has resigned from the Committee on British West Africa," he said. "It made the London papers. Apparently the committee's future is in doubt. Someone else must step forward to take its leadership."

"So Morvan won that battle," Raoul said. "But he has lost the war." He explained to the group what had transpired at the embassy, and that Morvan was being returned to France to face possible legal action. "Though I doubt he will be convicted of anything. He will probably be shuffled to a diplomatic position in another country, or in one of the provinces."

"And the co-conspirators?" Magnus asked. "I was unable to learn anything of their fates from the Foreign Office."

"All French nationals, and all to be returned to France." Raoul hesitated. "There is one more thing."

The other four looked at him.

"I have taken over Morvan's position. I am the new undersecretary for British affairs."

"Hurrah!" Toby said, and lifted his glass. "Another toast! To Raoul!"

Raoul blushed, but John's grin felt wide enough to split his face.

"There is one more bit to share with you," Raoul said. "Monday evening, Hugo Malherbe came to see me at my room." He took a sip of whisky. "He wanted to explain to me that several months ago, he was indiscreet, and Morvan discovered that he preferred men to women."

"As I assumed when he palmed my crotch at a soirée," Magnus said drily.

"Morvan began using Hugo to spy on the three of us, as well as anyone we met at embassy parties. He was hoping to find someone with leverage against the British government."

"He gives your countrymen a bad name," Toby said.

"I agree. Hugo reported on Alexandre's dalliance with a British woman, and he caught sight of John and me one day when we were walking. Once Morvan realized who John's father was, he transferred his evil intents to me." He shook his head. "Poor Hugo. He was merely a tool to Morvan's cunning."

"What will happen to him?" John asked. "Will he be sent back to France?"

"He was able to provide enough information about Morvan to negotiate a settlement for himself. He does not wish to return to France, so a position has been found for him with the French bank Credit Lyonnais."

He turned to John. "But you are keeping us in suspense," he said. "What will your father do now? And more importantly, how is his relationship with you?"

"We have come to a sort of agreement," John said. "He will remain in London, for the large part, and I have told him that I have no issue with his maintaining his relationship with Madame Wickes."

"You are a generous man," Silas said.

"Well, there is a tradeoff," John said, smiling. "We have both admitted that we share a fancy for the French, despite my father's long diatribes otherwise. So he will not put any impediment in the way of my continuing a relationship with Monsieur Desjardins."

"Another toast!" Silas crowed. "To Earl Badgely and his Francophile cock!"

John laughed as he raised his glass. "To two Francophile cocks!" he added.

Toby leaned forward. "But this still does not resolve the issue of your inheritance," he said. "Will your father keep you as his named heir?"

John put his empty glass down on the table beside him. "He will petition for a change to the entailment," he said. "Such things have been done in the past, so there should be no reason why it shall not be granted. Shorecliff House and its surrounding properties shall be granted to my distant cousin, William Marley, who is next in line for descent."

"But what does that mean to you?" Toby asked.

John understood his concern. Magnus's father had left Magnus with nearly nothing, based on his awareness of his youngest son's orientation.

"My father will retain Briar House for his lifetime, and I shall inherit it upon his death. He also will retain the bulk of his personal investments, which I am given to understand amount to a significant number, enabling him to live comfortably. Certain of those investments, however, will be made over to me."

He smiled. "Including several located in France. Apparently despite his disdain for the French government, I shall own a tapestry manufactory in Aubusson, a lace maker in Calais, and a vineyard in Burgundy."

He turned to Raoul. "As I mentioned to you earlier, it is not the one where your father labors, but it should give us an opportunity to visit your home in the future."

"What of your sisters?" Raoul asked. "Surely they are to be taken care of."

"It appears that a romance has begun between my younger sister, Lizzie, and our cousin Marley. Marley is to move into the dower property at Shorecliff House, where my grandmother lived after my father acceded to the title. It is quite possible that Lizzie will marry him and move in there, but there is no hurry. She is only fifteen, after all, and even if they do not marry, Marley has pledged to see her securely settled."

He coughed lightly. "My apologies, Magnus, but my throat has gone dry. Might I have another whisky?"

"Of course! My apologies for my hosting deficiency."

Magnus poured them all fresh glasses of whisky, and John whetted his throat. "Which leaves my elder sister Vanessa. As you know already, she is to begin college in London this year. My father will secure her appropriate lodgings, since he would like to be free to entertain Madame Wickes at Briar House."

He paused. "Despite an initial promise to do so, Vanessa is not inclined to take part in the social season, which is a relief to both my parents. My mother need not leave Cornwall, and my father's position with Madame Wickes can remain sub rosa. Should Vanessa wish to marry, my father will provide her with a dowry, but if she prefers to become an academic, as I feel is her most likely course, he will arrange an income for her."

Magnus looked at John. "How do you feel about becoming a man of business? Or will you hire someone to manage the properties your father has granted you?"

"I have given this some thought." John turned to look at Raoul. "I believe that you will often be busy at your work, and I would not seek to draw you away from it. I will continue writing my essays and hope they will be published, and perhaps initiate social change. Vanessa has shown me that I have some small talent in business, and with her advice I hope to be a more active manager, particularly of those operations in France."

He caught his breath, and turned to Raoul. "I came here, not knowing if you would still want me as your partner. Please rest assured that despite my outburst, my feelings for you have not dampened, and that I wish to be by your side in the future."

Raoul took his hand, raised it to his lips, and kissed it gently, and John felt a tremor of anticipation rise through his body. "Nothing would give me more pleasure," he said.

Toby and Magnus led a toast, and Silas banged a spoon on his glass and called for a kiss. John and Raoul shyly obliged.

"Here is a piece of advice for you both," Silas said. "Get yourselves a glass jar, and put a penny inside it every time you make love during the next year that you are together."

"Lovely," Toby said.

Then Silas's grin turned wicked. "After a year has passed, you must take a penny out of the jar each time you enjoy each other. I believe that the jar will never be empty!"

Everyone laughed, but John and Raoul blushed. Well, John thought, it would be up to him to see the jar filled, and then emptied—and then begin filling and emptying it again and again.

Author's Notes

Thanks for reading. I didn't expect *The Gentleman and the Spy*, the first of the Ormond Yard romantic adventures, to be the start of a series. But readers enjoyed the story of how Magnus and Toby came together, and that inspired me to write this book. If interest continues, then Silas will have a book of his own.

If you haven't read *The Gentleman and the Spy*, it's available at all e-book vendors. It's not a spoiler to know that Toby and Magnus end up together; after all, these are romances, and we expect our heroes to have happy endings. Other than that, you can easily read that book after this one.

I have another historical romance you might enjoy, set in the same time period but in the Pennsylvania countryside. *The Lock-Keeper's Heart* is set in rural southeastern PA where I grew up, as the United States recovers from the Civil War and two broken-hearted men are thrust together in a lock-keeper's cottage along the Delaware Canal.

The first reviewer wrote: "This book is perfect for those of us who enjoy MM historical romance. You will be happy to lose yourself in its pages."

Author's Notes

The second reviewer added: "This was an enjoyable read set in an American historical setting with interesting references to experiences I was unaware of."

Just what I wanted to do!

The Lock-Keeper's Heart is available at all e-book retailers.

I'd love to stay in touch with you. Subscribe to one or more of my newsletters, Gay Mystery and Romance or Golden Retriever Mysteries, via my website, www.mahubooks.com and I promise I won't spam you!

Follow me at Goodreads to see what I'm reading, at BookBub for bargains, and my author page at Facebook where I post news and giveaways.

If you liked this book, please consider posting a brief review at your vendor, at Goodreads and in reader groups. Even a short review help other readers discover books they might like. And there are often specific vendor promotions I can sign up for, only if I have a certain number of reviews posted at the vendor. Thanks!

References

London of to-Day: An Illustrated Handbook for the Season, by Charles Edward Pascoe (1892)

What Jane Austen Ate and Charles Dickens Knew: From Fox Hunting to Whist-the Facts of Daily Life in Nineteenth-Century England by Daniel Pool (1994).

Acknowledgments

Librarian extraordinaire Chris Caspar helped greatly with the research for this book. I appreciate the editorial work of Sue Trowbridge and Randall Klein, and beta readers Tim Brehme, Andy Jackson, Bob Kman, and Faith Lapidus Weiner. As usual, though, any undiscovered errors are my fault and I apologize.

Cover design by Kelly Nichols, who once again has done a great job of bringing together elements to convey the essence of the book in graphic form.

I don't think I could write about romance if it wasn't for the love of my husband, Marc. Special thanks for puppy kisses to Brody and Griffin.

Main and Supporting Characters

Alexandre ➤ Raoul's co-worker
Beller ➤ John's valet
Bitty ➤ Chestnut horse John rides
Desmond Wickes ➤ Louise's late husband
Earl Badgely ➤ John's father
Edwin Strong ➤ Africa reporter
Father Maurice ➤ Raoul's mentor/abuser
Gabriel ➤ Raoul's co-worker
Georges Morvan ➤ Secretary at the French embassy
Gervase Quinn ➤ Magnus's Eton friend, now at the Foreign Office
Hetherington ➤ estate manager at Shorecliff
Hugo Malherbe ➤ Raoul's co-worker
Jacob Lee ➤ drives a carriage from the railway station
John Prescott ➤ Lord Therkenwell, Earl's son, essayist
Lady Tregavethan ➤ Hostess of the ball
Lizzie (Lady Elizabeth Seales) ➤ John's sister, 15
Louise Wickes ➤ Dressmaker's model
Luella Tyne (Lady) ➤ Country neighbor
Madame Swaebe ➤ Dressmaker, employer of Louise

Main and Supporting Characters

Magnus Dawson (Lord) ➤ Gentleman partner of Toby Marsh
Maisie ➤ Housekeeper at Shorecliff House
Mrs. Fields ➤ Tenant wife and cheesemaker
Mrs. Hampden ➤ Cook at Shorecliff
Osbert ➤ Carriage driver at Shorecliff House
Otto ➤ Flirt at the Austrian embassy party
Parker, Miss ➤ Sylvia Cooke's companion
Ranulph Tyne (Lord) ➤ Country neighbor
Raoul Desjardins ➤ Assistant secretary at the French Embassy
Richard Pemberton ➤ Barrister
Samson ➤ The earl's elderly butler
Samuel Steingrob ➤ Wine merchant
Shoemaker ➤ French desk of the Foreign Office
Sid ➤ wine shop boy
Silas Warner ➤ Raoul's friend, law clerk
Sylvia Cooke, Honorable ➤ Childhood friend of Magnus's
Toby Marsh ➤ Tutor, translator, Foreign Office operative
Vanessa Seales (Lady) ➤ John's sister, 17
William Marley ➤ the heir after John, son of the earl's first cousin

Contents

1. His Father's Summons — 1
2. A Difficult Translation — 5
3. Distant Relations — 11
4. African Gold — 21
5. A Special Boy — 25
6. Encounter — 33
7. Appeasing Silas — 39
8. That Soirée — 43
9. Priapic Adventures — 51
10. As I Am — 55
11. The Wine Shop — 59
12. Lederhosen — 67
13. No Better Lie — 73
14. Weekend Encounter — 81
15. Pineau de Charentes — 87
16. Morvan's Allegation — 91
17. Unsavory Request — 97
18. Pawns — 103
19. In Love and War — 107
20. The Flying Dutchman — 113
21. Shorecliff House — 119
22. Special Friends — 127
23. An Unwelcome Guest — 135
24. Other Men — 149
25. Dancing Master — 153
26. A Ride with his Lover — 159
27. Dinner at White's — 171
28. Morvan's Decision — 177
29. Many Resources — 185
30. Louise's Assignment — 189
31. Rendezvous — 191
32. The Man in the Moon — 197
33. Louise Wickes — 205

34. An Old Shipmate	213
35. A Bed of Roses	221
36. Dossier	225
37. Proof	229
38. The Taste of Salt	239
39. The Badger	245
40. Quinn's Solution	249
41. A Grasp of Geography	253
42. Butterfly	257
43. Inconvenient Arrival	261
44. Jacob's Ladder	265
45. Revelations	275
46. An Awkward Affair	281
47. Quinn's Office	289
48. An Empty Jar	295
Author's Notes	301
References	303
Acknowledgments	305
Main and Supporting Characters	307

www.ingramcontent.com/pod-product-compliance
Lightning Source LLC
LaVergne TN
LVHW011945060526
838201LV00061B/4213